THE ATONEMENT MURDERS

An Agent Victoria Heslin Thriller, Book 7

Jenifer Ruff

Greyt Companion Press

THE ATONEMENT MURDERS
An Agent Victoria Heslin Thriller, Book 7

Copyright © 2023 Greyt Companion Press

ISBN ebook: 978-1-954447-26-4
ISBN paperback: 978-1-954447-24-0
ISBN hardback: 978-1-954447-25-7

Written by Jenifer Ruff
Cover design by Rainier Book Design

All rights reserved. No part of this publication may be reproduced, distributed, or transmitted in any form or by any means, including photocopying, recording, or other electronic or mechanical methods, without the prior written permission of the publisher, except in the case of brief quotations embodied in critical reviews and certain other noncommercial uses permitted by copyright law.

ALSO BY JENIFER RUFF

The Agent Victoria Hesin Thriller Series

The Numbers Killer
Pretty Little Girls
When They Find Us
Ripple of Doubt
The Groom Went Missing
Vanished on Vacation
The Atonement Murders
The Ones They Buried

THE FBI & CDC Thriller Series

Only Wrong Once
Only One Cure
Only One Wave: The Tsunami Effect

The Brooke Walton Series

Everett
Rothaker
The Intern

Suspense

Lauren's Secret

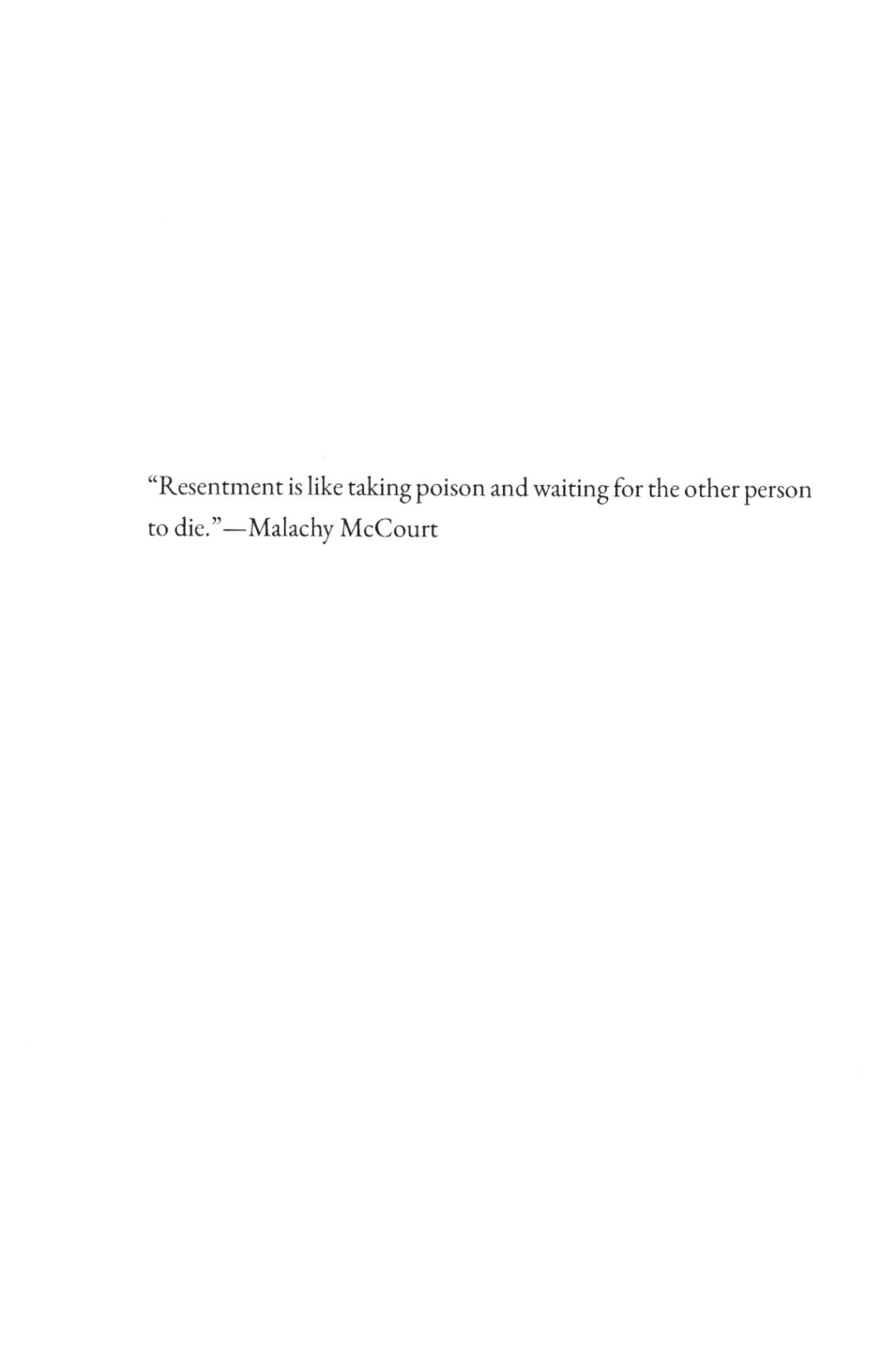

"Resentment is like taking poison and waiting for the other person to die."—Malachy McCourt

1

Two months ago, Charlotte, North Carolina

Sometimes the most unexpected things ruin what is supposed to be a perfect day. Real estate agent Paige Malloy was well aware of this and needed Wednesday morning's appointment to go exactly according to her plan. Stepping out of the elevator at Charlotte's Prestige View Condominium building, she said a little prayer that this property would be the one. Her clients would love the condo, and she would soon be free of them once and for all.

Philip and Tricia were challenging clients. Paige had taken them to three newish and nice listings yesterday, and several others the day before. They hadn't shown the slightest sign of excitement about any, though their criticisms were many and the hushed whispering between them almost constant. Buying a house was stressful...but still.

"You ready?" Paige asked, beaming at her clients from outside the door of the unit, just one floor down from the top of the building. "Two bedrooms. Two bathrooms. Floor to ceiling windows with absolutely amazing views of uptown. Hardwoods throughout. And it comes furnished."

Tricia scrunched her nose and scowled as she stared down the beautiful, clean corridor behind them. "Do you smell that? It smells like men's cologne out here. As if someone used way too much or just sprayed it right here in the hallway. Who would do that? Makes me wonder what they're trying to cover up."

Lord, give me patience, Paige thought, forcing a smile, though she smelled it too. Prepared to enter the code, she reached for the door, only to find it wasn't locked. It wasn't even fully closed.

"That's strange," she said, thinking perhaps the buyers from the previous showing hadn't shut the door all the way. Very unprofessional of their realtor. Except...Paige had selected the first showing of the day.

As they entered the condo, a phone began ringing from somewhere inside.

Tricia narrowed her eyes at Paige. "Do you think the owner is here?"

"He shouldn't be," Paige answered, stepping farther into the unit and calling out in her professional sing-song voice, "Hello? It's Paige with Carolina Realty Group. I scheduled a ten o'clock showing."

Paige waited for an answer. An apology really, because the owner wasn't supposed to be there.

None came.

Only silence.

The ringing ceased.

"There's no one home," Paige said. "Have a look around. See what you think. Take your time."

Her clients wandered toward the balcony, murmuring something Paige couldn't hear.

Dirty dishes in the sink and a glass on the countertop caught her attention. Even the smallest details mattered and contributed to an overall vibe. It really miffed her when a seller didn't clean up before a showing. After placing her business card on the stone countertop, she rinsed the used plates and glass and tucked them in the dishwasher. She wiped leftover crumbs into the sink with a paper towel and quickly scoured the basin. If she could prevent her clients from finding a single fault with the amazing condo, it was worth the small effort.

Finished with the cleaning, Paige turned to survey the space. The floor to ceiling windows were truly amazing. Very nice minimalist décor. Perfect for the unit. The owner, a man in his late twenties, must have used a high-end designer.

She eased through the living area with the comfy sectional couches and Carolina Panthers-themed bar and into the second bedroom, taking in the rest of the condo but staying out of her clients' way. Paige was admiring the view from behind a modern desk when she heard Tricia's blood-curdling scream and Philip's string of curses.

Hurrying to retrace her steps, Paige met Tricia and Philip in the center living area, where Philip leaned forward with his hands on his thighs, taking ragged breaths. Tricia's face was pale, her mouth agape. Unable to speak, she pointed down the hallway.

Paige moved past her clients and into the primary bedroom. She continued down a short hallway, her high heels clicking on the polished wood, and into the bathroom.

What she saw made her freeze in horror.

Submersed under a full tub of water…a naked man. His body was young and strong, but his skin had pruned and turned a grayish hue. His opened eyes stared upward. He was unequivocally dead.

On the polished Carrara marble tiles above him, written neatly in a thick red substance, were the words: THIS IS YOUR ATONEMENT.

Paige's scream was even louder than Tricia's.

2

Present day, Washington D.C.

First thing Monday morning, FBI Special Agent Victoria Heslin walked into her boss's office thinking she was about to get reprimanded. She'd thwarted protocol on her last investigation in Mexico, but only in pursuit of the greater good.

She loved her position as a special agent—specifically the opportunity to help desperate families who were often at their lowest point. Her professional accolades were many, and though she appreciated the credit, they usually came with a great deal of fuss she could do without. In almost ten years with the Bureau, she'd experienced few reprimands. Few in her entire existence, in fact. So the prospect of this looming admonishment did not sit well with her. Especially now, when everything in her life seemed fantastic. She'd been floating along in a bubble of happiness, and now her boss was about to burst it.

Stopping in front of Special Agent in Charge Murphy's desk, Victoria mentally prepared herself for what might come. Whatever it was, she supposed she deserved it. "You wanted to see me?" she asked her boss.

Murphy stood behind his desk with his phone in one hand and a Georgia Bulldogs mug in the other. The scowl on his face matched the mascot's. "Yes. Hold on."

She took a deep breath, wanting to get this over with. Instead, she had to wait while he set his phone down, sorted through a stack of papers, and selected one. His thick eyebrows pulled together as he scribbled a few lines in his messy penmanship. Finally, still holding his mug, he looked up at her.

"First, I hear congratulations are in order," he said, dropping his gaze to her left hand and the diamond sparkling on her finger.

"Thank you," she said, unable to contain her widening smile. After only a few days, Victoria wasn't used to the ring yet. Each glimpse ignited a spark of excitement inside her.

"You marrying a veterinarian makes sense. I'm happy for you, Victoria."

"Thank you," she said, thinking, *Is that all? Is that what he wanted to tell me?* Some of the tension weighing her down lifted away. Already she felt better about getting called into his office.

"That's not why I called you in here." Murphy's tone shifted to a more serious one.

So that's how this was going to go. He'd lowered her guard. Now he was going to hit her with a lecture, or worse.

"Did you hear Jerome Smith died over the weekend?" he asked, in what seemed a non sequitur because the topic wasn't anything Victoria expected.

"The NBA player?"

"All-Pro NBA player for the Celtics. It's all over the news. Twenty-nine years old and at the peak of his career. Although, who is to say what he might have achieved next?" Murphy looked away and stared out his office window while taking a drink from his mug. He sounded deeply sad, as though Jerome had been a close friend or personal hero.

"That's a shame," Victoria said. "Do they know what caused his death?" So young and healthy. If she had to make an educated guess backed by statistics, it was an unintentional overdose or a motor vehicle accident.

"This hasn't been confirmed to the public yet, but he was murdered inside his home in Boston."

"Oh, wow!"

"And we don't have a suspect. I just got off the phone with the Boston PD. We're going to assist them."

"Why is the FBI involved?"

"High-profile death, for one. But it's more than that. Jerome's death might link to an unsolved murder that occurred two months ago in Charlotte, North Carolina. A young man was found drowned in his bathtub. The same exact message was left behind at both crime scenes."

"A message?"

"*This is your atonement.* That's what the message said. We've either got a serial killer or a very big coincidence, and we've got to get a handle on it. The cops are already under tremendous pressure from politicians, the NBA, the Boston community, the victim's family, and every fan of Jerome's, of which there are millions."

Victoria nodded, imagining the urgency to find the perpetrator.

"You're going to catch the next commercial flight to Logan and see how you can help figure out who killed him."

"Why me?"

Murphy snorted and set his mug on his desk with a thunk. "That's something I've always liked about you, Agent Heslin. All that inherited money and you've never acted like you're above any of this." He shook his head. "How's this for why? You've got a reputation. An earned reputation. And you're very good at linking clues."

Victoria felt her face flush. She appreciated his words, but that was enough. If he continued, she'd be genuinely embarrassed.

"And besides all that, the Boston field office is slammed with casework. They need other hands and the detective working Jerome's case asked for you specifically. Her name is Suarez. Detective Lieutenant Lisa Suarez. She said she worked with you recently on your friend's case. That missing groom investigation."

"Yes. Of course. I like Suarez," Victoria said, picturing the native Bostonian with the grouchy personality. Suarez had proven to be an excellent and committed detective and a good team player. Victoria trusted her and welcomed the opportunity to work with her again.

Murphy picked up his mug. "What do you know about Jerome Smith?"

"Um...that he's a professional basketball player. An All-Pro. Plays for the Celtics. Twenty-nine years old. He might have been at the peak of his career when he died, but who is to say what else he might have achieved. He has lots of fans."

One side of Murphy's mouth curled into the slightest smile, the corner actually twitched, as Victoria finished repeating what he'd just told her. "That's what I thought," he said. "Your lack of interest in professional sports might give you an advantage. You can certainly be more objective than others. Right?"

"There's that. Yes. Objectivity."

"Grab your stuff and get to the crime scene while it's still relatively fresh. Meanwhile, I'm going to set up a task force here to support you. We'll work both atonement murder cases under one umbrella." Murphy was already turning to his computer as he gestured for her to leave his office. "Be on the lookout for the files on the Charlotte murder. We'll talk more once you're on your way to Boston."

"Okay. Thanks." Victoria left his office, thinking her meeting with Murphy hadn't played out the way she'd expected. Instead of an admonishment, she was on the hunt for a possible serial killer. Could an FBI agent ask for a better turn of events?

EXCERPT FROM JOURNAL ENTRY

I saw Jerome today. He was gloating at me from the television screen. It was more than I could bear.

3

Victoria parked her SUV in long-term parking at Dulles airport and took the shuttle to the terminal. Her fitted, lightweight black jacket had just enough length to cover her hips and her gun. The jacket came from a box of comfortable and professional clothing a stylist sent every other month, because Victoria avoided shopping whenever possible.

She moved her blonde ponytail out of the way and slid her arm through the straps of her black leather backpack, a gift from her father, something she wasn't sure how she ever lived without. After popping the back of her car open, she grabbed her go-bag, the carryon suitcase that was always there, so she was ready to go at a moment's notice. The suitcase contained a change of clothes, toiletries, and a snack stash. It also held an evidence collection kit in case an investigation necessitated the proper equipment. That wasn't really part of her job, but gloves, shoe covers, and evidence bags had come in handy so many times that she didn't do field work without them.

On the way to the airport, she'd called her fiancé, Ned, and left a message to let him know she was heading to Boston. Fortunately, she didn't have to ask him to take care of her greyhounds, foster dogs, and donkeys while she was gone. She could count on him to do so. They now seemed as much his animals as hers. And if he couldn't get home at a reasonable hour—he'd been working more and more hours at the busy veterinary clinic lately—he'd send one of the vet techs to the house to feed the animals.

Standing in line to board the flight, Victoria skimmed through her phone's news feed. Many of the featured articles were about Jerome. She read over several. Murphy was right about Jerome, and then some. He had enjoyed a fantastically successful career. Three-time All-Star. MVP of this year's NBA Finals. Spokesperson for an electrolyte beverage, a chain restaurant specializing in wings, and a luxury SUV. Thirty million followers on Instagram.

As she was closing her news app, she noticed an article titled *Eighty Percent of Adults Don't Drink Enough Water for Optimal Health*. Eleven cups was the recommended daily amount for women. Victoria wasn't even close. How much water had she consumed that day? A few gulps after her morning run. And if coffee counted, she'd had two cups. According to the article, not near enough for "optimal health." She vowed to do better.

During the short flight, Victoria had an entire row to herself and the privacy to do more research. She opened her laptop and combed through the digital case files from the first murder, the ones Murphy had sent from the Charlotte Police Department. The victim's name was Todd Eckstrom. He was twenty-nine years old when he died. Found drowned in his own bathtub by a realtor and her clients. Two months had passed since the crime, and it remained unsolved.

There was no water on the floor or on the side of the bathtub to indicate a violent death. The autopsy found ketamine in Eckstrom's system. The drug would have rendered him unable to fight back. The only sign of a possible struggle was a patch of hair missing from his scalp, torn from the roots.

After absorbing the crime scene photos, statements, interviews, autopsy reports, and toxicology results from Eckstrom's case, Victoria moved on to the information the Boston authorities had compiled so far on the murder of Jerome Smith. His death also occurred in his own home, and the message left behind—*This is your atonement*—linked the crimes.

One victim was white, one black. Despite the geographical distances between them, Todd Eckstrom and Jerome Smith had shared backgrounds. They both grew up in Charlotte and attended the same private high school, Charlotte Academy. They had played basketball together on the school team for four years. Todd and Jerome might have been best friends, or mortal enemies, Victoria didn't know yet. At the least, they were teammates and acquaintances. From the perspective of the investigation, that was good. The murders weren't completely random. Law enforcement already had a common thread from which to assemble the puzzle pieces.

By the time Victoria arrived in Boston on Monday afternoon, with folded pages of notes inside her purse, she was familiar with everything documented on the two cases, ready to help the police departments figure out what they didn't yet know. She would do her best to analyze every detail through the killer's eyes. She didn't expect any of it to be pretty.

4

Jerome Smith lived in a western suburb of Boston. His gated community, also home to several of his Celtics teammates, was an easy drive to and from the team's practice facility. When Victoria arrived, dozens of vehicles, news trucks, and at least a hundred people hovered around the neighborhood's front gate. Reporters were desperate for more information on Smith's death and eager to grab any new morsels. Jerome was a professional athlete and a celebrity. The fans who had set up chairs on the sidewalk, waiting for and demanding answers, might feel they knew him well. But did anyone know the real person behind the public persona?

Police officers, at least three of them, kept people away from the gate, preventing them from entering the neighborhood and from blocking the road.

Victoria's driver slowed as they approached the crowd.

"Pull up near that officer, please," Victoria told the driver as she rolled her window down. "Excuse me, officer, I'm with the FBI. They're expecting me." She lifted the lanyard from her neck and showed her identification.

The officer nodded and stepped away from the car. He moved temporary fencing aside before waving the vehicle through.

"Stop next to the gatehouse, please," Victoria said next.

The driver pulled up beside the white-brick gatehouse. Aware of the cameras and phones that might be recording things from only a short distance away, Victoria shielded her face with her hand when she emerged from the car. She showed her ID again, this time to the man working inside the small building. He seemed full of restless energy, eyes darting from Victoria to the people who were waiting for news. Working in a neighborhood full of celebrity athletes, he must have seen his fair share of gossip-worthy occurrences, but nothing so far had garnered more attention than Jerome's death and the questions surrounding it.

Victoria asked a few things about the neighborhood's security system, then headed back to the waiting car.

"Victoria Heslin? Agent Heslin? Is that you?" a reporter shouted. "Why is the FBI here? Was Jerome murdered?"

The bellowing questions increased. Cameras flashed nearby.

Without answering, Victoria ducked into the back of the car. Shouts of "What happened to Jerome?", "Was Jerome murdered?" and "Does the FBI know who killed him?" echoed behind her as the elaborate iron gate slid open and her driver headed into the neighborhood. While she was grateful to be involved in the case, it came with a giant share of media hype she'd much rather avoid than deal with.

"Is this where Jerome died?" the driver asked, following the instructions of his GPS down a tree-lined street.

"I can't comment on the case, but I can tell you it's where he lived," Victoria answered as she typed a message to Detective Lieutenant Suarez. *I just arrived inside Jerome's neighborhood.*

The driver seemed to take his time cruising through the opulent neighborhood, looking from side to side so as not to miss a single one of the large homes with immaculate, landscaped yards as they passed them. Finally, they reached Jerome's address and pulled alongside the curb.

Victoria got out of the car and stared up at the lavish mansion, set far back from the road. According to an Internet source, the ten-thousand-square-foot home had six bedrooms, eight bathrooms, cathedral ceilings, marble floors, a media room, a gym, a six-car garage, and a spectacular pool. A whole lot of house for a man who lived alone. It so happened that Victoria's own home was just as huge and surrounded by beautiful acreage. But, as of just a few days ago, she no longer lived alone. Ned was in the process of moving in. As far as she was concerned, it was *their* house now. Having thought of her fiancé and the recent and exciting change in their relationship, she was now standing outside the scene of a murder with a smile on her face. Not at all appropriate. She had to change her focus. No more smiles. Not for a while. It was time to think like a killer.

5

Victoria walked over to the officer standing guard in front of Jerome Smith's house. She showed her ID for the third time since arriving in the neighborhood. The officer recorded her name on the crime scene log. "Go on in," he said. "I'll make sure your driver leaves the neighborhood."

"Thank you," Victoria told him. She ducked under the police tape and walked through a courtyard, past a tall fountain, and up the large stone steps to the partly open front door. Residue from the mists and powders used to detect prints coated a large door knocker in the shape of a shamrock. She didn't touch the knocker or the doorbell. She nudged the door open with her shoe and went in.

Lt Detective Lisa Suarez from the Boston Police Department met Victoria in the entryway. The detective wore a stiff dress shirt buttoned up to her throat and no makeup. She'd pulled her hair back into a bun underneath a cap. With her phone against her ear and a worn notebook tucked high under her arm, she was no-frills, all-business.

"The FBI is here. I'll get back to you," Suarez said in an accent unique to native Bostonians. She lowered her phone and greeted Victoria. "Welcome back to Boston, Agent Heslin."

"It's nice to see you again, Lieutenant. I heard you asked for me. I appreciate that. Thanks for bringing me in on this."

Suarez grunted in acknowledgement. "You've seen the files? What we have so far and from the other case?"

"Yes. On my way here."

"Good. Then I'll show you to the crime scene." Suarez handed Victoria shoe protectors and gloves.

Victoria stretched the blue covers over her shoes and slid the first glove over her left hand.

"You weren't wearing that big rock the last time I saw you," the detective said.

"I wasn't. I just got it a few days ago. It belonged to my mother."

"Maybe you should put something over your finger to anchor it, you know, so it doesn't fall off. Be a shame to lose it."

Victoria's ring finger was a little more than an inch long. She'd lost the top half and part of two other fingers to frostbite after a plane crash in the Arctic. "It's not going anywhere," she said. As she pulled the latex glove over her ring, the plastic snagged and tore. When she got the ring, she'd thought the thin gloves might present a problem. Now she was ready with a plan. From a zipped, inner compartment of her backpack, she took out a small, airtight pillbox. The ring went into the box, and the box went back into the inner compartment.

"So, does that thing mean you're getting married or what?" Suarez asked, holding out another glove for Victoria.

"Yes, I'm engaged," Victoria said, snapping the new glove into place. "No wedding date yet."

Suarez grunted again. Seconds later, she added, "Congratulations."

Victoria followed the detective deeper inside the home. They stopped in the center of a spacious living room with a twenty-foot ceiling.

"The victim had a party Saturday night," Suarez said. "By our latest count, almost a hundred people came and went from this place. Friends. Teammates. Groupies. Food deliveries and catering."

"That's a lot of people to sort through," Victoria said.

"It is, and it gets worse. Jerome's cleaning crew arrived at eleven a.m. yesterday."

"They clean on Sundays?"

"Not usually. Jerome scheduled them because of the party. Paid them double time, they said. The alarm wasn't set when they arrived. They came in and conquered the mess with a vengeance. They scoured the lower living areas—this room, a dining room, the kitchen, a game room with a bar, and two bathrooms. They vacuumed, disinfected, wiped down every surface, collected bottles and cups and plates and napkins. You name it. The whole place is spotless because that's what happens, apparently, when you can pay people to clean up after you. All that very thorough destruction of potential evidence occurred *before* they found Jerome in the back of the house and called the police."

"Where did they find him?" Victoria asked.

"This way." Suarez said, pivoting to face a hallway. "This is where it gets interesting. And I can't wait to hear what you make of it."

6

Framed magazine covers featuring Smith lined the long hallway. Dozens of them at eye level and above. Some in his Celtics uniform and some in suits and dressy clothing. About halfway down the photo gallery, Suarez stopped beside a doorway marked with yellow tape and said, "This is a guest room. It's where they found him."

Victoria entered the well-appointed guest room. The first thing she noticed was the message on the wall above the tightly made, king-sized bed.

THIS IS YOUR ATONEMENT.

A careful, steady hand—not rushed nor trembling—had written the words in neat, block letters with a thick, red substance. It appeared identical to the message in the crime scene photos from Todd Eckstrom's file.

"I entered *this is your atonement* in the national homicide database and got a hit right away with the case in Charlotte," Suarez said. "Our handwriting experts say their analysis is pretty useless on those block letters, but the print sure looks similar. If it's written in lipstick, specifically Flirty Red by Mac Cosmetics, which was the brand used in the Charlotte murder, according to their Forensic Department, then we'll be certain it's a match."

A Boston forensic team had already processed the room, leaving behind colored tags, tape, and powdered residue. Jerome's corpse currently resided at the morgue. Homicide officers had found his six-foot-seven-inch frame on the floor between the fireplace and a leather ottoman. In death, he'd lain stretched to his full height. Not a usual way for a body to land in its final moments. The killer must have posed him.

"They found Jerome naked," the detective said. "But no signs of sexual assault or activity."

Victoria lifted her gaze to the ottoman. Polaroid photos, instant ones with white around the edge, were spread across the leather top.

"My family had a camera that made pictures like those when I was younger," Suarez said. "Apparently, the technology made a comeback. Some people enjoy the novelty of having an instantly printed photo. Great for parties, or when you murder someone and need to decorate the scene before you take off." Suarez punctuated her sentence with a loud huff.

"I don't think the camera company is going to be adding that little ditty to their ads anytime soon," Victoria said as she counted the photos. Nine covered the square ottoman in neat rows of three. Six more were taped along the fireplace mantle, hanging nearly equidistant to each and reminding her of macabre holiday decorations.

She kneeled to study each photo on the ottoman. All were close-up images showcasing body parts. Rippled biceps. A chiseled abdomen. A muscular thigh. "Did they verify all the photos are of Jerome?"

"Yes," Suarez answered.

Victoria studied the pictures on the mantle next. At first, she wasn't sure what she was seeing. Then she figured it out. Each photo captured a close-up image of Jerome's flaccid genitalia. Different angles, but the same body part.

"Forensics think the photos were taken after Jerome died," Suarez said. "They're all clean of prints. So is the tape. The killer wore smooth gloves. And if the cleaning crew's efforts throughout the house weren't enough, the killer did his own post-murder housekeeping in this room. Everything was wiped. Forensics have yet to find a single print in here. Not even one of Jerome's."

"Did they collect everything from the vacuums before they were emptied?" Victoria asked, because criminals always left something of themselves behind at the crime scene, either on purpose or inadvertently.

"They did. They'll be combing through it all for days. Believe me, they're being meticulous to a fault. Once we secured the scene, we brought the best of the best in to work it. We don't want to mess this one up."

"Cause of death?" Victoria asked.

"The medical examiner still has to confirm, but our working hypothesis is that the killer smothered him. Petechial hemorrhaging in the eyes. Bruising around the lips. The absence of other signs of death. No ligature marks."

"It would be difficult for anyone to overpower a guy like Jerome without some help. Might have been more than one person, or someone drugged him. I won't be surprised if the toxicology results indicate ketamine, like the forensics team found with Todd Eckstrom's case. A substantial dose of ketamine would have greatly reduced or eliminated Jerome's physical advantages."

Victoria surveyed the room again, taking in the scene and trying to figure out what it said about the person who created it. Neither of the women spoke for a moment.

"So, what are your thoughts on the killer?" Suarez asked.

Victoria rested her hands on her hips. "He's organized. Intelligent. Socially skilled. He carefully planned this murder and took his time. He'll have made a mistake, but it may not be an obvious one. And when I say *he*, know that I'm using it as a general pronoun, so I don't have to keep saying he or she or them. Most serial killers are male, overwhelmingly so, but let's not rule out either sex yet."

"I'm not," Suarez said, staring at the photos on the ottoman. "What the killer did, staging the scene, it sure looks personal to me. Both atonement murders seem like revenge killings."

"Definitely." Victoria looked around one last time. "If I wanted someone dead, I'd get the job done quickly, then get myself far, far away as fast as I could. That's the smart thing to do. I think this killer is smart, but that's not what he did. He stuck around. Took his time to send a message."

"And we need to know why." Suarez flipped through the pages of her notepad. "I googled the definition of atonement to make sure I wasn't missing anything. It means reparation for a wrong or injury. And in a religious context—an annual ceremony of confession and atonement for sin."

"Yes," Victoria answered. "I did the same. Which raises the obvious question: what does the killer think Todd and Jerome have to atone for?"

7
Twelve years ago - Todd

Todd wrapped a Carolina Panthers sweatshirt around a case of beer and stuffed it in his duffel bag, which left room for little else. No matter. The beers were more important than clothes. He could get by with just a bathing suit, socks, a few T-shirts, and his basketball shoes, but without the beer, they'd be bored out of their minds at night. His grandparents' guest room had a mini-fridge. He'd fill it with beer cans when they got there, so the drinks would be nice and cold.

Todd looked up and gasped when he glimpsed his father standing in the bedroom doorway under the *Play Like a Champion Today* banner.

"Sorry, didn't mean to startle you," his father said, shifting a stack of papers from one arm to the other.

"Yeah, well, you did," Todd said, stepping in front of the bed to block his father's view.

His father walked in, eyeing the sharp angles of the bulge inside Todd's bag. "What are you doing?"

"Huh? Nothing." Hardly a suspicious answer. Todd had a reputation for answering his parents' questions with as little information as possible.

"Looks as if you were packing."

"Yeah."

"Are you going somewhere?"

"Mountains."

"To visit your grandparents?"

"Yeah."

"Does your mother know?"

Todd crossed his arms. "Not yet."

"When are you going?"

"As soon as Jerome gets here."

"Oh, you invited Jerome? He's going with you?"

"Yeah. Why? You worried about your parents?" Todd asked.

"No. Of course not," he said with some indignation. "Why would I be worried?"

Todd shrugged.

"Your grandfather knows who Jerome is." Todd's father pressed the stack of papers against his chest and looked away for a few seconds, towards the large sign with a Michael Jordan quote. *If you push me towards something that you think is a weakness, then I will turn that perceived weakness into a strength.*

Just when Todd thought the discussion was over, his father sighed and said, "Don't be too crazy up there. Jerome has scouts coming next week, I heard. I'm surprised his parents are letting him go with you. Did he ask?"

"He doesn't have to get their permission. Besides, we'll play hoops the whole time. Not much else to do there."

"Then why are you going?"

"I dunno. Just thought it would be good to get away."

"How long are you staying?"

"Three days. Unless it gets super boring, and we come back sooner."

"Be careful driving in the mountains. Those last few miles. Stick to the speed limit."

"I know."

"How are you feeling? You doing all right?" Todd's father cast another glance at the duffel. He had to know what was causing the sharp-angled shape, but he said nothing about it.

"I'm fine."

"Does Jerome know about your...you know..." His father cleared his throat. "...your condition."

"My condition? No one knows, and I want to keep it that way. No one needs to know."

"Okay, but if something happens, wouldn't it be best if he understood what you were dealing with?"

"Nothing is going to happen. I'm fine." The volume of Todd's voice rose along with his frustration.

"Did you pack your meds?"

"Not yet. I was about to when you came in." That was a lie. He'd forgotten. But it wasn't as if he'd already left. He might have remembered on his own.

"Okay. Have a good time. Be careful. And be smart." His father turned away, took a step toward the door, then stopped short. He turned around and gave his son an awkward hug, accidentally poking the stiff corners of the papers into Todd's neck. "I love you, son."

"Yeah. Love you, too. And don't worry. We won't get into trouble, and nothing is going to happen."

8

It was almost nine p.m. when Victoria entered the Boston Police Headquarters with Suarez to discuss the two murder cases. Suarez held the front door open with one hand and stifled a yawn with the other. It had been a wild day for her, and it wasn't over yet. Her workload would get worse before it got better. If she had a life outside work, it would have to wait.

"You prepared to deal with all of this?" Victoria asked. "The pressure?"

Suarez blew out a loud breath. "It's not every case where the President of the United States calls our chief of police to make sure we have the resources we need. He's a basketball fan."

"That's good. That might help. But it's a lot of stress and scrutiny."

"We've got dozens of officers on the case already. No shortage of interest, that's for sure. Everyone here is gunning to be involved. We have a small team just to handle the press and communications alone."

Victoria heard the buzz of activity and chatter as Suarez led her to a room with long tables and partitioned cubicles. Despite the time, the room bustled with activity. Law enforcement officers working alone and in groups. Typing notes. Answering phones. Whispering. Everyone on overtime. A trashcan in the corner overflowed with empty coffee cups and Dunkin' Donuts boxes.

"This is our control room," Suarez said, her eyes roaming the space. "The officers have been fielding calls nonstop from people claiming to know something related to Jerome's death. We haven't even publicly announced he was murdered yet, and we already have hundreds of leads."

As Suarez entered the room, several of the people working there nodded or lifted a hand in acknowledgement. She returned their gestures without stopping.

She pointed to a long row of whiteboards completely covered in writing. "Any *promising* leads go up there. I'll make sure the information is available to you, along with any follow up we do." A gurgling, growling noise followed her statement, and Suarez placed her hand over her abdomen. "I have to eat something. You hungry?"

"Yes. I could eat." Victoria hadn't eaten since she got off the plane in Boston. They were too busy at the crime scene to think about food.

"Let's see if there's anything in the break area." Suarez headed out of the room and back to the corridor.

A bald man in a police uniform ambled toward them, eating a slice of pizza. He stopped and faced Suarez. "She Feds?" he asked, tipping his head toward Victoria.

"Yes, she Feds," Suarez mimicked back. "And she can hear you, Jimmy."

Jimmy's face reddened. "Anyone you like for this?" he asked Victoria.

"Not yet," Victoria answered. "It's too early. But I'll let Suarez know the minute I do."

"Any of that pie left?" Suarez asked him.

"Few more slices. Going fast," he answered, already walking away.

"We better hurry," Suarez said with the same seriousness she'd shown toward the investigation. "Come on."

After grabbing slices of room-temperature pizza, they walked to a door with a cheap metal plaque that said *Lt. Det. Suarez*. With a nudge of the detective's foot, the door swung inward, leaving only a few inches between its edge and the desk inside the tiny room.

"Make yourself comfortable," Suarez said, pushing aside a mug emblazoned with a gold police shield to set her paper plate down. "You can drag that chair over, but you have to close the door first."

Victoria closed the door, then wheeled a chair over from the corner. As she draped her jacket over the chair's back, she hoped the investigation would not only find the killer, but also earn the detective a decent-sized space to work in.

As she sat facing Suarez, she took her ring out of her backpack and its box and slid it back on her finger.

"You're not sure what to do with that thing yet, are you?" Suarez asked.

Victoria responded with a slight smile. She'd forgotten about it for a few hours, which made her feel instantly ashamed. It wouldn't happen again.

"I heard about your run-in with the cartel in Mexico," Suarez said, already having eaten half a slice of pizza. "And your epic escape."

"Not sure I'd call it that." Victoria was lucky to have survived overnight in the ocean, but she didn't want to talk about it or relive the nightmare. "On my way into Jerome's neighborhood, I talked to the man working at the gatehouse. He leaves at six p.m. After that, guests type a code at the gate. Jerome should have requested a special code that would work only for the evening."

"But he didn't," Suarez said. "He gave out his personal code. It was used twenty-six times."

"Only twenty-six? You said there were over a hundred guests at his home," Victoria said, picking the pepperoni off her pizza and dropping it onto her plate.

"Yes. Some arrived in groups. Some used codes that belong to other Celtics teammates who live in the neighborhood. There were two other parties Saturday night. Some cars followed others inside. Lots of food deliveries. The neighborhood was busy around the time of Jerome's murder. We're following up on everyone we can find."

"Does Jerome have a video security system?"

"Security system—yes. Video—no." Suarez grasped her second pizza slice but held off on taking another bite. "This is a guy who is used to being followed everywhere by the media and fans. In his own house, he wanted privacy. He worried about the security company spying on him."

"Do you think he might have been involved with something illegal or embarrassing that he wanted kept private?"

"Haven't found that something yet, but we're sure digging for it." The conversation paused as both women ate.

"A lot of Jerome's guests took photos and videos during the party," Suarez said. "We've got officers collecting those, and other officers combing through them."

"Does anyone stand out so far?"

"You mean a perp wearing gloves and a ski mask? Or someone hovering in the corner with a Polaroid camera?" Suarez laughed without smiling. "Unfortunately...no."

"Can anyone tell if something is missing from his home?" Victoria asked, since killers often took souvenirs from their victims, and those "trophies" could reveal the killer's motive.

"Jerome has a girlfriend who can tell us," Suarez said. "She doesn't live with him, but from the looks of their social media posts, they're serious. They've been together two years. She stays at his place often. She's a model. Cara Goodwin. She was in Italy for a photo shoot so she wasn't at the party. I'm the one who contacted her. Right after I called Jerome's parents." Suarez shook her head, probably recalling how difficult those tasks had been. "She gets back to Boston tonight. We'll escort her inside his place to have a look around."

Three short knocks on the door were followed by the voice of a woman with a strong Boston accent. "Hey. It's me. Blake. Heard you were back so I came in person. You in there?"

"Yeah. Hold on, someone's with me." Suarez made a half circle with her finger in the air, and the gesture alone was enough for Victoria to understand what she had to do. She got up, moved her chair aside, and stood by the corner of the desk.

"Okay, come on in," Suarez said, dropping her sauce-spotted plate into a trash can.

The door opened and a strikingly beautiful woman with a curvy figure stared at Victoria.

"Officer Missy Blake, this is Victoria Heslin from the FBI," Suarez said.

Missy gaped at Victoria and looked star-struck before flashing a stunning smile. The officer must have recognized Victoria's name from news coverage, either from a past case, or one of Victoria's personal tragedies.

"What is it?" Suarez asked, drawing Blake's attention away from Victoria.

Looking and behaving the opposite of Suarez in so many ways, Officer Blake continued to beam and seemed to almost bounce on her toes. "So, you assigned me to help interview guests from the party, looking for witnesses, and getting handwriting samples. And that's what I've been working on," she explained, apparently for Victoria's benefit. "Some of the guests flew out of town before we could identify them. We've got two guys at the airport in Los Angeles. One in Kentucky, one in Montana, and another in Colorado. Police at those locations are meeting them when they land or have already detained them for questioning." With a nervous smile, Blake's focus shifted to Victoria, then back to Suarez. "Anyway, that's not all. I thought you'd want to know this right away. We found out which guests were the last to leave."

"Who are they?" Suarez asked.

"Six people. Two of Jerome's teammates and their girlfriends. And then Jerome's former sports agent, Rick Haskin, and his date. They claim to have left together at 1:30 a.m. As far as they know, no one else was at the house when they left. But it's not as if they searched. And with a place so big, anyone could have been hiding inside."

Suarez nodded, and Officer Blake continued. "All six are acting shell-shocked about his death. Seems very authentic to all of us. I took notes and we've got a recording you can watch. What do you want to do? Should we hold them here?"

"Yes. Give me thirty minutes to finish up with Agent Heslin, then I'll look over what you have and talk to them. Thank you, Officer Blake," Suarez said, jotting something on her notepad.

Blake smiled at Victoria one last time before leaving and shutting the door behind her.

"She's a big fan of yours, if you couldn't tell. Some might judge Missy by her looks, but she's smart and a hard-working officer. It took me a while to appreciate that, but I do now."

Victoria pushed her chair back into place and sat down again. "So...the last guests to leave the party...that could be promising. Especially if one of them also knows Todd Eckstrom."

"I'll be shocked if it's that easy," Suarez answered. "But who knows? Like we talked about earlier, our perp is harboring some intense anger. Our interviewers are on the lookout for someone Jerome angered or betrayed."

"That's exactly what I would focus on," Victoria said. "Someone who feels he or she has been wronged. We'll need solid evidence to convict the killer, but figuring out his motive might be the quickest way to find him."

9

A strong wind whipped up tiny bits of debris on the sidewalk in front of the police station. Victoria wrapped her jacket tighter around her body to protect against the evening chill. Facts and unanswered questions from the two murder investigations had been swirling through her mind, but she'd sorted through the information enough to make a decision about her next steps. With that decision in mind, she called her boss for approval.

Just as Murphy answered, a nearby vehicle honked, someone leaning hard into the horn. Victoria could barely hear Murphy say, "Hey. Where are you?"

"I'm in Boston, waiting for a ride to my hotel. I have a strategy to run by you. Can you talk for a few minutes?"

"I can. What's going on?"

She filled him in on the details.

"So you think the crimes are definitely linked?"

"Yes, I'm fairly certain they are."

Revenge killings weren't uncommon. Victoria had investigated others. And the atonement message was a standard one. The killer hadn't left an unusual quote from an esoteric book or used cryptic symbols in the message. Based on those statistics, it was possible the message was a coincidence and the murders occurred independently of each other. But the victims' past connection—high school—and the staged crime scenes made a coincidence seem extremely unlikely.

"What about a copycat killer?" Murphy asked. "Though the victims weren't killed the same way."

"Could be," Victoria answered. "The Charlotte Police Department managed to keep the atonement message info from going public. A copycat killer would have to be intimately familiar with Todd Eckstrom's case. Someone in law enforcement. A close family member. Or one of the people who found the victim. We should look into all of them, find out if any of them were in Boston this week."

"After studying both crime scenes, what's your take on the killer so far?" Murphy asked.

Even though there was no one around, Victoria lowered her voice. "He or she has a job or a routine with some flexibility that allowed travel between Boston and Charlotte. I expect he's successful. We're likely looking for someone with psychological problems, though well-hidden."

"Very gutsy or very disturbed, murdering a celebrity and thinking they're going to get away with it."

"Agree," Victoria answered. "Your point also begs the question...does the killer want to be found? I mean, he's putting forth some effort to stage these scenes. I'm not yet sure who that's for."

"What's your plan to figure it out? The strategy you mentioned?" Murphy asked.

"As you would imagine, there are a lot of people investigating here. A huge team working different angles, interviewing people, sorting through the forensic evidence. Suarez is good. I'm sure the detectives in Charlotte are too. Now that they have evidence from Jerome's murder, they're looking into every aspect of the victims' recent histories. But the victims went to high school together. What if the answer lies in their distant pasts?"

"It might," Murphy said.

"I'd like to see what I can dig up going way back."

"How far?"

"Well, how far back can someone hold a grudge? The crimes are personal, and I see two likely possibilities for our killer's profile." The possibilities came to her as she spoke. "Option one, we've got a killer filled with fresh rage. Near or around the time of the first murder, the killer experienced a stress for which he blamed the victims. The killings may be a catharsis for that."

"Okay," Murphy said.

"Second possibility—the killer allowed years of animosity and anger to build up, and it eventually exploded. That anger might have been brewing since high school. I'm leaning toward the latter theory."

"Why?"

"I know it's early with Jerome Smith's case, but the crime in Charlotte occurred two months ago and the police there still haven't nailed down a strong lead. It's a big city with a lot of resources. If someone in Eckstrom's recent history was involved, wouldn't the Charlotte homicide detectives have identified that person by now? Also, these crimes were not pulled off in a fit of uncontrolled anger. Someone executed them after calm, careful planning. All of that takes time."

She waited for Murphy's response, but he kept quiet, so she continued. "I'd like to go to Charlotte, where the victims grew up."

A sedan that matched the description of Victoria's ride pulled alongside the curb.

"Hold on just a few seconds," she said. "My ride just got here."

Victoria checked the car's license plate before getting inside the vehicle and thanking the driver.

"I'm back," she told Murphy as she settled in against the leather seat.

"Okay," he answered. "Your plan makes sense. Keep me and the task force updated. The minute someone finds the perp through forensic analysis or any other means, you stop digging and take the first flight back to D.C. Until then, do your thing in Charlotte, or wherever you need to go."

Victoria flicked on the hotel room lights, set her suitcase on a luggage holder, and called Ned. Only a week had passed since she asked him to move in with her. His response still made her laugh. He'd answered by saying he needed to think about it, which really walloped her confidence. A few hours after Victoria asked him to move in, while she was stewing in confusion and he was supposedly considering her suggestion, he proposed with the engagement ring that had once belonged to

Victoria's late mother. Ned had asked Mr. Heslin for the marriage blessing weeks ago.

Ned answered her call right away, greeting her with the nickname her family used. "Hello, Tori. Long day?"

"Yes," she said, putting her phone on speaker and setting it on the desk. "I've still got some work to do. I'm flying to Charlotte early tomorrow morning."

"Charlotte? Oh. Are you going to reschedule the dinner with your family? That's tomorrow night."

"I'm only going to Charlotte for the day. What time is the dinner? Eight o'clock, right? I'll be back in time." As an introvert, she normally avoided dinners and parties whenever possible because they drained her energy. She had a lot of practice coming up with excuses to get out of social events. But this was her immediate family getting together. Her brother and his fiancée were arriving from Colorado and staying with Victoria's father for a few days. She loved them dearly and didn't get to see them often. She would definitely show up.

"They're calling Jerome's death a homicide now," Ned said. "I saw a television clip with a huge crowd outside his neighborhood. Then the camera focused on this gorgeous blonde woman. She was rushing to get into a car, blocking her face so no one could film her. Reporters were trying to get her to look their way. It had to be a huge movie star."

"Probably. I'm sure there are other celebrities in that neighborhood," Victoria said, flipping her laptop open.

Ned laughed. "I'm talking about you. You were the gorgeous blonde. It was a good five seconds of footage of you."

"Oh. Me? I can't imagine why anyone would consider my presence newsworthy, but whatever."

"I think you're newsworthy. I could watch you all day."

"Thanks," she laughed as she clicked to start a new file. "How were things at the clinic?"

"Busy. Bob had to leave early, didn't say why. I had to fit in the rest of his patients with my own."

Victoria loved the way Ned referred to his clients' animals as his patients. But she didn't like that Bob, the owner of the vet practice, kept leaving Ned to cover so many appointments. It seemed to happen more and more lately.

"There were no emergencies, so it worked out. But something is going on with him. He scheduled a meeting with me for next Friday after work. Which is odd. We always have quick exchanges throughout the day, so this must be...I don't know. Something important. I guess I'll find out on Friday."

"Hm...let me know. He's had to leave suddenly a few times this month, hasn't he? I hope he's okay." She also hoped he wasn't taking advantage of Ned.

A dog barked on Ned's end of the call. "That's Myrtle telling Oliver to get out of the way of the water bowl."

"So, what's next for you there?" Ned asked.

She could hear the smile in his voice. She wished she was home with him.

"What's next is that I have to type up some notes," she answered. "I'm doing it right now. Multi-tasking. Sorry."

"No need to. I'm proud of you, Victoria. And I also want to make sure you get some sleep. Focus on whatever you still have to do. I'll talk to you tomorrow?"

"Yes...wait. Did you arm the security system? The video cameras and the alarms for the doors...those should be on."

"I will."

"Good."

She felt better knowing the security system was on. Ned competed in triathlons. Muscles rippled through his lean body, and he could probably outrun almost anyone. But Todd and Jerome were also fit and strong and someone had murdered them in their own homes. That was enough to make Victoria want to protect those she loved the most. Better safe than sorry.

"I love you," he said. "Get some rest."

"I love you, too."

Victoria finished typing her notes, read them over, and then went to bed. She was asleep as soon as her head hit the pillow.

EXCERPT FROM JOURNAL ENTRY

I didn't intend to kill Todd, only to confront him. But the visit did not go as I planned. And now that he is gone, I feel better. Much better. I've come to realize that murdering them is the antidote to my pain.

10

Victoria arrived at the Charlotte Douglas International Airport at nine a.m. under a cloudless sky and walked into a confusing mess of temporary fencing, scaffolding, and construction work. It was early morning, but the people waiting around her looked exhausted. With the slew of recent flight delays and cancelations across the country, who knew how long they'd been traveling and what they'd been through to reach their final destinations. She felt grateful to have had a quick and uneventful flight.

A bus delivered her to the rental car area, where she picked up a Ford sedan that was a third the size of the Suburban she drove at home. There was nothing fancy about the rental, but she felt like a race car driver, low to the road and able to zip in and out of any available parking spot. She drove straight from the airport to the address of Ed and Sandra Eckstrom, Todd's parents, who were expecting her.

The Eckstroms lived on a beautiful street lined with enormous trees in an established neighborhood called Myers Park, near uptown Charlotte. Victoria parked in their driveway and walked a manicured path toward their stately home. The city's skyscrapers were visible to her left. To her right, a man with a wide-brimmed hat mowed the lawn, and another man edged the grass around a flowerbed.

Victoria rang the doorbell and waited. Todd had been gone for two months. His family would still be grieving. She hoped they would cooperate out of the desire to find their son's killer.

A woman in her late fifties with sad blue-gray eyes answered the door wearing slacks and a silk blouse, both with an elegant cut.

"Hi. I'm Victoria Heslin with the Federal Bureau of Investigation. I'm here about your son, Todd." Victoria lifted the identification card from around her neck. The woman's eyes went to the card, and inevitably, to Victoria's missing fingertips.

"I'm Sandra," the woman said, her gaze rising after a slight hesitation. "Please, come in. We're glad you're here."

Inside the lovely home, hardwood floors led from a foyer with an elaborate flower arrangement to a family room that also smelled of fresh-cut flowers. It was cool enough inside to warrant a sweater.

Todd's father, a tall, trim man with frameless glasses, introduced himself and extended his hand. "What can we get you?" he asked. "Sweet tea? Soda? Water? Something stronger?"

"Water would be great, thank you. I'm trying to drink more of it."

"Sparkling or flat?" Ed asked.

"Flat, thank you," she answered, taking a seat on the couch, setting her backpack down, and angling herself against two pillows to face Sandra.

At a bar across the room, Ed scooped ice cubes into a tall glass, got a bottle of water from the fridge under the marble counter, and poured it for Victoria. He poured himself a straight tumbler of brandy.

"Thank you," Victoria said again, accepting the cool glass and taking several sips. "First, allow me to tell you how sorry I am about what happened to your son."

"Thank you," Sandra said. "We still haven't come to terms with it. It's just..."

Her voice trailed off and her husband finished for her. "There's nothing more horrifying for a parent to experience than losing your child like this."

"I'm sorry," Victoria said, removing a notebook from her bag. She wasn't a parent herself, but she'd seen enough similar situations to fully understand their pain. "As I mentioned when we spoke yesterday, the FBI is working with the Boston and Charlotte Police Departments, assisting in the murder investigations of your son and Jerome Smith. We have access to all the case information, but I wanted to speak with you in person."

"We understand," Ed said. "And we appreciate your work. We'll do whatever it takes to find out who did this."

"As I mentioned earlier, we believe the cases are connected. With that in mind, do you have any ideas, any gut feelings about who might have killed Todd and his classmate?"

"None," Sandra said. "It's a mystery to us. An utter and tragic mystery. We're at a complete loss to understand why it happened or who could do such a thing to either of them."

Ed moved his glass in a small circular motion, swirling the remains of his brandy. "Maybe that's not quite true. Seeing who Jerome is. I can't say I'm as shocked about it as my own son's death."

Victoria remained quiet, hoping Ed would keep talking on his own and explain his comment. The silence didn't last long, before Ed continued with, "Being a celebrity, Jerome probably had a lot more people in and out of his life, is what I'm saying."

Victoria waited a few more seconds, but neither Ed nor Sandra said more on the subject. "Did you know Jerome well?" Victoria asked.

"We did," Ed replied. "Or we used to. We haven't seen him in prison...Oh, God," Ed exclaimed, his eyes opening wide. "I mean in person...we haven't seen him in person in...what...maybe ten years, Sandra?"

"That sounds right. He didn't come round much during college, and less after he joined the NBA. He was traveling. Sponsoring different products. But before his fame, he and Todd were friends."

"Close friends?"

"Yes. I'd say so," Sandra responded. "Todd always had a large group of friends, but Jerome was probably part of an inner circle of close ones. We took him with us to our beach house on Bald Head Island at least once when they were at Charlotte Academy. Remember that?" she asked her husband.

"They played pickup games on a tiny court for an entire day," Ed answered.

"Do you know when Todd and Jerome last saw each other?" Victoria asked.

"Only Todd could answer that for sure," Sandra said. "I don't remember Todd mentioning Jerome recently, but it's possible he saw him or kept in touch, and we just didn't know about it."

"Could you find out by looking at their phone records and their messages?" Ed suggested, his tone helpful rather than accusatory.

The killer had been careful with his crimes. Victoria didn't expect he'd called his victims from a traceable phone, but maybe if they searched back far enough, they'd find something. "The FBI is running their phone records through our systems, looking for connections," she answered.

"Good. Good." Ed drained his glass and set it down on a marble coaster.

"Can you think of anyone who would have had an issue with Jerome *and* your son?" Victoria asked, still hoping something important would suddenly occur to them.

Sandra shook her head. "The police asked us that question about our Todd a hundred different ways. Because of that message on his wall, they were sure he had hurt someone, emotionally or financially. He didn't. The homicide detectives thoroughly investigated Todd's past and present relationships, trying to sniff out his enemies. They didn't find anyone. Not a single person. Well, except for Jesse Glassman."

"Todd's classmate," Victoria said, referring to information from the murder case file. "Please tell me more about that situation."

"Jesse founded a company called InstaDX. He was developing a new medical diagnostic tool. He presented the opportunity to Todd and asked him to invest. Todd gave him quite a large sum, initially. In concept, it was a fine idea. But Jesse got ahead of himself before actually figuring out how to develop the product. He needed more money to continue and pay his developers. Todd imagined that happening over and over again. He thought Jesse would keep coming back for additional funding. Todd wanted to cut his own losses. He backed out."

"And Jesse was upset?"

"Yes. He'd put everything into the company and didn't want his dream to fall apart. He practically begged Todd for more money and other referrals. But Todd passed, and Jesse was angry. He got belligerent about the whole thing. Because of that, he became a prime suspect. But the police found nothing they could pin on him other than resentment."

The word *resentment* piqued Victoria's interest, as it had that of the Charlotte police department.

"Why was Todd selling his condo?" Victoria asked.

"He'd had enough of living in the heart of the city. The hassle that went along with it. Parking. The traffic. He lived near the stadium and every game day was a madhouse down there. He planned to sell his condo and move in with us for a few months while he looked for a house." Ed took his wife's hand and squeezed it.

"What about romantic relationships?" Victoria asked. "Did he have any?"

Sandra answered, "Todd was in a long-term relationship until a few months before he died. But Laura broke up with him, not the other way around. And not because of anything Todd had or hadn't done. He didn't cheat on her or anything like that. I know that's what some people probably thought later. There was a lot of speculation. But that's all it was. They were still friends. They had just...drifted apart in other ways. His death devastated Laura. She certainly didn't hurt him. And if you think Todd's murder is linked to Jerome's, well, Laura and Todd met in Charlotte long after college, so she wouldn't have known Jerome. She probably never even met him."

"The Charlotte Police Department seemed to have focused their investigation on recent interactions and relationships. What about going all the way back to high school?" Victoria asked.

Sandra tilted her head to one side, thinking. "There was one girl that both Todd and Jerome dated in high school. Bridget Arnold."

Victoria jotted down the name. "From what I've read about Todd and Jerome, they were popular in school. Did they ever bully anyone? Perhaps unintentionally, part of athletic hazing or something similar?"

"Oh, no," Sandra said instantly, before adding, "Not that I'm aware of. They were nice boys who turned into good men."

That's what both murder investigations indicated so far. Todd and Jerome were well liked. But someone out there seemed to disagree.

11

Twelve years ago – Jerome

The Jeep careened around the twisty mountain road. Next to Todd, in the passenger seat, Jerome gripped the door and let loose a nervous laugh. Without giving it much thought, he'd agreed to spend the long weekend with Todd.

"You get back from your SAT tutoring in time to see the end of the game last night?" he asked, to get his mind off the semi-nauseated feeling that came from the winding roads.

"Yeah," Todd answered. "Can't believe the Knicks won. That foul on Robertson was a horrible call. They didn't deserve the win."

"I know. They got ripped," Jerome said, taking in the country landscape. A dilapidated house sat oddly close to the edge of the road, though acres of land surrounded the structure. The next house was a sprawling estate on a hill set off by white horse fencing, followed by more crumbling homes with garbage piled on the porches and lawn. A quarter mile down the road, a giant metal sculpture of Bigfoot lurked alongside the front of a rustic cabin.

"Bigfoot could out dunk Robertson any day," Jerome said.

"Yeah. He'd make a good center. Be a real physical player. But he might not have the quickness," Todd answered. "Maybe we'll find a Bigfoot out here, bring him home and get him on our team. Work him through Coach P's drills."

"I call being his agent," Jerome said, staring out at a small house with a dozen or more rusting tractors spread around the front yard. "Hey, look at that. That would not fly in my neighborhood."

"You know anyone who owns a tractor in your neighborhood, dude? Anything goes along these roads. You've never been out here before?"

"Never."

"City boy," Todd said with a grin.

"This place where your grandparents live—is it a bunch of little cabins? You know, like a campground?" he asked, simply curious and not really caring if it was. "Or a country club golf course type place?" Where most everyone would be white.

"It's in between what you said. Most of the cabins are nice."

The roads narrowed and Jerome cringed again as Todd's Jeep hurtled around a hairpin turn. He looked down at his phone and saw the bars were gone. "I don't have cell service. Are we off grid out here?"

"Not really, but sort of. Cell reception is garbage out here. And it barely works where my grandparents live. Their cabin has satellite Internet. It sucks for gaming, but we can stream movies."

"What are we going to do there?" Jerome asked, wishing he'd asked more questions before agreeing to the weekend. It wasn't sounding so great.

"We're going to hang out. There's a hoops court. Clubhouse has a pool table. Hopefully, there will be a few hotties. If not, I've got a case in the back and my grandfather has a good liquor cabinet. We can put on our beer goggles."

"You can beer goggle all you want, man, but I'm not doing that. I've got a reputation to uphold." Jerome laughed. "Will your grandparents care if we drink?"

"Nah," Todd said as they rounded another blind corner. "They'll be fine if it's just beer and we don't act like idiots."

"You don't have to worry about me...only yourself." Jerome kept watch on the steep drop-off to his right. One slip of the tires and they'd be plummeting a long way down to certain death. That's about when he decided he wasn't too thrilled about being in the mountains. "You might want to slow down, huh?" he said.

Todd laughed without letting up on the gas. "Relax, bro. I've got this. I love driving these roads. Anyway, we're really close now. You know, my grandfather is excited that you're coming. He's a fan of yours."

"He's seen us play?"

"Yeah. He's seen a lot of games. He thinks you're going to be in the NBA someday."

"Gotta see how college ball goes first."

Minutes later, Todd took a left into the community and stopped before a single arm safety gate blocking the road. He coasted to a stop beside a gatehouse with a red metal roof. A man stepped out wearing a flannel shirt and brown pants, holding a clipboard. His age fell somewhere between Jerome and his parents. Maybe mid-thirties. He walked to the driver's side of the Jeep. His nametag said Crawford. Instead of speaking, he coughed and didn't bother to cover his mouth, though he turned his head to the side. His skin seemed an off shade of sickly gray.

"Can I help you, boys?" Crawford finally said, looking straight past Todd toward Jerome. He was sort of staring, yet not making eye contact. No hint of a friendly smile.

"How's it going?" Todd asked. "We're visiting my grandparents. The Eckstroms."

"Yeah. I know them. Done some repair work at their house." Crawford looked down at his clipboard, drew a line with his pen, and coughed some more. "Big anniversary weekend here. Lots going on. Don't cause any problems, you know what I mean?"

"No. What do you mean, exactly?" Todd asked, challenging the man.

"No throwing chairs in the lake. No tossing beer cans off Stone Ridge."

"Ah, got it," Todd said, with a good-natured laugh. "We'll just cross those activities right off our list. Thanks for the welcome, dude. Take care of that cough."

With one last stare in Jerome's direction, Crawford smacked his clipboard on the roof of Todd's Jeep and then backed away. A few seconds later, the gate arm opened upward with a clinking noise.

"So strange, that guy," Todd said as he drove through. "Lives here year-round. I don't think he gets away from this place much. Or ever. He's the resident handyman, too. But listen, I probably should have warned you about something."

The seed of discomfort already sprouting inside Jerome seemed to blossom then. "What should you have warned me about?"

"My grandparents grew up in the south, so you know, just don't let anything they say get to you, okay? I mean, I don't know that they'll be weird about anything, but just in case. We're not gonna change the way they see things. They're too old for that."

"Yeah, sure. Don't worry about it. I'll be cool. Thanks for the heads up, though," Jerome said, regretting that he'd agreed to the trip. If he was reading the situation correctly, he might have to deal with some old people's ignorant comments. Not his idea of a fun weekend.

A carved sign at the start of the driveway welcomed them to *The Eagle's Nest*.

Without knocking, Todd walked into the log cabin with huge windows. His duffel bag with the beer clunked hard on the shiny wood planks when he dropped it in the entry.

The couple who greeted them didn't look old at all, except for the silver streaks along Todd's grandfather's temple. Todd's grandmother had blonde hair and wore pearls with a matching cardigan sweater and shirt.

Todd hugged his grandparents one at a time, then pulled back. "Grandma and Grandpa, this is my friend Jerome. I don't think you've met yet."

Jerome wasn't sure what he was supposed to call them—Mr. and Mrs. Eckstrom?—or if he was supposed to hug them like Todd had. Lucky for him, Mr. Eckstrom stepped forward and gave Jerome a pat on the back and the grandmother smiled as if she were delighted to see them but clasped her hands in front of her chest to show they'd finished hugging.

"Glad you two could come," Todd's grandfather said. "I know you boys must have lots to do at home in Charlotte. Lots of friends. Girlfriends."

"Nah, no girlfriends," Todd said as Jerome answered, "Thanks for having me."

"So, son," Mr. Eckstrom said, focusing on Jerome. "You're even taller close up, aren't you? I hear you have offers from Duke and North Carolina and Kansas. All the big ones."

"Yes, sir."

"What are you thinking?"

"I'm still deciding, sir."

"And your father is an attorney?" Todd's grandma asked. "Is that right? Did I hear that right?"

"Yes, ma'am. My father and mother are both attorneys," Jerome answered at the same time Todd said, "I told you that, Grandma. You know they are."

"Really? How about that?" Mrs. Eckstrom touched her fingers to her chin and turned to her husband. "Isn't that something, dear? Both his parents are attorneys."

Something about her tone made the skin on Jerome's neck prickle. Was she seriously surprised to discover he wasn't at Charlotte Academy on a sports scholarship and his parents could afford to send him there? Or did she think only white people went to law school? Either way, it was the kind of stupidity he wished other people would keep inside their own heads, so he didn't have to know how messed up their thinking was. He took a deep breath to hide his irritation, just in time for what came next.

"Can you swim, Jerome?" Mrs. Eckstrom asked. "Because if you can't, there's a lifeguard at the pool during the day, so it's a good chance to learn."

As Jerome carefully chose his response, Todd blurted, "Oh, my God, Grandma. Do you get that he's one of the top athletes in the state? He doesn't need a swimming lesson."

Jerome offered a weak smile. The best he could do when all he wanted at that point was to bolt out the door and drive the twisty roads back to the highway and Charlotte.

Todd grabbed his bag off the floor. "We're going upstairs. I'll show Jerome where we're staying."

Carrying his suitcase, Jerome followed Todd through the large cabin. Solid beams crossed the soaring ceilings, and the wood gleamed everywhere. All the furniture looked rustic, and the art had a mountain theme—elk, bears, foxes.

They were halfway up the stairs when Todd turned to Jerome and said, "You *can* swim, can't you?"

"Yeah, dude. I can swim." Jerome punched Todd's arm hard. "You've been in my pool with me at my house before."

"Oh, yeah. Right," Todd said. "Duh. Forgot you have a pool."

Jerome let the offenses roll off him. If he didn't, his soul might grow heavy with the weight of other people's problems. He didn't want that. What he needed was a positive, forward-thinking focus. And besides, Todd wasn't anything like his grandparents. Never once had he said anything that made Jerome cringe. At least not with Jerome around. As more basketball-induced hype came his way, the media coverage and the big college offers, it got harder to tell who liked him for who he was, regardless of his basketball skills. Todd was a friend he could trust. And Todd's life wasn't perfect, though it may have seemed that way to others. Todd had his own problems. He didn't think anyone knew about them. But Jerome knew.

12

Victoria sat in an office chair with her jacket draped over her lap, facing Hugh Lambert, the lead homicide detective on Todd Eckstrom's case. In his charcoal gray suit and black tie, Hugh Lambert was less-than-average in height, with a compact, tightly muscled frame, glossy black hair, and a neatly trimmed goatee.

"I was one of the first to enter Eckstrom's condo after a realtor found him," Lambert said, taking a seat and lifting one leg to rest his ankle atop his knee. "We had a team on the case at first, then it was just me and two others. Now that we've got a second murder, I have more resources. When Suarez from the Boston PD called us about Jerome's death, it changed the entire trajectory of our investigation. I started screening for incidents involving other alumni of Charlotte Academy and other Charlotte basketball players."

"That's exactly what I would have done. And did you find anything?" Victoria asked, though she was eager to share something that her FBI colleague, Sam, had just discovered.

"Not with that angle, not yet."

"My colleagues on the Atonement Killer Taskforce just uncovered a link that's going to make you want to take another look at one of your primary suspects from before. Jesse Grassman. The founder of InstaDx."

"Right," Lambert said. "He's in Seattle, but we interviewed him several times. He had a solid alibi for the time of Todd's murder. He was across the country."

"Well, we just learned Grassman also solicited investments from Jerome, as well as Todd, as you know. We have a trail of messages to prove it."

"When did that happen?"

"I got word literally before I walked into your office," Victoria answered.

"Good work. Did Jerome invest in Grassman's company?"

"No. Grassman and Jerome spoke over the phone. Jerome heard the spiel, said he wasn't interested. Grassman didn't stop there. He followed up with additional calls and emails, sent more information. All those pitches went unanswered."

"That could make a guy pretty angry," Lambert said. "Especially if that guy is desperate for a break, and he knows how much extra money Jerome has sitting around, just piling up. Todd was doing very well for himself, too. They had what Grassman needed. But like I said, Grassman was in Seattle when Todd was murdered. And InstaDx is on the verge of bankruptcy. Not sure Grassman could have paid anyone to do the hits for him even if he wanted to. Did you already share all of this with the team working Jerome's case in Boston?"

"I will. Haven't had a chance yet."

Lambert glanced down at the paperwork on his desk. "When I talked to the Boston PD this morning, they were narrowing in on Jerome's former agent. Rick Haskin. That's what Suarez and I discussed."

"Haskin was one of the last people to leave Jerome's house," Victoria answered, recalling the information Officer Missy Blake provided when they were in Suarez's tiny office.

"Yeah, there's that. Last on the murder scene. But that's not all. A video just surfaced. It's from when Haskin found out Jerome was switching agents. Someone posted it online. It's since gone viral."

Victoria turned her phone over in her hands. "I haven't seen it yet."

"You need to. Go ahead. Take a look." Lambert dipped his head and nodded toward the phone in her hand.

Victoria typed her passcode, and then *Rick Haskin, Jerome Smith, video* in her Internet browser. She had multiple links from which to choose. She selected a video clip NBC News had posted two hours ago and pressed play. The video began with an enthusiastic male reporter sitting behind a studio's desk.

We've just been handed breaking news in the Jerome Smith murder case. The Celtics player's former agent, Rick Haskin, is being held for questioning after police discovered he was at Smith's home on the night of his death. Sources tell us there was bad blood between the sports agent and Smith that started after Smith ended his contract with Haskin and signed with another agent, despite Haskin getting several multi-million-dollar endorsements for the basketball star. Whether Haskin was angry enough to murder the NBA player remains to be seen. But the video speaks for itself. Here it is.*

The video switched to a clip of a white man in his forties. Rick Haskin. Hair disheveled and face twisted into an ugly snarl, he shook a fist and yelled. "That ungrateful son of a—. Karma is a bitch, Jerome, and it's coming for you." The way he slurred his words made clear he'd been drinking. This probably wasn't video footage Rick had intended to share with the public. His focus was toward the side of the camera, suggesting he didn't know someone was filming him.

Victoria looked up from watching the video. "Do you know why Jerome changed agents?"

"He went with a friend of his. He'd always promised to switch to his friend once the guy got more experience. Made no secrets about it. And Rick knew that. But that didn't stop him from being angry. He'd done a good job and thought he deserved to keep doing it. Can't say I blame him...for being so angry, I mean. Losing Jerome meant a major hit to Haskin's income."

"Do we know yet if Rick knew Todd Eckstrom?"

"Says he doesn't. Says they never met. We're trying to find evidence to the contrary."

At least they had suspects now. That was good. But until they had conclusive evidence against one of them, Victoria would keep digging. She thought through the notes she'd read in Lambert's files. "Your case information didn't mention anything was missing from Todd's condo. Is that still correct?"

"Nothing the family was aware of. Except, one odd thing was that he didn't have a toothbrush in his house." Lambert let his shoulders rise and fall. "The place was spotless. Maybe the perp used it to clean something from the tiles or grout—I know my wife does that—then took it with him."

"Perhaps," Victoria said, because at this point, almost anything was possible.

As she drove south from uptown Charlotte toward the suburbs, her phone paired to the Ford's speaker system, Victoria told Suarez about Todd Eckstrom's missing toothbrush, what the FBI had learned about Jesse Grassman, and Detective Lambert's doubts that Grassman was the killer. "And I just watched that video of Rick Haskin. You're building a case against him?"

"We are," Suarez answered. "Ever since that video went viral, information on Haskin has been pouring in. A woman who left the party with him changed the story she told us previously. Now she says Haskin was acting strange when they left Jerome's house. The rest of the group went to an after party, but Haskin said he had to take care of something. He took off for a while by himself and then he joined them again later."

"Is it true? Did you find out where he was?"

"He says he left the others to meet with a local dealer. He bought a few things to keep his friends feeling good through the night. When you're a prime murder suspect, you aren't real worried about getting busted for buying drugs, so he had no problem telling us that. We're trying to confirm it, but we haven't located the dealer yet."

"The video of him threatening Jerome—when was it recorded?"

"Right after Jerome switched agents. It's almost a year old."

"That's long enough time for resentment to build into something explosive, if Haskin was the type to hold a grudge," Victoria said. "Nothing on earth consumes a man more completely than the passion of resentment. That's a Nietzsche quote. But if there was so much bad blood between them, what was Haskin doing at Jerome's party?"

"According to Haskin, he'd forgiven Jerome, and they were repairing their friendship. He says there wasn't anything between them, and that video was one drunken rant on a super bad day. We've got to keep investigating him, mapping every step of his life between the fallout and the party, but I don't think he's our guy. And as far as we can tell, he doesn't even know Eckstrom. Unfortunately for

Rick, that video and his presence at the party convinced most of the public he's guilty."

"Only because they don't know what they don't know," Victoria said. "They don't know yet, at least." Anyone who disclosed information about the case would lose their jobs. But payments offered for information about the celebrity's death might exceed a law enforcement worker's annual wages, so there was a strong possibility the facts would leak out before the investigation uncovered the killer. So far, anyway, the facts remained under wraps, which left Haskin looking like a prime suspect in the public's view.

"Maybe you should provide some protection for him?" Victoria said.

"We have him in protective custody already. Don't need a vigilante killing on our hands," Suarez said. "You still with the Charlotte police?"

"No. I'm driving to Jerome's family's house. Where he grew up in Charlotte."

"If you're planning to talk to them, they aren't there. They're here in Boston, handling things. They flew up on the Celtics owner's private jet."

"I know," Victoria said, flicking her blinker on for a right turn. "I just want to see where Jerome lived while I'm here. I'm digging around in their pasts."

A rush of conversation came from people talking on Suarez's end of the call. "I have to go," the detective said. "But good luck with that, the digging around business. And let me know if you uncover something."

Victoria rolled her car window down and studied the memorial rising from the Smiths' front yard. A vibrant mound of flower bouquets, basketballs, jerseys, and stuffed animals. Hand-written signs proclaimed *Jerome is My Hero* and *Justice for Jerome.*

A beat-up Toyota pulled to the curb in front of her. A boy, elementary-school aged, climbed out from the passenger side and trudged over to the edge of the pile. He dropped to his knees and placed another jersey on the ground. He stayed there, his lips moving, his head hung low.

People all over the country loved and admired Jerome. They wanted answers. They wanted justice.

Victoria pressed her teeth gently against her bottom lip as she continued to watch the grieving child. Suarez didn't seem to think Rick Haskin was their guy. He didn't know the first victim. And Detective Lambert didn't think Grassman was the killer. Which left Victoria with more work to do in Charlotte.

What had the victims done to fuel such powerful vengeance? Could their Charlotte Academy classmates have the answer? Victoria hoped Bridget Arnold, the girl both victims had dated, might know something.

13

Bridget Arnold, who attended high school with Todd and Jerome, worked at a middle school located in a part of the city a few miles from the airport. Victoria pulled into a visitor parking spot and walked on a cracked cement sidewalk toward the one-story, red-brick building. Construction paper cut outs decorated the windows. They looked like snowflakes, though it was almost spring, and snow rarely fell in Charlotte.

A bell rang on an intercom as Victoria entered the office and waited for the woman working at the front desk to get off the phone. Victoria showed her identification, said she needed to speak with Ms. Arnold, then waited for her in a small conference room next to the principal's office.

Bridget arrived wearing a flowery wraparound dress with a red cardigan. Her skin had a healthy glow. Her dark hair was long and shining. The quick, uncertain smile she gave Victoria showed concern and warmth. Her students probably loved her.

"Thank you for meeting me," Victoria said. "I'm sorry I had to pull you from your classroom."

"It's okay. They'll be fine for a while. One of the other teachers is with them. You have questions about Todd and Jerome?"

"Yes. Their deaths might be related, though I can't get more specific than that right now."

"Oh." Bridget pulled her cardigan around her body and shifted back in her chair. "I still can't believe they're no longer with us."

"When was the last time you saw Jerome?" Victoria asked.

"Oh...it feels like I've seen him recently because I see him on television and hear about him so often. But in person...maybe six or seven years ago."

"You never visited him in Boston?"

"No. We're friendly, but it's not like he would invite me for a visit. I'm sure if I'd asked him, or said I was in town, he'd have me over. I think he would. But I've never been to Boston."

"Did any of your classmates visit him there...to your knowledge?"

"I wouldn't know. I'm sorry. His teammates were probably his closest friends. You could ask them."

Victoria nodded. Detective Lambert was already doing that.

"What can you tell me about enemies Todd and Jerome had? Mutual enemies."

Bridget raised her dark brows. "Enemies? I can't say much about that. Nothing, really. We've all been thinking about this, you know. Friends from high school. Todd's death and his funeral brought so many of us together again, talking about it, trying to figure out who could do that to him. And we just don't know."

"Were Todd and Jerome well-liked?"

"Oh, gosh, yes. Back in high school and now. Here's an example for you. We have an annual fundraiser here at my school. The money goes toward facility improvements and supplies—things every school should already have. We auction donated items. Each year, I send Jerome an email and ask him to contribute. He was always so generous. He sent autographed basketballs and jerseys and photos. Those are like gold to these kids. You wouldn't believe the amount of money parents will pay for them. Even parents who really don't have that kind of money to spend."

"That was kind of Jerome."

"It was." Bridget smiled and looked down at her hands for a few seconds. "Anyway, I made the mistake of gushing about his generosity to friends from high school, and then so many of our classmates started asking him for donations and gifts. Not for charity events, but to give to their friends and family members. Maybe to sell online. I mean, can you imagine what that was like for him? People asking for signatures and donations nonstop?"

"He probably had someone who handled that for him."

"Oh...I didn't think of that. I suppose you're right." Little lines crinkled on Bridget's brow. She lifted her hands from her lap and set them on the table. She had short, manicured nails and a simple silver ring. "But still...If anyone tells you that Jerome's head got big with his fame, it's probably because they didn't know him well before."

"Are you talking about anyone in particular?" Victoria asked, thinking of Jesse Grassman and wondering if he knew Jerome had been generous with so many others.

"No. I'm not thinking of any one person. It just seems as if everyone around here wanted a piece of him. He had to protect himself, you know? Put up a bit of a barrier. But with his real friends, he didn't forget us when he got famous."

"And Todd?"

"He was a good guy, too. I saw him out a few times at breweries in South End. Though he never drank much in high school, at least not senior year. I mean, he might have one beer, but compared to the other guys, not much at all. He was different in that way, and it definitely set him apart. Never got drunk or crazy at parties. Oh, and I saw him at a friend's wedding last summer. We haven't hung out much since high school, but it was always nice to see him."

"And neither you nor your friends from high school can think of anything Todd or Jerome did back then that might have come back to haunt them?"

Bridget looked to her left out the square window, one of the few that didn't have pieces of colorful art taped to the glass. Victoria kept quiet, letting Bridget think. After a few seconds, the young teacher swung her gaze back to Victoria and said, "Actually, there is something. Todd lost his license before his senior year. No one ever knew why. We figured it had something to do with drinking, maybe a DUI. And maybe that's why he didn't drink much after that. But Todd refused to talk about it. And somehow, Jerome knew the reason. I remember people really bugging him to spill the secret. But he never told anyone else. Jerome was a good friend."

Suddenly Bridget was crying. Tears rolled down her face. Her shoulders rose and fell gently with her sobs. She got up from the table and pulled a tissue from a box in the corner. Facing the wall, she blew her nose. "I'm sorry," she said, pulling a second tissue from the box and dabbing under her eyes. "We're all just so shocked and sad. And worried."

"Why are you worried?"

"Because, since no one knows why they died, everyone is wondering if one of us will be next. Especially the basketball team members."

"Why would they think someone else is next?"

"Because it already happened twice. Someone murdered Todd and then Jerome, and the police don't know who did it or why. And I guess the FBI doesn't know either or you wouldn't be here asking me questions. Todd and Jerome hadn't really hung out together since high school. What else do they have in common except basketball and Charlotte Academy? That's why some of us think that any of us might be next."

Victoria couldn't fault the logic, and she'd actually thought along those same lines.

"Do you have any good leads?" Bridget asked. "Do you think you'll find out who killed them and why?"

"That's why I'm here. There are a lot of other investigators working many angles as we speak. We'll find out who did this," Victoria said with complete confidence.

"But...do you think whoever killed them is done...or will there be more?"

Victoria did not have a definitive answer. She could only hope Jerome's death was the killer's last. "We have no evidence the killer has targeted anyone else," she said. And that was the truth.

14

Victoria had covered a lot of territory in Charlotte in less than a full day, but hadn't learned anything groundbreaking. She made it back to the Charlotte airport, went through security with her badge and firearm, and still had forty minutes before boarding. More than enough time to grab a coffee. A quick check of the airport map showed a Starbucks in every terminal. At the one closest to her gate, she scanned the menu for something new and sweet, though the chances of her trying something different were slim. She always ordered the same drink for weeks or months in a row before making a switch.

With a flavored latte in hand, she sat down near her gate. The first taste of her drink was marvelous. It was always that way, and she didn't want to spoil it. After a few more sips, when the initial rush of pleasure wore off, she got back to business and checked email messages on her phone. The first one she opened was from American Airlines. Flight delay. Her plane would leave an hour later than expected.

The gate attendant confirmed the message with an announcement. "Attention all passengers for Flight 899 to Dulles. Our plane is undergoing a maintenance check. As soon as that's complete, we'll begin the boarding process. We expect to leave an hour later than our originally scheduled departure time."

Better safe than sorry. One plane crash, the one Victoria had miraculously survived, was enough for her lifetime. The timing would be tight, but she could still get home, change her clothes, and head back out with Ned to meet her family for dinner.

After finishing her latte and making progress reading through her work emails, she got up to get a snack. Waiting in line to pay for an apple and a water bottle, a magazine titled *Bride* was tucked in the rack at eye-level. She picked it up and flipped through the pages. One of the first articles made her eyes roll.

Every woman has dreamed about her wedding day since she was a little girl. Make it the perfect day.

Victoria had not dreamed about her wedding day since she was a girl. Not even since her recent engagement. She had no preconceived notions about the day. She'd recently attended a wedding, which hadn't gone well considering the groom didn't show up, and her brother's wedding was coming soon. But she still didn't know what she expected from her own wedding day. Everyone needed to show up, that was for certain, but beyond that, she didn't want a colossal event with a lot of fuss. The simpler the better.

Planning a wedding would have been different if her mother were alive. Abigail Heslin would have planned a beautiful wedding without going overboard, respecting Victoria's need for privacy and her discomfort at being the center of attention for any longer than necessary.

Victoria slid the *Bride* magazine back into its spot, paid for her items, and returned to the seating area near her gate. She did a Google search for *wedding ideas*. She clicked on an outdoor image of a bride and groom with mountains in the background. That took her to another site full of wedding photographs. She scrolled through, trying to focus on pictures she liked and figure out why she liked them.

A notification popped up on her phone screen. Another message from the airline. A second delay. The man seated next to her grumbled before getting up and marching toward the gate attendant. At the attendant's desk, a different man spun around and stormed away. Victoria caught his gaze.

"They said it's a staffing issue now," the man said. "They're waiting on a pilot."

Disappointed, Victoria recalculated the time required to get from the D.C. airport to the restaurant where she was supposed to meet her family. If she went straight there and didn't go home first, she might still make the dinner. Some of it anyway. She called Ned and told him she'd meet him at the restaurant.

"Bob left the clinic early again. He didn't tell me why. I have two more appointments of my own and three of his to cover. As soon as I finish up here, I'll go back to your place—"

"Our place."

"What?" Ned seemed to skip a beat, and then his tone was less rushed and more charming. "Right. I'll go back to our place and feed *our* dogs. But I'll be at the restaurant at eight and we'll see you when you get there."

"Please tell them I'm sorry."

"I will. Don't worry. Be safe. I love you."

Her phone rang immediately after talking to Ned. Detective Suarez was calling back. "Hey. Jerome's autopsy and toxicology results are in," Suarez said. "I sent them to you. Can you talk a minute?"

"Yes. I've got plenty of time now," Victoria answered, sliding her PC out of her bag. She heard a constant flow of noise and chatter coming from Suarez's end of the call and pictured the busy task force room at Boston Police Headquarters.

"The medical examiner confirmed asphyxiation as the COD," Suarez told her. "The killer smothered Jerome with a pillow. His DNA and saliva were on the pillowcase. He had ketamine in his system. He was likely unconscious before he died."

Not surprising.

"A small patch of hair was missing. Smaller than a dime. Pulled right from his scalp. Same location as Todd Eckstrom. Above his right temple."

Interesting. And very significant. But why?

"And one other thing. Cara Goodwin, Jerome's girlfriend, got back from Italy and did a walk-through of Jerome's house with one of our officers."

"Did she say anything was stolen?"

"There's a locked safe in his massive closet. Not an unbreakable one. It's still intact. Nothing was taken from there. But Jerome usually wore a gold NCAA championship ring. It wasn't on him when forensics arrived, and Ms. Goodwin couldn't find it anywhere in his house. It's gone."

The ring was engraved and easily traced back to its owner. Not an easy item to sell, even on the black market. It represented something important to Jerome. For that reason, the killer might have taken it.

"Did you ask Cara to check for Jerome's toothbrush?"

"Yes. That was good info you passed us from Detective Lambert. There might be something to it. Jerome's electric toothbrush wasn't in his bathroom. Cara says he could have tossed it after she left for Italy. He went through toothbrushes often, liked to switch them up every few weeks, but usually he just switched out the heads. And the toothbrush wasn't in the trash picked up by the cleaning crew. So basically, his toothbrush is also missing. Not sure what that's about or if it's relevant, but…"

"We'll find out if it is," Victoria finished.

15

Victoria hurried inside the cozy restaurant, one of her father's favorites. The maître d' led her toward a back corner where her father spotted her first. He stopped talking mid-sentence and waved. Soon everyone at the table was smiling in her direction.

Victoria made her way past other tables to join her family. Ned was incredibly handsome in a dark sports coat, and Minka, who would soon be Victoria's sister-in-law, looked gorgeous in a black dress.

"Glad you could make it, Tori," her father said.

"Sorry I'm so late." She put her hands on Ned's shoulders and bent down to give him a quick kiss. A salad with blackened salmon graced the place setting beside him.

"Only an hour and then some," Alex said, grinning. Her brother got up, wrapped his arms around her, and pulled her into a bear hug. She laughed as he crushed her against his chest, something he did whenever they hadn't seen each other for a few months.

Victoria welcomed his embrace. In her arms, he felt well-toned with powerful muscles. Not surprising for a man who spent most of his days outdoors on the Colorado slopes. His face was tanned from his work as a ski instructor, paramedic, and a member of an elite avalanche patrol rescue team.

He let her go, took her hands in his own, and stared at her fingers. "Last time I saw you, you still had bandages. And you didn't have mom's ring. Looks good on you. She'd love that you're wearing it now."

Victoria wiggled her fingers around, focusing on her ring. Light from the chandelier above glinted off the stone.

Minka got up from her chair. Standing next to Alex, her fair skin was several shades lighter. A busy attorney, Minka spent most of her time indoors.

"Congratulations on your engagement," Minka said as the women hugged. When they moved apart, Minka's gaze dropped to Victoria's hand. "It is beautiful."

"Thank you," Victoria answered, smiling back and taking her seat.

"Hope you don't mind we've finished eating," her father said. "But Ned ordered for you, if you're hungry."

"Yes. I'm famished, so excuse me while I devour this. It looks great. Perfect. Thanks, Ned." She picked up her fork and knife and got started on the salad.

A server came by and asked if they wanted anything else. Victoria asked for bread. Alex ordered a cocktail, Minka a coffee, and Ned and her father ordered slices of chocolate pie.

"We heard you're working on the Jerome Smith case," Alex said. "Wow! Really, that's got to be something. We were talking about it before you got here. Do you think his former agent is the guy?"

Victoria shook her head. "I really can't talk about the case. Sorry."

"Right. Of course. So why were you in Charlotte?"

"I was looking into another homicide with some similarities," Victoria told them. That was about all she could share. She resumed eating, hoping everyone would take the hint that she wasn't going into details. Fortunately, they did.

"Have you chosen a day for your wedding yet?" Minka asked. "And I'm sorry if everyone is asking you, but I wanted to set the date aside on our schedules, and Alex wasn't sure."

Finished with her meal, Victoria crossed her utensils over her salad plate and shook her head. "Not yet."

"We have to get going on that, I guess," Ned said, slipping Victoria's hand into his and resting them on the table space between them.

"Do you have some place special in mind?" Minka asked.

Ned and Victoria looked at each other. They broke into smiles. Neither had an answer.

"Looks like you've really given it some thought," Alex joked. "You should hire someone and tell them what you want or it's never going to happen."

"That's a good idea," her father said. "I can find out who Brett Hamilton and his wife hired for Sofie's wedding. That was nice. And I can make some calls to help you get in somewhere."

Alex snorted. "Yeah, I don't think Victoria and Sofie have a lot in common, Dad. Sofie's a huge snob. Her wedding was probably as show-offy as it gets. Not the same taste at all. If I'm wrong, Victoria, say so."

Victoria looked over at Ned and smiled. "We still have to talk about it. And maybe your mother would like to be involved?"

"I'm sure she would if you want her to," Ned answered.

Victoria didn't know Ned's family well yet. But her father had gotten to know them when Skyline Flight 745 was missing for days. They'd bonded over their shared fears.

Mr. Heslin settled back in his chair, commanding their attention with his gaze. "I'm grateful our family is growing. If Abigail were alive, I know she'd be thrilled." He smiled at Minka and Ned.

"Thank you," Minka said, beaming, followed by Ned commenting, "It's an honor."

Victoria squeezed Ned's hand.

"Why don't you tell the rest of us what you two have planned for your big day," Victoria said, grinning at Minka and Alex. "I want to hear all about it. Maybe we'll just copy everything you do."

She happily listened to her brother's wedding plans for the next fifteen minutes or so. At one point, she was embarrassed to find herself yawning. She covered her mouth with her napkin and hoped no one would notice. She wasn't bored, but the last few long days of work and travel had finally caught up with her.

Outside the restaurant, when they said their goodbyes, Alex took her aside.

"Dad couldn't be happier about both of us settling down, huh?"

"I know. Well, we both got lucky. Minka's great, Alex."

"Ned's a good guy, too. Perfect for you and your crazy dog obsession. But it seems as if you and he are both working long hours. Life goes by fast...you know the saying. You've stopped enough crimes or criminals already, haven't you?"

"What's that supposed to mean?"

Alex shrugged. "I guess I'm saying you should try slowing down and enjoying life a little more."

She knew his words stemmed from brotherly love and concern. "I do enjoy my life," she told him.

"I think Dad feels a little responsible for your career choice. If Mom hadn't been abducted, if he hadn't left her alone at the house when we were at the lake back then, you'd have a nice, safe job somewhere."

This surprised Victoria. She'd never thought about it before. "Did Dad say something to you?" She'd been so careful to shield her father from learning about the perils she'd faced in previous investigations, precisely so he wouldn't worry.

"I just know he adores you and he worries."

"Then what about you? Your job isn't exactly what I'd call safe, Alex. Dropping into an avalanche zone and trying to dig people out without getting yourself buried in the process. Heading out during the worst blizzards to search for people stranded in the mountains. You couldn't even buy life insurance if you tried. That's how dangerous your job is." Victoria wasn't upset, but she wanted to make sure Alex saw the irony of his advice.

"Right. But...it's different."

"How is it different? I try to help people. So do you."

"Okay. Okay. Look, you know how proud I am of you. I only mentioned this because I love you. We all do. Someday you'll be saving the world's mistreated animals full-time. We all know it. Maybe a few trips to the White House and Congress. You are somewhat of a celebrity, you know." He gave her an affectionate sideways squeeze. "Anyway, you've obviously got a lot going on in your life. Hire someone to do the wedding planning since it's not your thing. But definitely have one. We want to be there to celebrate with you and show our support. I'll be a married man by then and I'll get to flaunt my incredible, accomplished and amazing wife to all your friends who didn't want to date me when we were younger."

"That's why you want me to have a wedding?"

"One of the reasons."

Victoria laughed. "I love you, Alex. It's really great to see you."

Alex gave her another chest-crushing hug before leaving with her father and Minka.

On her way home from the restaurant, driving in separate cars but following not far behind Ned's 4-Runner, Victoria thought about what her brother had said.

Ned was working more and more hours at the veterinary clinic. It was a busy practice and only about twenty minutes from her house. He loved it there. Victoria's schedule was consistently unpredictable and often took her away from home. As a self-professed homebody that should have been a problem. But it wasn't. She loved her job and the autonomy that usually came with it. As long as they were enjoying their work, everything was good. She and Ned were fortunate to have fulfilling careers, and each other.

But as she cruised down the Virginia highway in the dark, Victoria would only let herself feel happy for a short while. Because there was still a killer on the loose.

16

Victoria took a seat in an FBI conference room across from Sam, one of her favorite colleagues. Sam wore his usual work uniform of a dark hoodie and jeans. He greeted Victoria with a warm smile that crinkled the skin around his eyes. Victoria appreciated his good-natured attitude and how he always seemed to make her requests a priority, though she had a feeling he was like that with everyone. In her opinion, he was the most agreeable, most capable, and perhaps the smartest intelligence analyst in the D.C. office.

"Good morning," she said.

"Morning," Sam answered before taking the last bite of a breakfast sandwich.

Victoria got to work setting up her computer. "We've got that conference call in an hour."

"Got it," Sam said, wiping his fingers on a napkin. He crumpled it with a foil wrapper, tossed them toward a bin in the corner, and missed by several inches.

Victoria logged into the FBI's server and reread everything in the case files to prepare for the conference call. Forensic evidence had failed to move the cases forward. Law enforcement officers were dutifully exploring every potential lead until alibis or contrary evidence brought their efforts to a dead end. Sam and others working with him had cross-referenced everyone the police had interviewed—friends, colleagues, neighbors, employers. They'd watched videos from Todd's funeral service and memorial, and of the crowds surrounding Jerome's neighborhood.

Six days had passed since Jerome's murder. With so many law enforcement personnel working the cases, it really bugged Victoria that the killer was still out there enjoying his freedom. What were the authorities missing? What could Todd and Jerome have done to provoke their murders?

An hour later, Victoria and Sam and a few others from the FBI team joined Detective Suarez from Boston, Detective Lambert from Charlotte, and representatives from those investigations. With little progress made, the mood was somber. For lack of other suspects, they had narrowed their persons of interest to Jesse Glassman and Rich Haskin, who had strong motives to commit murder.

A police captain from the Boston PD was making the case to arrest Haskin when Victoria temporarily turned off her video screen. With her connection muted, she waved to get Sam's attention. "Nothing connects Haskin to Todd Eckstrom's murder. Do you think this guy actually believes Haskin is our killer? There's just no way."

Sam didn't respond. He was staring intently at his laptop. He leaned closer, his nose mere inches from his screen. She could hear the rapid pressing of his fingertips against his keyboard. Whatever he was doing had fully captured his focus.

Victoria returned her focus to the video conference call. After discussing next steps, mostly a continuation of their current efforts, the meeting concluded.

Across the table, Sam's jaw dropped open. "Oh, wow! We just got something," he said. His eyes beamed, yet he wasn't smiling the way he should have if they'd gotten a break in the case.

"What is it?" she asked.

"Another atonement murder. And not one, but two."

"Two more murders?"

"Lilly Fuller and Cassandra Fuller Rowe. They were sisters. Same message written on the wall."

This was not the type of break Victoria hoped to receive, yet with the information came a spark of renewed energy. Two murders. Surely fresh evidence from the crimes would lead authorities to the killer.

A revolting twist in her gut accompanied her excitement. Everyone wanted the murder spree to end with Jerome, but apparently, the killer had other plans.

"When did it happen?" she asked.

"They found the victims last night."

Two months separated the murders of Todd and Jerome. Now, only a week had passed since Jerome's death. If it was the same killer, he had escalated the pace of his work.

"They died in North Carolina," Sam said. "A detective there read the bulletin we sent to law enforcement, recognized the atonement message at his crime scene, and contacted us. He thinks his case matches the others."

Victoria pressed her fingers against her temple. "North Carolina. That state keeps coming up. So far, it's the only common denominator. Was it in Charlotte?"

"No. Durham. It's about a hundred and fifty miles northeast of Charlotte. Home to Duke University."

"Lilly Fuller? Was that the first name you said?" Victoria asked, already typing it into her browser to start a background check. She was certain the recent victims had grown up in Charlotte or lived there as teens. A few minutes of research proved her wrong. Both sisters were born in Durham. Their address history showed they had spent their entire lives in the Durham area.

"I have to get to the crime scene," she told Sam. "Call me as soon as you find a connection between the Fuller sisters and the previous victims. I'll do the same."

Not wanting to waste any time, she packed up her laptop and left the conference room. She went straight to Murphy's office and gave him an update on the situation. With his approval, she booked the next flight to Durham.

Who were the victims this time? What connected them to an investment banker in Charlotte and an NBA player in Boston? That question would vex her all the way to North Carolina.

17

Victoria purchased two large water bottles at the Raleigh-Durham Airport. Called the Research Triangle, the area consisted of Chapel Hill, Durham, and Raleigh. She picked up a four-door Hyundai sedan, plugged the newest crime scene address into her GPS, and drove off. Her destination was a few miles away from Duke University. She arrived in an area with apartment complexes, duplexes, and other buildings that looked like student housing. Police tape cordoned off the perimeter of one yard, and cones blocked the driveway, making the crime scene location obvious.

Victoria parked across from the yellow tape, behind a marked police vehicle. She stayed inside her Hyundai, forcing herself to finish one of the two water bottles she'd purchased, as she took in her surroundings. Clues might be anywhere, everywhere, or if the authorities were incredibly unlucky…nowhere at all.

She stared out her window at the duplex behind the yellow tape. The building was a simple, rectangular shape, with vinyl siding and small windows. There was no lawn to mow, only patches of weeds and spindly bushes sprouting up through the dirt. A border of trees surrounded the sides and possibly stretched across the back of the units. So different from the upscale condo development where someone had murdered Todd, and from the neighborhood of ultra-luxury homes where Jerome had taken his last breath.

Lilly Fuller, age twenty-nine, the older of the two sisters, rented the side where the murders occurred. Lilly worked as a bartender at a dive in downtown Durham called The Goal Post, a place where college kids could get away with fake IDs. Cassandra, age twenty-seven, a dental hygienist, was supposedly visiting her sister when the murders took place.

Victoria placed her ring in the pillbox and then inside her backpack before getting out of the car. Three young adults lingered on the side of the road, staring at the crime scene. Victoria approached them.

"They know how they died yet?" a man wearing a cap asked. Though Victoria's jacket concealed her Glock, he'd correctly assumed she was some type of law enforcement, and for that, she gave him credit.

"I just arrived," she said. "Do you live nearby?"

"Across the street." A woman in a baggy Duke sweatshirt pointed to the box-shaped, multi-unit building behind them. "And we're sort of freaked out, you know?"

Victoria didn't know if they had good reason to be wary yet, but any murder, never mind two, had the power to send waves of fear through a neighborhood. "Have the police questioned you?" she asked them.

The young woman nodded and the man with the cap answered, "They did. But none of us saw anything. We were at school when it happened."

Victoria took business cards from her pocket and handed them out. "Let me know if you think of something later." She dictated their names and numbers into her phone in case she wanted to speak with them once she knew more. With a polite thank you, she left them and headed toward a tall, solid man with dark skin and the posture of a military man. Wearing a sports coat and jeans, he'd watched her the whole time she was talking to the students and continued doing so as she walked toward him.

"Victoria Heslin with the FBI," she said, showing her credentials.

"I know. Hello. I'm Detective Patrick Durst." Stubble had sprouted over the detective's chin and along the sides of his face. Considering the situation, it was not surprising that he hadn't found the time to shave. He shook her hand, completely encompassing it with his own. "Your boss called mine, said to expect you. I understand this case might connect to two others."

"Please show me what you've got," Victoria said.

"Double homicide. Causes of deaths are undetermined. Though we know the killer did not shoot, stab, or strangle the victims. There might have been a robbery. Some things are missing from the house."

"What sort of things?" Immediately Victoria thought of toothbrushes.

"Televisions. Possibly other items. But the televisions are what we know about for sure."

Victoria followed Detective Durst to the front door, where they pulled covers over their shoes before going inside. At eye level on the living room wall, exposed wires stuck out through an empty television mount.

"We had to air the place out in case it was a noxious gas that killed them," the detective said, gesturing to an open window. "Can't rule that out when we aren't sure of things yet. Forensics wore gas masks earlier, just in case."

Victoria moved deeper into the apartment. The kitchen had just enough room for a small table and two mismatched chairs, both turned over on the floor. Natural light streaked through a small window in the back door. A gray film covered the glass. A Styrofoam container sat open on the dirty countertop with a thick accumulation of crumbs in the seam between the counter and the sink.

A few steps away from Victoria, the detective cleared his throat. "There was hardly any food in the house. The refrigerator was basically empty, but our team hauled out two bags full of empty liquor bottles and took them to the lab." He shifted his weight in the doorway and cleared his throat again, as if something agitated it. "Cassandra Rowe, the younger sister, died in this room. She lived with her husband in a neighborhood about thirty minutes away. Been married for almost two years. She had the day off and came over to check on Lilly, who wasn't feeling well. She wasn't here long before someone killed her."

Yet the kitchen walls were unmarked. The killer had not left a message there.

"Tell me how Cassandra was found," Victoria said, in case the detective mentioned something that wasn't included in the initial reports.

"When Cassandra didn't come home or answer her phone, her husband drove over. He found her lying right here." Durst pointed to the tile floor next to the table. "There was a towel spread over her head. Broken dishes and shattered glass surrounded her, suggesting she fought her assailant. Forensics took the shards away to test for prints. She had vomited, and they're analyzing that now. Her husband started CPR, only stopping long enough to call the police. He stayed on the phone with the dispatcher and performed mouth to mouth and chest compressions until medics arrived."

"Did he report any symptoms of sickness or not feeling well after doing mouth to mouth?" Victoria asked.

"No. Not that I know of. We can check on that to be sure. But the guy is in shock. We have the recording of his 911 call. You can listen to it. It's very emotional. He never left Cassandra's side, held her hand as they carried her away on a stretcher. The medical examiner said she'd already been dead for hours by then, but obviously the husband didn't know that. While all of this was going on in the kitchen, waiting for the ambulance, he was shouting for his sister-in-law, asking for Lilly's help. He didn't know she was dead in the next room. She was killed first, probably right before Cassandra arrived."

"You've ruled the husband out as a suspect?"

"He was at work all day surrounded by colleagues. Never left his office. We're questioning him, but we know he didn't do this. He's a total wreck. Doesn't know who could have killed his wife but had plenty to say about the prospects associated with his sister-in-law. He says Lilly knew some shady characters. We've got names and we're following up with them."

Victoria didn't think anyone would describe the Atonement Killer as a shady character. Probably the opposite, or they would have caught him by now. He was disturbed, but not in a way people might detect on the surface.

"What about Lilly?" Victoria asked. "Who found her?"

The detective's eyes darkened, and the tension in the tiny apartment seemed to rise. "The medics found her in the bedroom." He turned to face the hallway. "It's this way. And it's where things get really creepy." His choice of words was similar to what Detective Suarez had said before leading Victoria to the room where Jerome had died.

Victoria had already seen the crime scene photographs from when forensics first arrived and entered Lilly's bedroom. The coroner had since delivered Lilly's body to the morgue, but the rest of the haunting scene remained, and the time had come to study it in person.

18

Victoria followed Detective Durst down a short hallway with worn, stained carpet to the bedroom where someone had murdered Lilly Fuller less than twenty-four hours ago. They passed a tiny, cramped bathroom. Victoria could have used a moment in there alone, thanks to the bottle of water she'd consumed, but since the whole place was a crime scene, a bathroom break would have to wait. She popped in for long enough to see if Lilly's toothbrush was missing. It didn't appear to be. On the back of the sink, a pink cup held two green-handled brushes.

From the bedroom doorway, Victoria studied the room. The message written above the metal bed frame drew her gaze. THIS IS YOUR ATONEMENT. To the best of Victoria's memory, everything about the words on Lilly's wall—the letters, the size, the color—seemed to match up with the messages at the other crime scenes.

In addition to the full-sized bed, the room also contained a dresser with chipped paint and two nightstands. One nightstand lay on its side on the floor. Someone had cut a twelve-by-twelve patch out of the carpet near it.

A single window with a dingy shade rolled halfway up faced the woods behind the house. Crime scene tape streaked the room, along with the evidence markers forensics had left behind. On the wall across from the bed and the atonement message hung another television mount, minus the television, again with wires protruding from the wall.

"Lilly was found in her bed. She'd also vomited, like her sister," Durst said. "There was a large bottle of Jack Daniels on the floor under the knocked-over nightstand. It was empty, though some of it had spilled onto the floor. We're testing the bottle and a patch from the carpet."

Victoria caught a whiff of something unpleasant, perhaps the vomit.

"The strangest thing is that Lilly's hair was cut off and lying all around her," Durst said.

Stepping inside the bedroom for a closer look, she pictured Lilly Fuller on the bed in the green tank top and polka dot pajama pants she'd been wearing when she died. In the crime scene photos, Lilly's eyes were closed, her expression tortured. Her shorn hair lay splayed out over her chest and arms, as if someone had stood over her and let the fibers fall onto her body, strand by strand.

As with the other two murders, there were no signs of physical torture or sexual abuse. No blood or anything else to suggest violence, though the overturned nightstand suggested Lilly had struggled for her life.

Victoria imagined herself as the killer taking a last look around. Had he done what he'd set out to do? And what was that, exactly?

Detective Durst waited silently in the hallway and didn't speak again until Victoria finally turned to him. "Thoughts?" he asked.

"Cutting off Lilly's hair was meant to further degrade her. The killer wants us or someone else to know he's in charge now. He's taking back the power he once lost...or never had. And in the kitchen...the younger sister's death wasn't staged. The killer didn't feel good about taking her life. That's why he covered her head with a towel. He didn't expect her to be here. The atonement message wasn't intended for Cassandra, only Lilly. She's the one who angered him."

Victoria looked around again and said, "Make sure your ME checks both women for patches of missing hair. The other victims were missing a small patch above the temple where their hair was torn from the scalp."

"Will do," Durst said as someone shouted, "Hey!" The sound came from behind the house.

Victoria caught movement at the window and looked straight into an older man's fat face. He had a bulbous nose and hair that needed a trim months ago. His brown eyes widened as he stared back at her. Then he was gone.

A spike of adrenaline hit, and her nervous system lit up, muscles and blood vessels contracting. Victoria and the detective raced from the bedroom to the kitchen. Victoria flipped the lock on the back door, and they burst outside.

A uniformed officer was already chasing the man across the backyard, toward the woods. "Police. Stop running!" the officer shouted.

The heavyset man in cowboy boots had no chance of outrunning the young officer and had enough sense to admit defeat and turn around. "I didn't do nothing. I swear," he said, puffing and wheezing.

Victoria and Detective Durst joined the officer as he handcuffed the man. "He snuck through the backyard," the officer said.

The man dropped his head and didn't deny the accusation.

"You think the crime scene tape doesn't apply to you, huh? Who are you?" Durst asked him.

"I'm Lilly's boss. She was sick, I heard. I just came to check up on her. Did she die or something?"

No one answered his question.

Killers were often fascinated by the power they had over their victims' lives. They enjoyed returning to crime scenes and attending memorial services. But no one capable of carrying out the atonement murders would be as careless as this man. Not with the police and FBI around. And he didn't fit the profile of an organized, meticulous killer who had so far eluded arrest.

The handcuffed man turned his head to one side and spit on the ground before he spoke. "If someone hurt Lilly, check out that ex-boyfriend of hers. He banged her up good a few times. She wouldn't say he did it, but we all knew it was him. He came around the restaurant one night, shouting and hollering at Lilly in front of everyone. Told her she would pay for what she'd done."

"Pay for what?" Detective Durst asked.

"I don't know," the man said, his gaze dropping to his scuffed boots.

"What's the ex-boyfriend's name?" Victoria asked.

Lilly's boss looked up again. "Alan Bushy. Spelled B-U-S-H-Y. Lilly said she broke up with him a few weeks ago. He stormed into her house and stole some of her stuff. Her televisions. Claimed she owed him a lot more than what he took."

"Put him in your car and we'll interview him downtown," Durst told the officer.

The officer led Lilly's boss toward the front of the property. When they were out of earshot, Victoria said, "That guy is not the killer. But see what he knows. Someone may have been following Lilly. Watching her at work."

"I will. But before we do that, I'm going to find the ex-boyfriend. See if he can tell us what was going on in her life before she died. Because this is the first we've heard of him."

"If you don't mind, I'd like to go with you."

"I don't mind at all," the detective said. "I'll drive."

EXCERPT FROM JOURNAL ENTRY

Lilly hasn't changed much since I saw her last. Except for her looks. Hard to believe I ever thought she was beautiful. She deserves what's coming. What I've done to her so far isn't enough. I need to watch her die, and when that happens, she needs to understand why.

19

With the windows cracked to let in the cool air, Detective Durst drove to Bushy's address. Victoria sat in the passenger seat with her phone cradled between her hands and used the time to research Lilly's ex before they questioned him.

"Looks as if her boss was right," Victoria said, after scanning a recent police report involving Lilly and Alan. "There is a history of abuse. Six weeks ago, a 911 operator dispatched officers to Lilly's address in response to a domestic violence report. A neighbor heard shouts and screams coming from Lilly's house and called the police. The responding officers found Lilly there with Alan. They saw evidence of physical violence. Bruises on her face. Choke marks on her neck. But Lilly refused to press charges. She denied that Bushy had hurt her and insisted he had nothing to do with her bruises."

Victoria looked up from her phone and out the window, trying to avoid the headache that often followed an extended period of reading in a moving vehicle.

"Here it is," Detective Durst said, slowing the car to a stop. Looking over his shoulder, he maneuvered the vehicle into a parallel parking spot and cut the engine.

Bushy lived a few miles away from Lilly Fuller, on a street with duplexes, all as plain as could be. The white siding on his unit needed a power wash, as did two mildewed plastic lawn chairs on the concrete front porch.

Detective Durst rang the doorbell. They waited. He rang it again. Finally, a lock turned, and the door jerked inward. A man glared at them.

Victoria recognized Bushy from photos she'd seen on their way to his house. But in his Carolina blue T-shirt and sweatpants, he looked younger in person. The messy state of his hair suggested they'd woken him.

Bushy rubbed his hand over his chin and the beginning of a beard as he looked from Durst to Victoria. "Who are you?"

They showed their badges. "We're looking for Alan Bushy," Durst said.

"I'm him. Why are you here?"

"We have to ask you some questions. Where were you yesterday afternoon?"

"Here," he answered immediately. "I was here all afternoon and all night. I was studying. Why are you asking?"

Durst frowned. "You're a student?"

"I'm getting my GED. Then I'm going to be a cop."

God help us, thought Victoria, recalling the police report that mentioned Lilly's bruises. If only Lilly had pressed charges, Alan would have a record that would make it harder for him to join the force.

"Why are you here?" Bushy asked.

Durst ignored the question and posed another. "Was anyone with you when you were studying?"

Bushy rubbed his face again and left his hand cupped over his chin. "No. I was alone, and I didn't leave here. But I ordered from Door Dash. So you can check that."

"Any trips to Boston recently?" Victoria asked.

"What? No. Why would I go there?"

"Charlotte?" she asked next.

"No."

Durst pressed one hand against the side of the house and leaned forward. "If you're lying, we'll find out pretty fast." Durst presented an intimidating figure, but Alan didn't seem fazed.

"I'm not lying. I went to Myrtle Beach last summer and haven't been anywhere else except around here. Why are you asking? What is it you think I did?"

"Lilly Fuller and her sister died yesterday," Durst answered. "Someone murdered them."

Bushy's lips parted. He stared at Victoria and blinked several times. "How?" he asked.

"You don't seem shocked," Durst said.

"I am. I mean, the girl was a hot mess. And I don't mean good looking either. Not anymore. Red flags all over that one, with her drinking. But I didn't expect her to get herself killed. The sister, too, you said? Someone killed Cassandra? Were they together or something?"

"We heard you had some issues with Lilly," Durst said. "You thought she owed you."

Bushy shifted his weight from one foot to the other. "It's not like...look, you don't understand what it was like dealing with her. She stole some things from me, man."

"What did she steal?"

Pressing his lips together, Alan narrowed his eyes. "Just...things."

Whatever Lilly stole from him wasn't something he could share without digging himself into a deeper hole.

"Were you angry enough to want her dead?" Victoria asked.

"No. I told you I'm going to be a cop. I didn't kill her. And I had nothing to do with whatever happened to her. I haven't talked to her in weeks. Haven't been near her or her place. I'm seeing someone else now."

"But you used Lilly as a punching bag in the past," Durst prompted.

"No. That's bull. That's not how it went down."

"You also showed up at her place of employment and threatened her," Durst continued. "You said she was going to pay for what she did to you. What was that about?"

"She was screwing around with her boss! The ugliest guy you've ever seen. Made me sick."

Victoria pictured the man they'd just arrested at Lilly's place. The story of that woman's life grew sadder by the hour.

Bushy snorted. "You know, instead of harassing me, you should go do your jobs elsewhere. Lilly has a lot of loser friends who could have killed her."

"Any of those *loser friends* ever threaten her like you have?" Durst asked.

"I dunno," Alan said dismissively, before his expression suddenly changed. "Hey, you know what? Two weeks ago—" Alan stopped mid-sentence. He looked away.

"What happened two weeks ago?" Victoria asked.

"Look, I'm going to tell you something now only so you hear it from me and don't think I'm hiding stuff. Because I'm not. I took her TVs. And I took 'em because she owed me big time. So let's just get that out of the way. But before that, the day before, she calls, and she's crying and yelling. Says I broke into her house. And I ask her what the hell she's talking about. She says she left the lights on when she went to work—she always leaves the lights on, she's afraid of the dark. I don't know what the hell she thought was gonna happen that can't happen with the lights on, but she was afraid. So this time, she gets back from work and the house is dark. No lights on. And because of that, she's sure someone was in her house. But nobody stole anything, so I figured it was just Lilly being a paranoid drunk. But maybe not. Maybe someone was creeping around in her house when she was at work."

Victoria dictated a note that someone might have broken into Lilly's house approximately two weeks ago.

Bushy shook his head. "She could have been so hot, you know? I've seen pictures of her. Used to be a real knockout before she let her life turn to crap."

"Can we come in and look around, Mr. Compassion?" Durst asked.

Bushy had the worst poker face. He grimaced as he scrambled to think. "No. You can't," he answered after a few seconds. He closed the door until only a small crack of space remained. "I don't have to let you in unless you've got a warrant."

"If you've got nothing to hide, might as well let us come in and get this done," Durst said. "We have witnesses saying you threatened Lilly. Then she was murdered. We're going to have to rule you out for sure before we can leave you alone."

Bushy shook his head. "I'm not stupid, man. You're gonna plant something here so you can blame me for this because you obviously don't know who really killed them. Because you suck at your job. Don't you?"

Victoria focused on maintaining her composure while Alan piled on the reasons to dislike him. She vowed to help make sure he didn't become a cop.

"Appreciate your opinion," Durst said deadpan, expressing none of the animosity brewing inside Victoria. "We'll get a warrant and come back. Don't go anywhere. We'll be watching."

Bushy slammed the door closed. The lock clicked into place.

"He's awful, to put it mildly, but he's not organized enough to pull off that killing," Victoria said, her voice quiet as they headed down the front path to Durst's vehicle.

"He's not smart enough either," Durst added. "Unfortunately for us, he's got no alibi, and he wouldn't let us in, though I'm sure it's because he's got drugs and stolen merchandise in there. So, you know how it is. My department has to waste more time investigating him."

The detective was right. He had to follow up with Alan Bushy until he could thoroughly document ruling him out of consideration. 'Not smart enough' wouldn't fly if the killer ended up on trial and a defense attorney found Alan hadn't been thoroughly vetted. Not when witnesses had heard him threaten Lilly.

"I'll send his name to my colleagues and see if they can find anything that connects him to the other victims," Victoria said. "But I'll be shocked if anything turns up."

"I know the victims are all about the same age, but they're spread out geographically. Do you really think one person killed all of them?"

"Yes. I do. Someone with a flexible job, since Todd's murder occurred on a Wednesday night and the Fuller sisters died during the day on a Tuesday."

"Or someone with no job at all," Durst suggested.

Victoria shook her head. "No, I think the killer has a stable career. Though it's possible he had one and no longer needs to work."

Durst pressed a button on the side of his phone and glanced at the screen. "It's almost eight o'clock. Since you're by yourself, um, would you like to have dinner together?" He moved his finger around the inner cuff of his sports coat as he waited for her reply. Was he nervous because he was thinking about more than just a professional dinner? That was the vibe Victoria got. Her engagement ring was still in her backpack. Again, she'd forgotten to put it back on after leaving the crime scene. Durst had no way of knowing she wasn't single.

"I can't," she replied. "Would you mind dropping me off at my car? I have to find a hotel for the night and update the task force in D.C. And let my boyfriend know where I am," she added, so there was no confusion. She also really had to find a bathroom.

"Are you going to be in town tomorrow?" Durst asked, unlocking the car doors with the key fob.

"I'm leaving in the afternoon. Before then, I'd like to meet with Lilly's and Cassandra's parents. I have some questions for them."

Victoria and Durst discussed the murder investigations until they reached her rental car. She handed the detective her business card. "Thanks for the hospitality. Please keep in touch with any updates and call me when the autopsy and tox results come back."

"I will. The autopsy report will come soon. And good luck interviewing the Fuller parents. They're kind of destroyed right now."

Victoria could imagine, and it made her that much more motivated to stop the killer before he claimed a fifth victim and caused heartbreak for another family.

20

Twelve years ago - Cassadra and Lilly

From the backseat of her parents' SUV, Cassandra Fuller watched the landscape pass by in a peaceful display of pastures, creeks, and black cows. On the seat beside her, her seventeen-year-old sister Lilly, older by two years, stared out the opposite window, twisting a section of her blonde hair into a spiral.

"We're almost there," their mother said, pivoting around to look at them between the seats.

"Yay. Can't wait to climb a rock," Lilly said, her penchant for sarcasm going strong.

Their mother let out a loud, frustrated sigh. Her patience with Lilly was near its limit. "Try to leave your poor attitude behind when we get to the cabin. Can you do that? Is that too much to ask?"

Lilly responded with a huff and a snort. She wasn't interested in another family vacation. Anyone could tell that with one look at her, thin arms crossed, face hardened in defiance. "It's a challenge to be pleasant when the last thing I want to do is go anywhere with you," she said.

Cassandra didn't think the *you* category included her, but she wasn't entirely sure it didn't, so the comment stung.

Still twisted around and leaning through the seats, their mother pointed her finger at Lilly. "Every time we leave you alone for a weekend, you throw a party and let your friends trash our house and throw up on our carpet—"

"That was one time," Lilly hissed. "Someone had the flu."

"Sure they did." Their mother huffed. "We weren't born yesterday, Lilly. My point is, we don't trust you to stay alone overnight in our house anymore. And that's all on you."

Lilly rolled her eyes before turning back to her window.

Their parents didn't know the half of it, or their worries would go far beyond mere annoyance. Because it wasn't just the drinking. Not anymore. It was pills, too. Appetite suppressants. Lilly took them every day. She'd lost a lot of weight. Her body was all sharp angles now. Her pants hung low off her jutting hips. And Lilly's weight wasn't the only thing plummeting downward. Her grades were slipping. No surprise there. How could anyone sit through school all day and learn when they'd snuck out of the house the previous night, carrying heels and tiptoeing so the floors wouldn't creak and alert their parents?

For reasons Cassandra wasn't privy to, Lilly's last boyfriend, Tom, the quarterback on the football team, had broken up with her a few weeks ago. Cassandra didn't know who Lilly had recently met and stayed with until five in the morning. Casandra had asked, but her sister hadn't told her.

At school, Lilly had earned the reputation of a party girl who was up for anything. Cassandra rushed through the hallways between classes to avoid hearing the gossip when her sister's name came up. She still heard some rumors, though she tried not to. No one wanted to believe their sibling wasn't a nice person.

And though Cassandra worried and cared, she hadn't mentioned her concerns to their parents. Lilly wasn't one to forgive anyone who betrayed her trust. Instead, Cassandra racked her brain for ways to help get her sister back to the girl she used to be.

They'd had fun on past family vacations. Taking the thrill rides side by side at Disney World. Biking together at the beach. Horseback riding in the mountains. Maybe this trip would change things, bring them all together. Maybe Lilly would cheer up once they reached the cabin, and they'd feel like a family again.

As her father slowed yet again for another curve in the never-ending road, Lilly desperately wished she could grab the bottle of Captain Morgan rolled up in a sweatshirt inside her suitcase. Booze warmed her insides and spread through her limbs, making her smarter and more confident, making life better. It was all she needed to get through the day. A few giant swallows could help her tune out the rest of the ride.

She should have mixed rum into a Diet Coke bottle before they left home. But instead of planning for the annoying, most boring ride ever, she'd been scheming to get out of the vacation until the very last minute. At least the Captain Morgan was waiting. Along with two bottles of vodka and a few minis. Something to look forward to. Her fake ID was in her purse, in case she ran out. They probably didn't even card people around here. Looking out her window at the sprawling old farms, she bet there were people making moonshine in barns. If only.

She dreaded spending so much time in close quarters with her family, but she and The Captain would make the best of it. To hell with the rest of them. Unless there were others at this so-called fun vacation community who wanted to party with her.

She hoped there were.

21

Three days ago - Lilly

Slumped over her kitchen table with her phone, Lilly wrapped an arm around her aching abdomen and wondered if she'd throw up again. Maybe then she'd feel better.

"If you aren't here by the end of the week, I'll have to find someone new," her boss threatened.

"Real supportive, thanks a lot. Glad I can count on you when I need help." Lilly glared at her phone, wishing it was her boss, not her, feeling as if a truck crushed his body and his insides were put back together all wrong. Then he'd know she wasn't faking.

"And if I find out you weren't really sick…"

"Why would I lie about it? You know I'm short on money. It's not like I get any paid sick days." In her mind, Lilly was fierce and shouting. In reality, she barely had the energy to hiss at him. Talking to her pervert boss, picturing his ugly face, and recalling his repulsive body odor made her sicker. He only wanted her to come to work so he could feel her up in the storage room. For weeks now, she had to pretend she didn't mind his meaty hands on her breasts and his hot, disgusting breath on her face if she wanted her daily *bonus*—a liter of this or that. Sometimes two. It was worth it. Unlike him, she didn't get a wholesaler discount on her booze. With her measly income, she needed all the help she could get.

When her unsympathetic boss ended their call abruptly without saying *feel better* or *get well*, she wanted to throw her phone across the room but couldn't muster the strength. Good thing, too. A spiderweb display of cracks already covered the screen from when Alan hurled it at the wall. She'd been so out of it, she couldn't remember the reason, but as bad as she felt then, it was nothing compared to now.

She really was sick. Sicker than she'd ever been before. Worse than the time she tried to stop drinking cold turkey and lasted four miserable days.

Leaning heavily on her cheap table, feeling as if she couldn't move, sweat dampened her green tank top and coated her forehead. Her hands trembled. Pins and needles made her fingers numb, a regular occurrence for days now. Her heartbeat seemed erratic, beating too fast at times. What was happening? Did it have to do with the booze? After all these years, was her body screaming *enough*? Her liver or kidneys failing and toxic waste building up inside her? Her family would leap straight to that conclusion, regardless of her symptoms. Their past admonitions replayed in her head. *Stop drinking and let yourself heal. Your body is going to reach a point of no return…it's coming. You're ruining your health, and you look awful.* Blah, blah, blah. She'd heard it all too many times. It meant nothing to her anymore. Why should she believe them, anyway? Year after year, she got up every morning, drank, and made it through another day. Until now…

I will stop drinking.

I will.

Eventually.

She'd quit just about everything else. Alcohol was her last leg to stand on. And she never drove drunk. It helped that she didn't own a vehicle. Not since the police arrested her for DUI and the courts took her license away.

No. This couldn't be the alcohol. This was different. Something else entirely. A terrible flu or some other virus. It would pass. It had to.

I will stop drinking. But I cannot quit today. There is no way. Not when I'm this sick. Can't heap on more pain.

Walking away from booze would require a monumental effort and her utmost physical and mental strength. She'd doom herself to failure if she tried now. She had to wait until she felt better.

Lilly forced herself to her feet, swayed, and managed the few steps to the cabinet, where she gripped the counter to keep herself upright. When she was steady enough, she grabbed a bottle of Jack Daniels. She'd earned that one after a particularly humiliating groping exchange in the refrigeration unit at work.

With the slightest twist of her hand, the top came off the bottle, the seal already broken. Strange. She could have sworn she was saving this one and hadn't opened it yet. In fact, when had she started a bottle and not finished it lately? Not in a very long time. But she didn't give the situation any more thought. The bottle was full. That's all that mattered.

She took generous gulps, welcoming the familiar warmth that coated her throat and slid through her insides, then trudged the few steps down the short hallway and into her bedroom. She cursed her ex, remembering she couldn't turn on a television to help take her mind off her misery because he'd stolen them. Who knew when she'd be able to afford a new one? Maybe her sister had an extra TV sitting around her house.

After collapsing on the bed, Lilly tipped the bottle and swigged again. It was already working its magic, dulling her pain and discomfort. She closed her eyes, ran her hand through her hair...and froze. Something didn't feel right. Panic racked her emaciated body. Was she hallucinating? No, it was real. With dread, she withdrew her hand, and with it came a clump of her long blonde hair.

Her heart hammered, expressing pure horror at the strands slipping through her fingers and onto her bed. Her hair! This was her worst nightmare. Worse than missing classes and being naked in front of an enormous crowd. It was playing out in real life and she was powerless to stop it. She wanted to cry. But crying never helped. Not when she tried to borrow more money from her parents or her sister. Not when her jerk of an ex-boyfriend pummeled her face. Nor when her self-proclaimed "good friend" stole the last of Lilly's savings from under her mattress and tried to lie about it. And according to her ex, the tears made her face so ugly and puffy he couldn't stand to look at her. She couldn't bear to look at herself either, so they agreed on that.

So Lilly held back the tears. They weren't what she needed. Only one thing could help her get through this.

She let the remaining blonde tresses slide to the floor, shook her hand free of them, and took another long pull from the Jack.

22

Victoria woke in her room at the Durham Marriott feeling rested. She had to admit she'd slept better than usual. No random barking or licking had woken her like it did at home. Not from Ned, of course, from the dogs. She could count on them racing from her bedroom in the middle of the night and running outside. They'd wake her again on their return, where they would lick their paws and other parts until Victoria was wide awake and begging them to stop. As much as she missed them, she didn't miss that.

After an energizing workout and shower, she headed out to visit Lilly and Cassandra's parents. The Fullers hadn't been available to meet with her the previous night. A doctor had prescribed Mrs. Fuller a strong sedative to get her through the first few days of shock. Earlier in the morning, they'd met with their pastor.

At ten a.m, Victoria arrived at their house, a two-story with blue vinyl siding. She stood on a *Welcome Y'all* doormat and rang the bell.

Hank Fuller came to the door wearing dark-framed glasses, a dress shirt, and khaki pants. He might have been on his way to the office where he'd worked as an accountant for the past thirty years, except for his bloodshot eyes and the mask of intense anguish distorting his features.

Denise Fuller stood behind him, disheveled in pink sweatpants and a worn gray sweater, as if she'd picked her clothes up off the floor and gotten dressed in a daze. Her eyes were red and swollen, her face drained of color except for her red lips. Perhaps applying it gave her some semblance of normality, but the lipstick's dark red hue created an unsettling effect against her pale skin.

Victoria identified herself as an agent, and said, "I'm very sorry for your loss."

"Don't be sorry, just find out who killed them," Denise answered in a monotone that suggested heavy medication.

"A lot of people are working on that right now," Victoria answered. "We'll do our best. That I can promise you."

"Come inside," Hank said, standing aside while holding the door open.

The Fullers' home was modest compared to the Eckstroms'. They'd pulled the shades down and closed the curtains, blocking out the daylight.

Denise moved through the house with the limp fluidity of someone on muscle relaxants, while Hank walked beside her with a stiff, short step. Victoria followed them into a living room with an upright piano against one wall.

Denise sank onto a slip-covered couch. Her husband sat close to her.

Victoria chose an upholstered chair facing the couch. "Do you play?" she asked, gesturing to the piano.

"No," Denise answered. "Cassandra was the only one in this family with any talent. She played beautifully."

Victoria was no stranger to speaking with heart-broken families, but the grief emanating from the Fullers weighed so heavily it seemed to suck the air from the room. Compounding their horror, they'd not lost one child, but two. The interview wouldn't be easy. Nothing would be easy for this couple for a long time.

"I know you've already talked to detectives, so please bear with me," Victoria said.

Denise dropped her head against her husband's arm and squeezed her eyes shut. "It doesn't make any sense. You need to find out how this happened. You need to find who killed my babies."

As Victoria waited for the Fullers to regain some of their composure, her eyes were drawn to a series of family photographs hanging on the wall. "Do you mind if I look at those pictures?" she asked.

"Go ahead," Hank told her.

The Fullers had arranged the photos in chronological order; the girls growing from toddlers to young adults over the years. In the earlier photos, Lilly seemed to love the camera, playing up to it and outshining her younger sister. Over time, that dynamic changed. Cassandra grew more radiant, exuding charm and confidence, while Lilly seemed to disappear into herself, getting thinner and appearing more worn out than anyone her age ought to look. As her natural beauty diminished, her most notable characteristic became a hollowing gauntness around her eyes. Only her blonde hair continued to shine.

From the couch, Denise moaned and said, "It's my fault Cassandra is dead."

Surprised by the comment, Victoria pulled her gaze from the photos and sat down again across from the family. "What makes you say that?" she asked.

Denise lifted her head from her husband's shoulder and stared down at her hands. "Lilly wasn't feeling well. She was so sick she hadn't gone to work for almost a week."

"What sort of sickness did she have?"

"We don't know." Denise seemed more focused now. "But it was serious. Nausea. Vomiting. Abdominal pain. The first few days, it sounded like a stomach bug, but it went on too long. She couldn't stop shaking, so it sounded neurological to me. Some sort of palsy. Because of her drinking. Which is no secret. And she wouldn't see a doctor."

"Why wouldn't she visit a doctor?" Victoria asked.

Denise sighed, slid her hands under her thighs, and went on. "Only Lilly could explain, not that she'd care to if she were still with us, but I can make an educated guess. Lilly's drinking problem started years ago when she was in high school. She's done several rehab stints over the past ten years. None went well. She'd beg and cry to leave before the program ended. And we couldn't keep her in there. Each stay was expensive, drained our savings. Not one of those places delivered on their promise of recovery." Denise shook her head, swallowed, and started up again. "I think Lilly equated all medical care with being locked in rehab. She outright refused to go to a doctor, not even for an annual physical."

"Do you think she was using illegal drugs and didn't want anyone to know?" Victoria asked.

"It's possible," Hank said, speaking for the first time since his wife began sharing her thoughts. "Her drinking escalated to drugs before. But alcohol was always her preference. She'd knock it for a time, then start up all over again. I'm sure you and all the other investigators are looking into her background. You'll see for yourself. Multiple arrests. Petty theft. Indecent exposure. Public intoxication. DUI. But none of that was really Lilly. It was the alcohol. The lack of judgment it caused."

"Why did you say Cassandra's death was your fault?" Victoria asked Denise, since they had veered from the topic.

"I asked Cassandra to go over there, to Lilly's house, and talk some sense into her sister. Take her to an urgent care center, or even the emergency room if necessary. Because sometimes Lilly listened to Cassandra even when she wouldn't pay attention to anyone else." Denise choked back a sob. "And now Cassandra is dead. All because I asked her to go over there and help Lilly. Cassandra didn't deserve this. She's done nothing wrong in her life. And she's practically a newlywed. If she hadn't been there…"

"Whoever did this…" Hank said. "I just don't understand."

"Do you know Lilly's ex-boyfriend?" Victoria asked. "Alan Bushy?"

"No," Denise answered. "The police asked us about friends and boyfriends. We couldn't tell them who she'd dated or if she was currently dating anyone. We really didn't know. Lilly stopped introducing us to friends and boyfriends a long time ago." Denise took a deep breath. "Anyway…are you going to find the person who did this?"

"The message that was written on your daughter's bedroom wall—*this is your atonement*—does it mean anything to you? Any significance to those words?"

"No. Not at all," Denise answered.

Victoria turned to face Hank.

"No. It means nothing to us," he answered. "I don't know who would write those words or why they would kill both my daughters…why they had to kill Cassandra, too."

"I know the detectives already went over this with you, but we'd appreciate it if you don't tell anyone about that atonement message."

"That's what they told us, but why?" Hank asked.

"The public doesn't know this, but detectives found those same words at two other homicide scenes," Victoria answered. "It's critical that we keep the information from the public so that there are things only the real killer would know about."

"What?" Denise slid her hands out from her thighs and covered her mouth. "I don't understand...what are you saying? Who else?"

"The other victims are Todd Eckstrom and Jerome Smith."

"Jerome Smith the...the basketball player?" Hank stammered. "The police didn't tell us this. You're saying the same person who killed my daughters killed Jerome Smith?"

"We don't know that for sure, but there is a strong possibility that the same person who killed Jerome Smith and Todd Eckstrom killed your daughters." Victoria pulled a file from her backpack and took out a photograph. "This is Todd Eckstrom. Can you tell me if either or both of your daughters knew him?"

"I don't know anything about that man. I've never heard his name and I've never seen him before," Denise answered.

"Neither have I," Hank said. "But we know who Jerome Smith is. My daughters even met him once."

"They did?" Victoria asked, straightening in her seat. Could this be the break they needed? Or did the Fuller sisters have a fleeting interaction with Jerome, perhaps asking for an autograph after an NBA game? "When and where did they meet him?" she asked.

"It was years ago," Hank answered. "Before Jerome was in the NBA. Before he played for Kentucky. He was still in high school. We were on vacation. The girls told us they met a top college basketball recruit. Cassandra searched for his name online and confirmed it was true. Later, when the NBA drafted Jerome and there was so much press about him, Cassandra reminded us they knew him. Because they didn't just meet him. They spent time with him, befriended him, if I recall correctly."

Little sparks of excitement fired inside Victoria, and yet, what he'd said didn't make sense. When she'd last checked with Sam that morning, the FBI had yet to find any record of communications between the Fuller sisters and Jerome or Todd. There were no phone messages. No emails or social media connections. Facial recognition found nothing in the way of online images linking the victims together. There didn't seem to be much of a friendship because they hadn't stayed in touch."

"Where exactly did they meet him?" Victoria asked.

"We were on vacation," Hank answered. "We rented a cabin in western North Carolina, the mountains, near Boone." He turned to his wife. "What was the name of that place where we stayed with the girls? It was only for a long weekend. Your boss told you about it. Deer Crossing? Bear Creek? No. Something with mountains in the name."

"Oh, I don't know. What does it matter?" Denise dropped her head into her hands. Just as quickly, she lifted her head. "Stone Ridge Mountain," she said. "It was Stone Ridge Mountain."

Her husband nodded. "Right. That's it. And there was something going on there. Some special event that weekend."

"There were fireworks over the lake. It was the Fourth of July weekend and the anniversary of their opening. Maybe their twentieth or twenty-fifth anniversary jubilee," Denise said, wiping her finger under her eye. "I remember because I have a photo with a jubilee banner in the background. The girls were in high school. Lilly was going to be a junior. So it was...um, twelve years ago. We had a good time together. Maybe one of the last." With that, Denise Fuller's eyes closed to slits, and her tears flowed.

"Do you remember anything else about that weekend?" Victoria asked. "Anything significant?"

"Someone got hurt," Hank said. "I don't remember who, only that Cassandra came home all upset about it one night."

"Hurt how? Physically?"

"I can't recall. I only remember Cassandra's reaction. She was young then. And she's always been a sensitive soul. I think it spooked her. I'm sorry, that's all I've got. Though whatever happened, no one died or got maimed. Nothing on that level. That's not something any of us would have forgotten."

Victoria asked more questions, but the Fullers couldn't recall anything else from that weekend over a decade ago. When she left their house, her mind echoed with Hank Fuller's cries of grief.

23

Victoria climbed into the driver's seat of the Hyundai, looked back at the Fullers' blue house, and thought about what she'd just learned.

Lilly and Cassandra Fuller had met Jerome twelve years ago. Was it just a coincidence? And what about Todd? How did he fit in?

Victoria called Todd Eckstrom's parents. She hoped they might know.

Sandra Eckstrom answered.

"Hello. This is Victoria Heslin again. With the FBI."

"Yes. Have you found something? Has there been a break in Todd's case?"

"No break yet, but we're getting there," Victoria said, staying positive and praying that the Eckstroms could help. "I have a few more questions for you and your husband. Do you know Lilly and Cassandra Fuller? Two sisters from Durham?"

"No. I've never heard of them."

"Can you ask your husband? Perhaps you or he met their parents. Hank and Denise Fuller."

Victoria listened to Sandra repeating the question. She heard Ed say he wasn't familiar with those names. He didn't know them either.

"You said Jerome and Todd vacationed at your beach house," Victoria said. "Did they go on any other vacations together? The mountains maybe?"

In the background, Ed was asking, "Who is it? Who are you talking to?"

"It's the FBI agent." Sandra answered, her voice sounding far away. "She has a question about Jerome and Todd going to the mountains together."

There was silence on the other end of the call. Victoria stared through her window, away from the sun, and wondered if it was normal for Sandra's response to require so much thought.

"My in-laws owned a vacation cabin in the mountains," Sandra finally answered. "Todd took Jerome there. Just once."

"Where was their cabin located?" Victoria asked. "Was it in a neighborhood?"

"Yes. In a community near Boone. It's called Stone Ridge Mountain."

Bingo! Victoria felt a rush of excitement. She'd found a place that connected the victims. "When did that trip occur?" she asked. "Do you remember the date?"

"Todd's grandparents sold the place during his senior year of high school. Which means it was…it was the summer before his junior year of high school."

"Do you know when exactly?" Victoria asked, trying to rein in her anticipation but imagining Sandra answering *Fourth of July.*

"No. I couldn't tell you about the month or the day. Only that it was in the summer."

That still left the Fourth of July as a possibility. And though Sandra couldn't pinpoint an exact date, she didn't seem to have trouble coming up with the year of the trip. That seemed unusual, and Victoria needed to understand why. "Todd and Jerome's friendship began in middle school. What made you remember their trip occurred before their junior year of high school?" Victoria asked.

"Because Todd drove to the mountains himself. With Jerome. We weren't with them. I don't understand why you're asking about a trip they took over a decade ago. How is that going to help find out who killed them?"

"I think something might have happened on that trip." In fact, Victoria was sure of it now. She couldn't imagine what it was, but something had occurred. "Is there anything you can tell me? Did Todd mention anything unusual while he was there or after he got home?"

Sandra's response wasn't immediate. Victoria had to wait again. "Todd had an…incident, and Jerome helped him through it."

"An incident?"

"It's…I assure you, it's personal, and it's not relevant," Sandra said. "If it was, if it could help you with your investigation, I would tell you."

"I'd like to be the judge of that," Victoria said. "Sometimes the smallest things end up being relevant in an investigation."

"I'm sorry. Todd didn't want anyone to know, not then and not now. And while I don't think it's anything to hide, the least I can do is respect my son's wishes now. It had nothing to do with breaking the law or harming anyone. It's not related to his case or with Jerome's case. I'm certain of that. So please don't ask again. It was so long ago. And I'm sorry, but if you don't have any news for us, I have to get going."

"I understand. But I need to find out more about what happened on that trip. Can you call me back to talk about it as soon as you have a chance?"

"That seems like a waste of time. I'm sorry, but I have to go. Please let us know if you have any more information on who killed our son."

Victoria decided it was best not to press Mrs. Eckstrom any further. Not over the phone. Even though the woman knew something. Perhaps the Smith family would have more to say about the trip and give her exact dates. Victoria had yet to question them, but Detective Suarez had spoken with them several times.

Victoria tapped Suarez's name in her contacts. The call went to voicemail. Not surprising. The detective was probably answering dozens of calls, handling her giant task force, and running on pure caffeine at this stage of the investigation. Victoria typed up a quick summary about the connection to the girls. She asked Suarez to find out if the Smith family had information about Jerome's trip to Stone Ridge Mountain with Todd Eckstrom before their junior year of high school.

Now Victoria had to wait for Suarez to get back to her. And that gave her time to wonder. If an incident occurred that compromised their children's reputations, would Jerome's parents be willing to disclose that information? Or would they be as evasive as Sandra Eckstrom?

Victoria propped her phone on the steering wheel and searched for *Stone Ridge Mountain community, Western North Carolina* within the time frame Todd and Jerome went there.

She scanned the results, looking for information about a criminal occurrence, and found nothing of the sort. If a life-altering event occurred there involving the murder victims and the killer, it hadn't made the news. Perhaps something happened, but no one reported it.

Victoria sank back against the cloth driver's seat to think. Something must have happened at Stone Ridge Mountain, and she intended to find out about it. Did it have anything to do with the incident Sandra Eckstrom wouldn't reveal? The supposedly *not relevant* incident. Todd and Jerome came from affluent families. If they got into trouble as teens, their parents could have paid attorneys to expunge the juvenile records. That would successfully hide the arrests from college admissions committees and prospective employers. Fortunately for Victoria, the FBI could uncover those files. She sent a quick email to Sam, asking him to look for concealed juvenile records.

She returned to her Internet browser and found the community's website.

Stone Ridge Mountain, as beautiful as a national park with the amenities of a friendly neighborhood and vacation community.

Our gated community, built on 1,000 wooded acres, features lakes, hiking trails, waterfalls, and breathtaking vistas. The neighborhood boasts a competition-sized outdoor swimming pool, tennis, basketball courts, and two lakes for fishing and boating. The clubhouse includes a fitness center, a ballroom, and meeting rooms.

With over four hundred cabins nestled in the woods and around the majestic Staghorn Lake, Stone Ridge Mountain offers privacy and seclusion. Just off the Blue Ridge Parkway, the convenient location is a short drive from the towns of Boone, Blowing Rock and West Jefferson, close to Grandfather Mountain, ski slopes and other outdoor recreational activities.

If you visit, be sure to check out the 300-foot quartz monzonite dome the community is named after. Formed 250 million years ago, the lookout point provides a stunning view of Staghorn Lake.

Whether you are looking for the perfect primary home, an idyllic retreat to transport you from the hectic pace of everyday life, or a memory-making vacation spot, Stone Ridge Mountain offers something special for everyone.

A killer had targeted four of the community's visitors, and special was not a word Victoria would use to describe what happened to them.

Victoria called the phone number on the website. When a woman named Mabel answered, Victoria asked if she had lived or worked in the neighborhood twelve years ago.

"I'm one of the original homeowners here. I can tell you almost anything you want to know about Stone Ridge," Mabel said. "I've got photos and newsletters going back to when we first opened. Come on up and I'll show you. I'll give you a tour."

"I'm in Durham right now," Victoria answered, intending to convey that she was too far away.

"Great," Mabel said. "Not too far, then. Not too far at all. We have guests from Durham just about every week."

Victoria took a few seconds to think about her situation before deciding. It was eleven thirty in the morning. According to her GPS, she could reach Stone Ridge Mountain in three hours.

24

Victoria's investigative efforts might pay off, but they came at a steep price—time away from home. Something she could never get back. Though there was one good thing about traveling for work—it really made her appreciate what was waiting for her back in Virginia. Ned and her animals. She missed them and couldn't wait to see them again soon. But with the time it was going to take to get to Stone Ridge Mountain and back, she wasn't going to make her flight home to Virginia.

Cruising west on State Highway 421, she called DTI, the government's travel department. After giving her name and identification number, she said, "I'm currently booked on a flight out of Durham tonight. I need to reschedule that. I'm heading toward Boone. I think the closest airport might be Charlotte." She waited while the travel agent confirmed Charlotte was indeed closer.

"Can you book my departure on the latest flight out of Charlotte tonight?"

"Sure," the operator said. "Do you want to hold while I look up the departure options?"

"Yes. I can hold." Victoria concentrated on maneuvering through highway construction until the operator returned and said, "All flights from Charlotte to Dulles tonight are full."

"Okay. What is the first flight out in the morning?"

"There's a 6 a.m. and a 10:25 a.m. Which would you prefer?"

Tomorrow was Saturday. Victoria had planned to hike with Ned and the dogs and then relax at home together. The earlier she got back to Virginia, the better. "I'll take the 6 a.m. flight. I'll also need a hotel room in Charlotte for tonight when you have a chance. The closer to the airport, the better." She thanked the agent and said goodbye. A confirmation for her hotel would arrive in her inbox.

The steady hum of her tires on the pavement and the whoosh of cars and trucks became her soundtrack for the long drive. Victoria didn't mind being alone. In fact, she rather liked it. It allowed her time to think and recharge her energy. She kept the radio off and focused on her thoughts—details from the three different crime scenes, all the questions that still needed answers. Every so often, the sun shone through the window onto her hands and glinted off her engagement ring. That made her think about Ned, which made her smile.

After two hours on the highway, she exited to country roads and sloping pastures dotted with cows grazing on the first green sprouts of spring—a landscape that brought her inner peace. Though Victoria had grown up in nearby McLean, Virginia and gone to college in Washington D.C., it was always the countryside that felt like home. The quiet. The open space. More cows and horses than people.

On one property, rusting tractors littered an enormous front lawn, making it seem like a cemetery for yard equipment. A little farther down the road, an amusing sculpture of Bigfoot caught her attention.

Any whimsical pleasantness disappeared in an instant as she passed two long, windowless buildings with signs for Happy Farms Chickens on them. Her stomach tightened and turned. She'd seen similar buildings and knew what was inside. Those chickens weren't happy. Cruelty had profoundly disturbed her for as long as she could remember. And now, the thought of thousands of chickens cramped together in those dark buildings made Victoria miserable. Her small car suddenly seemed claustrophobic, the roof and windshield too close to her face.

She knew there would always be some cruelty lurking in the shadows, no matter where she went. But sometimes the reminders came crashing down, almost suffocating her, and it felt like she couldn't do anything to help. Not enough, surely. In those times, she honestly hated humanity—its treatment of animals and of people. Humanity's shortfalls were too often on full display in her investigations, and yet she continued to sacrifice a lot to find justice for its members. She couldn't stop all needless suffering, and yet she wanted to try. That desire explained her drive to the North Carolina mountains in search of a killer's motive before another person died, and another family got destroyed.

Who could ever have imagined this career for her? Certainly not the privileged people who made up her inner circle of family and friends when she was younger. And not Victoria. Not until she was in college and criminals abducted her mother, hoping to score a ransom. That's when her world exploded, and her priorities changed.

The GPS had Victoria only five miles away from Stone Ridge Mountain—though the estimated travel time for that distance on the winding, narrow roads was twenty-five minutes—when her phone rang. It was Detective Durst from the Durham Police Department.

In her distress, she'd been gripping the steering wheel hard. She took one hand off now and shook it as Durst's voice came over the phone.

"Hey? How did it go with the Fullers?" he asked.

She told him what she'd learned. "I'm on my way to Stone Ridge Mountain now to look for answers."

"Really? What do you think you might find there?"

"I don't know. It's a long shot. But I have a gut feeling. I just have to look into it while I'm here."

"Well, I hope you find something. Let me know if you do. I'm just calling you now because we got an update. Forensics are still examining fibers from the house and the victims' clothing, but we got the autopsy report and the toxicology results back. Record timing for both reports, by the way. I forwarded them, but wanted to call you myself with a heads up that they're in."

"The FBI really appreciates that," she said with full sincerity. A professional way of letting him know his cooperation and helpfulness floored her.

"Sure. Anytime."

"Did they find the cause of death?"

"Yeah, they did. Wait until you see it."

"Since I'm driving, would you mind summarizing for me? If you have time?"

"I'd be happy to. It will just take me a minute to log back into the system."

While she waited, the possibilities she'd considered stormed to the forefront of her mind, ready to be shot down or stand victorious when the detective read her the cause of death. She'd had so many ideas, at least one had to be correct.

"By the way, I specifically mentioned the patch of missing hair on the other victims," Durst said. "The medical examiner took another look. He didn't find one on either victim."

"Thank you for asking him to double check." Victoria wondered why both male victims had missing patches of hair, and missing toothbrushes, but not the female victims.

The detective cleared his throat. "Okay," he said. "I've got the report up."

Victoria quieted her mind to listen to the results.

"Lilly Fuller and Cassandra Rowe died from acute poisoning."

This did not come as a giant surprise considering the vomitus and the lack of outward signs of murder. But it was unusual for a serial killer to employ a different means of death for each victim. Drowning Todd Eckstrom. Smothering Jerome Smith. Poisoning Lilly Fuller and Cassandra Rowe. Each murder and manner of execution meant something to this killer.

"What was the poison?" Victoria asked.

"Thallium sulfate."

"I'm not familiar with the chemical."

"Neither was I."

"What do you know about it?"

"It's odorless, colorless, tasteless, and deadly. We can absorb it through our skin, but that's not how Lilly and Cassandra died. They ingested it. The ME found the evidence in their gastrointestinal tracts."

"Do you think the killer forced them to drink it?" Victoria asked, thinking aloud, and imagining scenarios where that would occur. Had the killer aimed a gun at the women? If the killer carried a gun, it would have been easier and quicker to shoot the sisters. Though perhaps killing them quickly wasn't the point.

"With Cassandra, yes, that's what we're thinking. The evidence of a struggle in the kitchen supports it, though we aren't sure how the killer forced her. With Lilly—yes and no. She ingested a fatal dose, that's what killed her. But her poisoning began over a week ago."

"Over a week ago?" Victoria repeated.

"Yes. Her alcohol supply was contaminated with thallium sulfate. Forensics found traces of it in empties they took from her recycling bin. She'd been ingesting the poison for almost two weeks, which explains the illness she experienced in the days leading up to her death."

"Hmm. Denise Fuller told me her daughter had been seriously ill."

The detective cleared his throat again. "Thallium poisoning accounts for all the symptoms Lilly experienced. It causes GI problems, vomiting, abdominal pain, neurological issues, a pins-and-needles sensation in all extremities. And alopecia, which is hair loss. That begins around ten days after the exposure and is complete within one month."

"So, Lilly was already succumbing to the poison. She was losing her hair, or about to. But then the killer gave her a lethal dose and cut her hair off. He wanted her to die, and he wanted her to die hairless. That means something."

Victoria thought back to the photos she'd seen on the Fullers' wall. As Lilly's beauty yielded to her addiction, her hair lost some luster, but remained long and thick. She always wore it down rather than pulled back. Lilly was proud of her hair, and the killer wanted to take that from her. That act indicated hatred or envy.

Victoria swallowed, relieving pressure in her ears caused by the higher elevation, and racked her brain to think of poisoning cases she'd studied. "Where would someone get thallium sulfate? Can anyone purchase it?"

No answer.

"Detective?" Victoria continued driving through a few seconds of silence. She shot a quick glance at her phone. No reception bars. She had no choice but to wait for cell service to return before learning additional details. She was about to hang up when the detective's voice came through the phone again.

"Agent Heslin? You still there?" he asked.

"Yes. Sorry about that. I've got half a bar for cell phone reception. I might lose you again. Not sure if you heard me. I asked if you have information on where the chemical comes from."

"According to forensics, thallium sulfate is the primary ingredient in rat poison. The U.S. outlawed it decades ago. You can't purchase it here. But it's available in other countries and easily enough made in a lab."

"That should make it easier to find the source," she said.

"Yes, it should. I've got someone on it, but the FBI might have more resources."

Again, she appreciated the way the detective seemed to welcome the FBI's help rather than view them as an interfering party. "Forward the information to my colleague. He'll get on it as soon as possible. He's great." She rattled off Sam's email address. "So, we already know what the poison is. What else?"

"Cassandra...ingested...of the...died," Durst answered.

"Sorry, I didn't catch all of that. I'm losing our connection."

"We think the killer—"

The detective never finished his sentence. Victoria had lost him again. She waited, hoping the call would return, but her phone had zero bars. Losing her cell service meant her GPS couldn't function, and her directions had ceased. She hadn't brought a satellite phone, a mistake on her part. But she didn't have to worry for long. Around the next turn, a large sign offered directions to Stone Ridge Mountain. It wasn't much farther. A few more miles on the same road. She could feel that she was getting closer to finding out what they needed to know.

25

The last few miles to Stone Ridge Mountain seemed to take forever. The speed limit on the winding one-lane road was thirty miles per hour, and for good reason. Losing control around one of these turns wouldn't end well. Not with the steep drop on one side of the road.

When Victoria arrived at the community, a single horizontal bar crossed the entrance road, serving as a gate to keep out unauthorized vehicles, although anyone could walk around it. She put the Hyundai in park next to a gatehouse with a sloping red roof. It was a cute structure resembling a tiny cabin. She rolled down her car window, and the wind rushed in, making her shiver.

The man working inside the little house had thick silver hair, a face lined with deep wrinkles, and a pipe clamped between his teeth. The words *Stone Ridge Mountain* were stitched in black thread on the pocket of his flannel shirt. Below that, his name—*Frank*.

Through the gatehouse window, Victoria watched him grow taller as he stood from whatever he'd been sitting on. He set his pipe down and exited the building through the single door. "Can I help you?" he asked, walking toward her car.

Victoria flipped open the case with her badge and held it up for him. "I'm meeting Mabel Hans at the community house."

"Does it involve the community or is this Mabel's personal business?" he asked, shielding his eyes, though the skies had clouded over during Victoria's drive. "Cause I can't think of anything Mabel might have done wrong. She's a kind soul. Everybody knows her."

"I'm hoping she can help me with historical information about the neighborhood."

"Then you got yourself the right person. Mabel has been the communications director here for as long as I can remember. It's a volunteer position, and she's in charge of all the community history. Old newsletters, back when they didn't go out in emails and got delivered to people's real mailboxes. And pictures. Lots of pictures from over the years and from so many events."

"Great. We're meeting at the clubhouse. And I don't have cell service. Can you give me the directions?"

"Only one service works up here, and that's spotty. Internet isn't too great, either, depending on the weather. Satellites don't have a clear view with all the mountain ridges. We're supposed to have high-speed fiber optic installed. But they've been saying that for a few years now. Don't bother most of us much. We came here to get away from it all. Anyway, you don't need directions to where you're going. Just follow the signs." He took a step back and his gaze ran from the front of her car to the back. "Not all the roads are paved, but you'll be fine going to the community center."

"Okay. Thank you."

He backed away, but kept his eyes on her. "Hope you find what you're looking for."

"Me, too."

He returned to the small structure and went inside. A few seconds later, the bar that was blocking the road lifted. Victoria waved a thank you and drove in, traveling mostly uphill for another mile on a road lined with thick pines. Log cabins were visible through the woods. Along the winding road, directional signs pointed the way to the clubhouse and the tennis courts. She passed markers for *Forest Cove Trail*, *Resting Doe Loop*, and *Looking Glass Falls*. Usually, mountain trails transported her away from her work, allowing her to breathe easily, enjoy fresh air and strenuous exercise. But this mountain area visit might take her right to the heart of the atonement murder investigation.

At the clubhouse, she parked the rental car in front of the building and walked onto a deck surrounding the building. She stretched her arms overhead, necessary after the long drive. A gust of wind whipped her hair back and delivered the smell of deep pine woods, a scent Victoria loved.

Below the deck to her left, a green tarp with puddles and leaves covered the pool. Smaller tarps covered stacks of chairs, identifiable by the few on the bottom that weren't fully covered.

Victoria walked to the back part of the deck and looked out over a large lake with miles of curving shoreline. She appreciated the view for a few more seconds, arms wrapped around her body for warmth, then went inside. After a quick trip to the restroom, she found Mabel Hans in a back office.

Mabel stood beside a solid writing desk, next to a leather chair. Gray streaks ran through her black hair, including her thick bangs. She looked warm and comfortable in a long cable-knit sweater with jeans. Eyeglasses hung from a braided cord surrounding her neck. She was wiping a lens on her sweater when Victoria said hello.

After introductions, Mabel said, "You came! In all my life, I've never met anyone from the FBI before. You're the first."

Victoria smiled back. "Then I hope I represent the Bureau well."

"You already have. I didn't expect you to drive all the way here from Durham just to talk to me! Are you kidding? But you did! And I'm so glad you came. And I'm happy to show you what we've got and share what I know."

"Thank you. I'm interested in the Fourth of July week twelve years ago. There was a jubilee event at the same time."

"Our jubilee event! I was here! I remember it well. We have pictures of the celebration in our old newsletter. Most of those photos I took myself, with my trusty Nikon. I know exactly where they are. The photos and newsletters are organized by year."

A tall man wearing work pants and a flannel shirt walked past the office. Mabel called out, "Crawford?"

He backtracked to the doorway. "Yeah?" he asked, eyeing Victoria. He was approaching middle age, probably in his forties, though he might have been younger. It was hard to tell because of his weathered skin. He had the look of a man who chopped cords of wood every day.

"Did anyone tell you about the leaking spigot by the pool?" Mabel asked him.

"It's dripping. Better make sure a pipe or valve didn't crack."

"Yeah. I'm going to look at it now." With that, Crawford walked away, his boots clomping across the wood floors.

"Oh, Crawford, wait, come back," Mabel said.

Crawford's noisy steps returned. He stuck his head in the doorway again. "Yeah?"

"I should have introduced you." Mabel smiled. "This is Victoria Heslin. From the FBI. All the way from Washington D.C. And this is Crawford Naught. He's our resident maintenance worker. Mr. Fix-It we call him. He can do just about anything that needs doing. And he would have been at the jubilee as well. His father was one of the first residents, just like me." She turned back to Crawford. "You remember the jubilee, don't you, Crawford? Our twenty-fifth anniversary event."

Crawford grunted. "What about it?"

"I'm investigating four murders that might trace back to that event," Victoria said.

Mabel gasped. "Murders? I didn't know that's what your visit was about. Well...my word. But wait, there's been no murders at Stone Ridge."

"No one ever got murdered here," Crawford said from the doorway.

"He's right," Mabel said, crossing her arms. "We've had deaths, unfortunately. Heart attacks. A drowning in the lake once. An unfortunate accident. But no murders. That I can guarantee."

"The murders didn't occur here," Victoria clarified. "They took place elsewhere. But the only thing the victims seem to have in common is they were together here at Stone Ridge Mountain twelve years ago. I need to find out what happened, and who else is involved."

"What happened?" Mabel asked. "I still don't understand what on earth could have occurred in this community that would cause four murders."

"Nothing," Crawford said, followed with another grunt. "Every few years someone gets hurt out on the stone lookout on account of acting stupid. Slips and breaks an arm or an ankle. But none of them died."

Mabel turned to the maintenance man. "Only time we've ever had authorities out here that I recall is because of you, Crawford. When you refused to pay your property taxes for so many years and got yourself arrested."

A flash of anger darkened Crawford's eyes. "I didn't pay because I was disputing the charges. The government was stealing from me."

"I know, I know," Mabel said, waving her hands through the air before turning back to Victoria. "Anyway, that's all resolved. No other trouble here."

"I'd like to see your pictures," Victoria said, hoping the trip hadn't been a colossal waste of her time.

"I still can't believe this is about a murder," Mabel said, putting her eyeglasses on and facing the bookshelves above the cabinets. "I don't know what I thought, but not that." She bent over and opened a cabinet drawer, rifling through the contents inside. "And not just one murder, but four. How were they killed? And why are you investigating now if the crimes occurred twelve years ago? Or did you say they were recent?" The questions shot out one after another as she pulled out a stack of glossy newsletters.

"I can't really discuss the details of an ongoing investigation," Victoria answered.

Mabel gave up on her questions and focused on the newsletters, spreading them out over the desktop. "We used to put out two newsletters every year to commemorate the community events. My friend and I took most of the photographs. He's passed now. Heart attack on the Appalachian Trail. Can you believe that? At least he died doing something he loved. I miss him." Mabel sighed. "Then someone decided the newsletters should all be digital, to save money. But it's not as fun as holding it in your hands and going through the pages one by one, hoping to find a picture of yourself or your friends to cherish, is it? Oh, here it is. Our jubilee issue." She lifted one copy away from the others and held it out for Victoria.

Victoria flipped through the magazine-sized, sixteen-page newsletter. It contained articles about improvement projects and upcoming events, but mostly photographs showcasing community activities and residents. A cheerful caption accompanied each photo.

Sam Robertson at the newly graveled entrance with his trusted labradoodles.

Mimi Gates and Greta Ruffin win ladies' doubles for the third straight year.

The centerfold featured the jubilee celebration.

A beautiful fireworks display to commemorate twenty-five years of an extraordinary community.

Jackson and Harry Lindberry, enjoying the barbecue.

Joey Lafond, one of Stone Ridge's first residents, helps to serve the cake.

The photographs showcased older individuals. Victoria turned another page. Under a blue sky, six teenagers stood together at the far end of the clubhouse pool. Victoria recognized four of them. Younger versions of Todd, Jerome, Lilly, and Cassandra.

A jolt of energy rocketed through her veins. The proof was in her hands. All four victims were together at Stone Ridge Mountain for the jubilee event.

In the photo, Jerome stood farthest to the left, next to Todd. Both were over six feet tall and towered over the two blonde girls beside them—Lilly and Cassandra Fuller. Victoria easily recognized them from the photos hanging on their parents' wall. Wearing a black bikini, Lilly had one hip jutting forward in a sultry pose as she cast a knowing smile over her tanned shoulder. Cassandra stood slightly behind her, her smile less certain, and a towel wrapped around her lower body.

There were two others in the picture. A male and a female. Victoria didn't know who they were, but the photo's caption provided one name.

Karen Strauss (second from right), one of Stone Ridge's newest community members, with friends at the pool.

Slightly pudgy compared to the Fuller sisters, frizzy red hair to their blonde, and with sunburned shoulders, Karen looked the youngest of the teens. She faced the camera head on. No sexy sideways pose.

Next to Karen, to the far right of the group, stood a young man with dark hair. Same approximate age as the others. He wore a black T-shirt and sunglasses. He didn't have a tall, athletic build like Todd and Jerome, but he had the lean look that often accompanies youth. Unlike the rest of them, he wasn't smiling.

Six teens in the photo. Four of them recently died.

Did the other two know what happened? Were they the next victims? Or had one of them grown up to be a vengeful killer?

EXCERPT FROM JOURNAL ENTRY

A few surprises recently, but can I really trust the information? None of it really matters in the grand scheme of things, anyway. My plan is falling into place perfectly. Each of them deserves what they get. Everything I've done was meant to be.

26

Victoria continued to stare at the picture. She could hardly believe her luck, finding a photo of all four victims together. Though it wasn't merely luck. Pursuit of the information had involved intuition, multiple interviews, and a drive all the way to the western Carolina mountains.

"Um, did you find something helpful?" Mabel asked.

"Do you know the people in this photograph?" Victoria spun the newsletter around on the table so Mabel could see the six teens right side up.

"You're interested in *that* photograph? These children?" Mabel slid her reading glasses over her ears again and lifted the photo to eye-level. "Oh, I think I took this shot. Yes, I did. But no, I don't recognize any of them. Although it says right here that the girl on the end is Karen Strauss."

"What about the boy with the sunglasses standing next to her? Do you remember his name?"

"No. Not that I recall. You have to understand, not everyone staying in Stone Ridge Mountain lives here. Some are guests who are renting, although many families return year after year to rent the same cabins."

"Is there a list of renters? For the jubilee week specifically?" Victoria asked.

"Uh, no. Definitely not. Many cabin owners manage their rental situation by themselves. There's just no way to get that information from twelve years ago."

"Okay." She'd thought as much, but it was still worth asking. "Can you get Crawford back here so I can show him this picture, please?"

"Sure." Mabel dipped her head and stared out over her glasses. "But he won't know them. Crawford is a good maintenance man, and otherwise, he mostly keeps to himself. He always has. But we can ask him. See what he says."

Carrying the newsletter, Victoria walked alongside Mabel through the clubhouse, out a back door, and onto the deck overlooking the pool area.

Crawford's tall frame hunched over something just outside the pool's gate.

"Crawford! Can you come up here?" Mabel shouted with a set of lungs so powerful she startled Victoria.

Without standing, Crawford turned and looked up at them. Mabel beckoned with her hand until he straightened and dropped a wrench into a toolbox with a clatter that resonated all the way to the upper deck.

Victoria watched the first few strides of his approach. She was still uncertain about his age. As he got closer, she shifted her attention to the lake and the forest of trees around it. "Any surveillance cameras on the property?" she asked Mabel.

"We have cameras in the pool area, to keep people from swimming after dark. And on the far side of the lake, around one of the picnic table areas. You can't see it from here. We installed those after some terrible renters destroyed some of our outdoor furniture and we couldn't prove who did it. No one seems to know the cameras are out there now. Or they just don't care. We catch people relieving themselves constantly. They have sex, too." Mabel widened her eyes in amusement. "On the ground, on the picnic tables, in the work shed, of all places. Imagine that. Lots of mosquito bites in strange places, I'm sure." Mabel shook her head. "Anyway, the cameras went up four or five, maybe six years ago. We didn't have any at the time of our twenty-fifth jubilee if that's what you're getting at."

Crawford joined them on the deck, not the least bit winded from his trek up the stairs. "What do you need?" he asked.

"The FBI needs to know if you recognize anyone from this photo," Mabel said, pointing to the picture with the teens.

Crawford stared for several seconds before shaking his head. "No. Don't recognize any of them," he said, but the look in his eyes told Victoria otherwise.

"You sure you can't tell me anything about them?" she asked.

"A lot of rich entitled kids come here on vacation and drink and vandalize stuff. Most of them are jerks. This group probably wasn't any different."

"Crawford!" Mabel exclaimed. "What a terrible thing to say about our guests!"

Crawford shrugged. "Sometimes you gotta call it like you see it. Mostly it's true."

"But do you remember any of these kids specifically?" Victoria asked.

"No. Why should I?" Crawford answered. "They're all the same."

"One of these kids was Jerome Smith," Victoria said.

"The basketball player?" Crawford looked genuinely surprised. "No way."

Mabel moved closer, taking another look at the picture. "Well, I'll be! I photographed a celebrity. Oh...he wasn't famous yet, not back then, was he? But all this time and we didn't even know. That picture needs to be framed on our wall in the community center. We've had other celebrities here, of course. Actors and actresses. An Olympian. But a famous basketball player...he's the only one I know of."

"You might not want to showcase this photo, considering Jerome recently got murdered," Victoria said.

Mabel's beaming expression disappeared. "Jerome Smith is dead?" she asked, eyes wide and mouth gaping.

"I thought I might 'a heard somethin' about that," Crawford said.

"Three others in this photo are also dead," Victoria said. "I need to identify the two who are still alive."

"All of them got murdered?" Mabel asked, wringing her hands.

Crawford crossed his arms and scrunched his eyes. "That may be, but we don't know anything about that. It's got nothing to do with this place. We can't help you."

"Is there anyone here who might know these two?" Victoria pointed to the unidentified teens.

"I've got an idea." Mabel turned to Crawford. "You know who we should ask? Joey! We should ask Joey!"

"Joey isn't going to remember a name from so many years ago," Crawford muttered, uncrossing his arms and stuffing his hands into his pants pockets. "She's getting forgetful. She can barely remember her own day-to-day comings and goings lately."

"That's not true. Joey might help. And she'll love having a visitor." Mabel twisted her wrist to check the plastic watch she wore. "Oh, no. I can't go with you right now. I have to give a tour soon. It shouldn't take more than an hour. Can you wait for me?"

"I need to get phone and Internet service as soon as I can," Victoria said. "I'm afraid I can't wait."

"Oh. Right. My apologies. Of course, you must be very busy. Your job is to solve murders. Obviously, that can't wait. I'll just show you how to get there. The driveway to Joey's cabin is steep. And it's not paved. Do you have four-wheel drive?"

"Not with me. I've got a rental car from the airport."

Mabel looked out the window. The Hyundai was the only car parked in front of the clubhouse. "That little thing?" Mabel asked. "Hm. Well, the roads are dry. Just drive slowly. Stick to the inside edge and you should be fine. If not, someone will come and help you. It happens. Last winter, someone rented a cabin and showed up in a fancy sports car. Lamborghini? I don't remember exactly. Something ridiculous for these roads. That didn't go well."

A Subaru pulled into a parking spot next to Victoria's rental.

"That must be my appointment. For the tour. They're considering holding a family reunion here."

"Thank you for your help," Victoria said. "I might be in touch again."

"Anytime," Mabel answered. "It was wonderful to meet you. Good luck with your work. And if Joey can't help, get back to me. I'll see if there's anyone else around to ask. Oh, I know you're in a rush, but while there's some daylight left, visit our famous lookout point, the stone dome. It's worth a quick stop before you go."

Victoria left the clubhouse, got back into her car, and drove the main road further up the mountain. She hadn't come to sightsee, yet when she spotted the sign for the lookout point, she pulled over to check it out before dark. If the view was that special, everyone who visited had probably seen it. Including the four murder victims.

A short walk and she was standing on a giant stone formation. Signs cautioned against walking too close to the edge, though that wouldn't discourage some from doing so anyway.

In the fading twilight, Victoria took in a bird's eye-view of the community. Colored metal roofs in red, green, and gray peeked out from the trees around the banks of Staghorn Lake. Beyond the lake, a small clearing contained picnic tables that looked dollhouse sized from above. That was probably the area that now had video cameras.

Victoria moved closer to the edge and stared down the side of the steep cliff. A beer can was resting on a ledge approximately thirty yards below. There was no way to get there without climbing equipment. Someone must have dropped it. Victoria recalled Crawford's comment about kids drinking and vandalizing. She pictured the six teens in the photo. They seemed the age when kids experimented with alcohol. Had they come up here together to drink all those years ago? So much could go wrong at this height if people weren't careful. And excessive alcohol made people careless. A fall from the stone dome would prove fatal. But no one had fallen that July 4th weekend, or it would have made the news. Wouldn't it?

Beyond the jagged cliff, the woods were dense, the lake wide and dark.

If Stone Ridge Mountain held secrets, it was hiding them well.

27

Victoria didn't linger at the stone lookout point. Minutes later, she was crawling around a blind curve at five miles an hour, navigating the mountain peak that was Joey's driveway. Twigs and debris littered the road, but nothing so large the car couldn't drive over. Based on Crawford's comment about Joey's memory, Victoria assumed Joey was an elderly woman. If she navigated the road to her house regularly without incident, she was an excellent driver.

As slow and frustrating as the route might have been, Victoria would not miss the chance to talk to someone who might recognize the people in the photo. In-person interviews were always better than over the phone or on a video call. She planned to show Joey the picture of the teens and find out if she knew more about them. As soon as she took care of that, Victoria wanted to get back on the road to Charlotte, hopefully before the twilight sky changed to darkness.

The driveway ended at a large, graveled area in front of a log cabin. Two mixed breed dogs barked from the cabin's porch. One raced toward the car and stopped a few yards away, teeth bared. His front legs jumped off the ground with each full-body bark. A pronounced limp slowed the other dog, but his bark was deep and fully invested in proclaiming the property as his territory.

As much as Victoria loved dogs, these two didn't know that yet, and they were big enough to tear her throat out if they wanted. She stayed inside her car.

The cabin's screen door opened, and a large woman came outside. She had wiry gray hair and wore a colorful, tie-died sweatshirt with jeans and Birkenstocks. "Calm down, boys. Come. Come," she yelled.

The dogs spun around. One ran back to the porch, the other ambled. Both kept their eyes on Victoria once they got there.

"Hi. Joey Lafond?" Victoria asked, getting out of her car but staying close to it.

"Yes. And who are you? I don't get many people coming up here." She didn't sound unfriendly, just surprised to have a visitor.

Victoria introduced herself, having to almost yell across the distance. She took a few minutes to explain why she was there, and that Mabel had sent her.

"I'll have to get my glasses if I'm going to help you," Joey said. "Come on over. The dogs are big sweethearts. They won't hurt you unless I tell them to."

Victoria met Joey on the porch, stopping to greet the dogs on her way. They seemed fine with her now that their owner had spoken.

A wall of windows formed the back of Joey's cabin. Even with the thickening clouds and the darkening sky, the view from inside was as spectacular as the view from the lookout point. Joey moved past antique furniture that predated the cabin by at least forty years. She went into the kitchen area and returned wearing glasses. "Now let me see what you've got."

Victoria set the open newsletter on a tabletop, over a jigsaw puzzle in its early stages of completion. "Mabel took this picture twelve years ago at the jubilee anniversary event. I'm trying to identify this man here. He'd be in his late twenties today."

Even with glasses on, Joey squinted at the newsletter. Victoria was already thinking about making a quick exit and scanning the photo into the FBI's facial recognition software once she had cell service. But Joey straightened and surprised Victoria by saying, "Oh, yes. It's been a long time, but I recognize him. That's Rita's nephew. Rita Markle. She's no longer here. She moved to a retirement home in Winston-Salem. But we used to be in a neighborhood book club together."

Victoria felt a rush of gratitude. "That's great, that you recognize him. Do you know his first name? Or where he and his family lived?"

"No. I don't know his first name. But he has the same last name as Rita. His father was Rita's brother. Rita got a divorce and took her maiden name back."

Rita Markle's nephew. That might be all the FBI needed to identify the young man. But the more information they had to work with, the easier it would be.

"Anything else you can remember about him? The state and town where he grew up?" Victoria asked.

"He lived somewhere in North Carolina. I remember he was a smart young fellow. And a quiet one. He always had his face in a book when he was here. He was never one of those boys that had to run around hollering as if the house was on fire to get their energy out. Not like that at all. Rita bragged about him. She used to buy him T-shirts with chemistry jokes. She showed them to me, part of her Christmas shopping, because she thought they were so clever."

"That's great. Anything else?"

"He went to a very good college. Rita mentioned it often, but I can't recall the name of it now." Joey smiled then. "Rita adored him. We'd be right in the middle of a book club discussion and then Rita would go off out of nowhere with an update about her nephew Jeffrey, the chemistry major, and how he planned to cure cancer someday. His mother was sick with cancer, you see."

"You just said his name was Jeffrey."

"Oh. How about that?" Joey looked surprised. Then her smile grew. "There you go. Jeffrey Markle."

Victoria took a moment to jot down everything Joey had told her.

Jeffrey Markle. Nephew of Rita Markle. North Carolina family residence. Quiet. Bookworm. Competitive college. Chemistry.

It was more than enough to confirm they had the right person once they identified him.

"And Karen Strauss, the girl standing next to Jeffrey in the photo," Victoria said. "Do you know her or her family?"

"I've met her father and stepmother." Joey's mouth seemed to curl up with distaste, but then the expression was gone. "Didn't know them well. Like most people here, their cabin wasn't their primary home. Just a vacation place. I know they had a daughter, and that must be her in the photo, but I never met her. Some young people don't care much for our community. They're too attached to their phones and electronic gadgets, and we don't have great internet service around here. The mother, a stepmother actually, seemed to be a little uptight. She complained about a lack of supervision and security at Stone Ridge Mountain.

She wanted more rules, especially in relation to youngsters and what they could and couldn't do. I was on the board then. She had her share of issues about moral values. Live and let live. That's what I say. It's what I've always said. But some people think they know what's best for everyone."

Victoria agreed with Joey's thinking, but kept her thoughts on the matter at hand. "Do you recall where the Strauss family lived, their primary address?"

"I'm not sure of that," Joey answered. "Oh, can I get you something to drink? Coffee? Tea?"

"Thank you so much. You've been so helpful, but I really should go now. I'm driving back to Charlotte. And I really need to get my cell service back."

"Be careful driving out of here," Joey said, staring at the now dark sky. "The rain is coming, and with it comes the fog. At this elevation, visibility on those roads can be a real challenge. The clouds really surround you something thick."

"Thanks," Victoria said. "I'll be careful."

28

When Victoria was a few miles away from Stone Ridge Mountain, full darkness descended, and the sky unleashed a torrential downpour. Alone on the unlit mountain road, she slowed to less than ten miles per hour. Heat blasted from the defoggers, and the windshield wipers slashed a frantic rhythm but could not get the job done.

Joey had warned her about the weather and Victoria understood why. Thick fog closed in, reaching all the way to the ground. Combined with the heavy rain, visibility dropped to the small space directly in front of her headlights. The high beams made things worse, and the rental didn't have fog lights like her Suburban. Victoria leaned forward, straining to see out. A precipitous drop on the side of the narrow road left no margin for error. Thinking about the possibility of an accident on a remote road with no cell service made her extra wary. She imagined herself home with Ned, curled up together in front of the fireplace with a soft blanket and a nice warm dinner. Roasted vegetables. A glass of white wine. She wondered what he was doing right then. Wasn't this the day he was meeting with Bob after work? If there hadn't been any veterinary emergencies, Ned was in the meeting now, or already on his way home.

Since she couldn't call him, or anyone else, her thoughts returned to the atonement murder case. The visit to Stone Ridge Mountain convinced her something happened there that was at the center of the murders, but she still needed solid evidence to back her theory. Finding the two others from the photo, Jeffrey Markle and Karen Strauss, was critical. Until then, Victoria could only continue to wonder why someone had murdered the other four. They were only teenagers. Had they stumbled upon something they shouldn't have seen? No. It was more than that. The atonement message implied they'd been more than just witnesses. They'd done something. But what?

The rain intensified, battering the windshield, and blurring everything outside the car. Her neck and shoulders tensed as she focused on the road.

She glimpsed an embankment and pulled over to wait out the worst of the rain, assuming it had to let up soon. She checked her phone. Still no service. With nothing to occupy her time, her empty stomach clenched. Rummaging through her bag produced a protein bar, which she broke into small bites and ate slowly to make the meal last. Her suitcase in the trunk held more snacks, but she wasn't hungry enough to get drenched in the relentless rain.

For ten frustrating minutes, she sat in the idling car with the heat running and the hazard lights blinking, thinking about all the calls she desperately needed to make to update her colleagues and the detectives working on the homicide cases. The rain wasn't letting up. Out of habit, she reached for her phone to check her messages again, as she'd done three times already, before remembering there was no connection.

A rumbling sound separated itself from the pounding rain and howling wind. Thunder? The rumble grew louder. A truck with glaring lights materialized from the mist like a glowing halo. Victoria put the Hyundai in gear and pulled back onto the road, following the truck's blurred red tail lights as the vehicle crawled around the tight bends. Even the most prepared drivers seemed to respect the treacherous conditions.

When she descended from the mountains and emerged from the fog, the part of the drive that should have lasted approximately twenty minutes had consumed over an hour of her evening. Rain continued to pelt her vehicle as she cruised down the highway, but she could see ahead. Best of all, cell service had returned. Her phone chirped repeatedly with incoming notifications.

She exited the highway and pulled into a gas station. Under a roof next to the gas pumps, where she finally had shelter from the rain, she checked her phone. Patrick Durst had left five messages since she spoke with him last. An unsettling feeling brewed inside her as she stared at the list of notifications bearing his name.

He'd left the first voicemail shortly after their connection dropped in the middle of their conversation near Stone Ridge Mountain.

She pressed play, and his voice broke the silence in the car. "Hey, I lost you. Call me back when you can."

The second message had come a minute after the first. "Hey. This is Detective Durst again. Not sure if your phone died or you still don't have service, but call me back when you can."

The third call came two hours later. "Hey. It's Patrick. Patrick Durst. I haven't heard from you and I'm a little worried."

Worried? Did he forget she was a federal agent?

The last call had come thirty minutes ago, probably while she was inching along the fog-drenched roads.

"Victoria. This is Detective Durst from the Durham Police Department. I need you to call me as soon as you get this message."

The first message was perfectly normal, coming after their call cut off. She supposed the second was as well. But the two that followed made her shift uncomfortably in her seat. What was going on? Something about the detective's tone made her tense. And for that reason, she put off calling him back and contacted Sam in the FBI's D.C. office instead.

Sam picked up on the first ring, and Victoria told him what she'd learned at Stone Ridge Mountain. She spoke rapidly, barely taking time to catch her breath, which meant she was truly excited. "We've established that all four victims knew each other, or at least were at the same event together twelve years ago."

"*You* established that. No reason to let others take the credit. Great work, by the way."

"Thanks. We've got two people to find now. The first is Karen Strauss, who could be married by now and have a different last name. She looked a little younger than the others, but not by much. She's still in her late twenties. I'd start looking in North or South Carolina."

"Got it."

"The male's name is Jeffrey Markle. Same approximate age." Victoria repeated the information Joey had given her on Jeffrey.

"I'm on it," Sam said. "Safe driving."

"Thanks, Sam. Oh, wait. Did Patrick Durst from the Durham Police Department send you the info about the thallium sulfate poison?"

"He did. I've got someone looking into it. If only a few places sell the chemicals, or only a few people have recently purchased them, we'll be in luck."

They said goodbye, and Victoria filled her gas tank and moved the car away from the pumps. She parked again and sprinted through the rain to the convenience store. Inside the restroom, as she was sliding the metal lock from one side of the door to the other, it jammed her fingertip. She jerked her hand back, shocked by the sudden, sharp pain. At the sink, she held her finger under the water, pushing the top of the faucet every four seconds to keep the cold water flowing.

Outside, after purchasing a banana and yogurt, she hurried between parked cars to get back to her own. What looked like a sliver of water turned out to be a deep puddle when her foot splashed into it, leaving her shoes, socks, and feet as soaked as the rest of her. And in her surprise, she'd dropped her plastic spoon onto the dirty pavement.

What next, she thought, sitting inside her car a few minutes later with a second spoon, steam rising from her drenched clothes. Her finger pulsed with pain and the nail bed was already turning a deep shade of purple.

For a few minutes, she let her grouchiness take over, though she knew life could get worse. So much worse. She'd seen it all. And for that matter, she could be a Happy Farms chicken. That's all it took to end her short-lived pity party and feel miserable for other reasons.

Before leaving the gas station, she checked her work mail and opened one from DTI with a one-night hotel reservation for the Charlotte Airport Hilton. The location sounded promising for returning the car and catching her super early flight. Back on the highway, with the hotel's address programmed in her GPS, she called Ned.

"How was your day?" he asked.

"I'm still driving. It's taking longer than I expected. But I think it might be worth the trouble. I'm looking for that one thing that will make sense of all this. And I think I'm going to find it."

"Do you want to talk about the case?" he asked.

"I want to talk about your day," she told him.

"My day, huh? Well, I have a new client with two greyhounds. I told her all about our dogs and your rescue. She already knew about you."

Victoria focused in on the first part of his last sentence. He's said *our dogs*. A wave of happiness hit her. Less than a minute talking to Ned, and she felt so much better.

"How was your meeting with Bob?" she asked. "That was tonight, right?"

"Yes. It was…interesting. And something we need to talk about." His words would have sparked concern, if not for the tone of his voice. Victoria thought it suggested something positive, and that had her intrigued.

"We can talk about it now," she said. "I've got plenty of time." She glanced at the GPS. "Another hour to my hotel."

"I'd rather wait until we're together."

"Is everything okay?"

"Yes. Everything is fine. And this can wait until you get back."

"All right then," she said, her curiosity piqued. Ned didn't play head games. Whatever he wanted to talk about had to be important. "I've got the first flight out of Charlotte in the morning. I'll be home before ten. We can take a long hike and talk then."

"Sounds great."

"You up for a challenging climb? Because I need one. I've been sitting on my butt for two days."

"I'm always up for a challenge. I'll swim early, then pack lunches and get everything ready for the dogs."

"Looking forward to it. I miss you."

"I miss you, too."

"I've got to check on today's lab results, but call me later, once you're finished working."

When they said goodbye, she wondered what Ned needed to tell her. She trusted him when he said everything was okay, but still, she wished she already knew what he was going to say and didn't have to wait.

It didn't take long for her sense of duty to nag at her. She could procrastinate no longer.

She called Detective Durst back.

29

Patrick Durst answered his phone after one ring. "Victoria!" he exclaimed, as if she'd been lost alone in the wilderness for weeks. His tone made her uncomfortable.

"Sorry about earlier," she said. "I told you I had poor reception and might lose you."

"I know. You did. Are you...can you stop by the precinct tonight?"

"No. I'm headed to Charlotte. Why? Did something happen with the case?"

"Yes. We have some, uh...some additional evidence."

She was relieved this was business and not personal, yet something in the detective's tone still sent up a red flag. "What new evidence?"

"We found something in Cassandra's purse and only just realized what it is a few hours ago."

Victoria was coming up on a construction area with concrete blocks on her left while passing an eighteen-wheeler to her right. Her arms were tense, and her hands held a tight grip on the wheel. "What did you find?"

"A Polaroid photo."

"Like the type of photos at Jerome Smith's crime scene?"

"Might be from the same camera. We're checking."

"Was it body parts?"

"No. I'll scan it to you, with the enlargements we made, so you can give us your thoughts."

"I'm on the highway. Do I need to pull over and look at it now?"

"I think you should. Call me back once you do, okay?"

"Okay," she said, and ended the call.

She put on her blinker and switched to the far-right lane. For the half mile it took to reach the next exit, she was concerned but also mildly annoyed with the way the detective had presented the new development, creating more drama than might be necessary. Everyone seemed to have secrets tonight.

Victoria left the highway and pulled off the road into the parking lot for a fast-food restaurant. She selected a spot in an empty row of spaces. Behind her, an SUV and a minivan waited in the drive through line.

With the car in park and the motor running, Victoria typed her phone password, then her email password, and opened the message from Detective Durst.

This photograph was in Cassandra's purse at the crime scene. We enlarged the image.

Victoria downloaded the first attached image. It was a Polaroid with white edges, the same type as the ones left behind in Jerome's guest room. Someone had taken the shot outside in daylight and from far away. Only after a long stare could she make sense of it. In the center of the background, she recognized the white-brick gatehouse and the scrolled iron gate in front of Jerome's neighborhood. That's all she could see.

She downloaded another image from Durst. An enlarged and enhanced section from the first photo. The graininess had worsened, but she saw what she needed to see—a woman in a black jacket getting into an average-sized sedan. She'd lifted her left hand, shielding her face. The hand bore a large diamond ring and was missing two fingertips.

A bolt of fear struck.

Why was there a photograph of her? Who had taken it? Had the killer hidden in the crowd of reporters? Why was it in Cassandra's purse? Was it a threat, or was the killer just messing with their heads, letting them know he was ahead of them?

Unpleasant memories returned. This wasn't the first time a serial killer had taken an interest in her. It also happened a few years ago, during a previous investigation. Beth Dellinger, the so-called Numbers Killer, had become obsessed with Victoria and her colleague Dante Rivera. Beth was deeply disturbed and delusional. She'd conjured up a romantic relationship between the FBI agents. One that didn't exist. Not then, anyway. The obsession ultimately led to Beth's capture. It hadn't ended well for her, but at least her killing spree ceased. Was something similar happening again?

Victoria read the rest of Detective Durst's message.

Call me when you get this. Cassandra was not in Boston recently. She could not have taken that photo. No prints on it. We identified the location as Jerome Smith's neighborhood, as you probably already know. I checked with Detective Lisa Suarez to find out if the Boston PD filmed everyone in the crowd outside the neighborhood gate. They did the first day of the investigation, but not throughout the second, which is when she said you arrived. They're looking through security camera footage now.

His message ended with: *We don't know who the killer is yet, but the killer knows you.*

Victoria didn't need the reminder.

30

An hour after learning the killer had photographed her, Victoria walked to the entrance of the Charlotte Airport Hilton, her suitcase bumping up and over the curb behind her. She wasn't feeling her best. She didn't know what to make of the photo they'd found in the victim's purse. The long day of driving had left her with a headache. Her socks and shoes were still wet, and her feet were cold. Her finger ached where she'd jammed it in the restroom. She still had to type up her notes, then she planned to take a hot shower, go to bed, and eke out as many hours of sleep as she could before her alarm went off at 4:00 am. At least the hotel was close to the airport.

She waited at the reception desk while a man wearing a suit checked in and got a key. When he left, Victoria stepped up to take his place.

"Hi. I'm checking in. Victoria Heslin. One night."

"Oh…I'm sorry," the woman behind the desk said. "We don't have any available rooms."

Victoria didn't quite understand. Had the DTI operator or system messed up her reservation and booked the wrong night? She entered her passwords, scrolled through her messages, and found the hotel confirmation. "Here it is. Would you like my reservation number?"

"I'm sorry. It's just we really don't have any rooms left. We're fully booked and when you didn't show…it's so late, we assumed you weren't coming. We gave your room away."

"But…I didn't cancel."

"I really am sorry."

Victoria huffed, thinking about the man who had just left with a room key. If she'd arrived a few minutes earlier, would he be the one without a room? "You don't have one room?" she asked. "A single? A double? A suite?"

"We don't have anything."

"I didn't realize I had a deadline to check in." Victoria narrowed her eyes at the woman, wanting to say so much more, but managing to hold it all back before she started acting unreasonably. Although...she had a reservation. That should be enough to guarantee a room. She took a deep breath and stepped back. It wasn't the employee's fault. Or maybe it was. But that didn't matter now. Victoria couldn't control what happened to her. Past investigations had proven that beyond a doubt, but she was always in control of her response. For the second time in a short while, she reminded herself that her current situation was light years away from her most challenging moments.

The faster I forget this happened, the better.

"I can give you the name of nearby hotels and you could try those," the woman suggested.

"Great. Thanks, that would be helpful." Victoria forced her mouth into a tight smile. She didn't need a mirror to know it wasn't a pretty one.

You in Charlotte yet or still driving? Sam's text message asked.

Rather than type a response, Victoria stepped into her new hotel room, flicked on the light, and called him.

"Hey. How are you?" Sam asked, sounding full of energy.

"Why can't things ever be easy?"

"What happened?"

"I had a hotel mishap. Not what I needed after a long day, but whatever. I'm fine now. Just a lot farther from the airport than I wanted to be," she said, realizing she'd have to set her alarm for 3:30 am. "Your chipper attitude is making me feel like an old lady for being so tired. What's got you in such a good mood?"

"Me? When am I not in a good mood?"

"True. Are you still in the office?" Victoria asked, flinging open a luggage rack and tossing her carryon suitcase on top.

"Yes. Because I didn't want to call you and say I have good news and bad news. I was trying to get to a point of only having good news. But unfortunately, I still have good news *and* bad news. So, which do you want first?"

"The bad news," Victoria said, as she removed a wet and dirty shoe.

"I haven't found a Jeffrey Markle who is the right age or fit with the information you gave me. So, I'm still looking."

"That's not so bad," she said, grimacing as she peeled off her wet socks, though it was strange that Sam hadn't located Jeffrey yet. "What's the good news?"

"I found Karen Strauss. She's Karen Green now. And she lives in Charlotte."

"Perfect," Victoria said, excitement giving her a sense of extra energy. "Send her address and I'll try to meet her in the morning. Maybe she'll know where we can find Jeffrey Markle." Only after Victoria spoke did it sink in that she'd just derailed her plans to travel home on the first flight to D.C.

"I'm putting together a background file on her," Sam said. "I'll send what I've got soon. Then I'm outta here."

"Okay. Thanks, Sam."

The investigation was getting somewhere. Speaking with Karen was top priority to understanding what happened then and what was happening now. At least one thing was going Victoria's way. And it was an important thing.

She washed her face and changed into pajama bottoms, a camisole top, and dry socks. She sent Ned an apology note with her change of plans and a promise to hike and picnic on Sunday.

Ned responded with, *That's okay. Do what you have to do and be safe.* A second message came, *Dogs about to get their bedtime snacks,* followed by a picture of her entire pack crowded together, big dark eyes gazing up at the camera. That made her smile. And then she got back to work.

Sitting at the hotel desk with her legs tucked underneath her, she uploaded the scanned photo that included the four victims, Karen Strauss, and the man she listed as *potentially Jeffrey Markel-need to confirm.*

Without intending to, Victoria spent another hour and a half reading the email updates coming in from the other investigations.

The FBI team was all over the thallium sulfate research. By Monday, they expected to have a list of places where one could order the chemical components in the United States along with a list of who had purchased them. Information on sales of the product from other countries would take much longer.

Though forensics had made progress, there were no new leads in the suspect department. The information Victoria recently found seemed to offer the most promise. She hoped following those clues would prove her right.

It was after midnight when she was finally ready for bed. She took a swig of warm water, because she'd had almost nothing to drink all afternoon. She'd make up for it tomorrow by drinking extra. Unless she said the same thing then, and the next day, and the day after that. She might as well start her quest to do better now. She'd refill the bottle and get some ice to make it palatable. Yawning, she grabbed the ice bucket from the counter and the hotel key card from the front of her backpack. Since her shoes were sopping wet, she left the room in her pajamas and socks, and headed toward the ice machine she'd spotted earlier near the elevator.

After filling the ice bucket, she returned to her room and placed the keycard on the sensor. A tiny red light glowed. She tried again. Still red. She looked down at the brown keycard. Not the blue one the front desk clerk had handed her this evening. She was holding the card from her hotel room in Durham.

She squeezed her eyes shut for a second and gathered her composure. Getting locked out was not a big deal. She'd go down to the lobby and get a new key. It was late. There wouldn't be anyone else around.

Carrying the ice bucket in one hand, she rode the elevator to the ground floor. As she walked into the lobby, the hotel's automatic front doors slid open. In a rush of movement and animated conversation, a throng of people entered. Behind them, a steady flow of passengers emptied out of a bus.

Wearing only socks on her feet, Victoria hurried to the front desk to beat the crowd. "I just got locked out of my room," she said, offering the desk clerk a weak smile. Her comfy camisole suddenly seemed tiny and flimsy without a bra.

"It happens," he said. "Room number?"

"Uh, I'm sorry. I don't remember. My name is Victoria Heslin," she said, keeping her voice low.

The area behind her was filling with people. Apparently, everyone on the bus needed to check in. Their boisterous laughter suggested they'd been drinking. Maybe they were coming from a sports event.

"You have any ID with you?" the desk clerk asked next.

"Nope. It's just me and the ice bucket."

"Okay. What did you say your name was?"

"Victoria Heslin."

"Sorry, I couldn't hear you." The desk clerk raised his voice. "Victoria Heslin? Heslin with an h?" he asked while staring at his computer screen and typing.

"Victoria Heslin?" a woman behind Victoria shouted, somehow hearing the clerk over the buzz of noisy conversations. "Isn't that the name of the FBI agent from that plane? The missing plane? Is that her?"

The woman was too insistent and demanding for Victoria to pretend she hadn't heard. She slowly turned to look over her shoulder. Many sets of eyes stared back at her. Oh, how she hated attention, even if she weren't in her pajamas. She smiled quickly and offered a curt wave before crossing an arm over her chest and turning back to the desk clerk.

Could the night get any worse?

Out of the corner of her eye, she caught phones lifted and aimed in her direction. People were taking her picture as if she were a celebrity.

The desk clerk held out the replacement key for Victoria, but she didn't take it. Not yet. She turned around again and slowly, carefully scanned the crowd behind her, person by person.

No Polaroid cameras in sight.

But if the killer was already watching Victoria, evident by the photo in Cassandra's purse, what if one of the lobby photos got posted online along with Victoria's location?

She'd be looking over her shoulder more often until the atonement murder investigation resolved. Not because she was afraid, though a healthy dose of fear was both warranted and wise if it kept her alert. If the killer was near, she intended to grab him before he got to anyone else, including her.

31

Instead of waking at 3:30 a.m. for the early flight, Victoria had slept until six. With the sun still rising, she'd gotten in a long run, exploring quiet, unfamiliar streets in the chilly morning air. Running seven-minute miles had left her drenched with sweat and renewed in the best possible way. When she returned to the hotel, her reflection in the lobby mirror showed a flushed face and Rudolph-red nose. Eagerness pulsed through her body, some of it from endorphins. Staying an additional day in Charlotte would be well worth the personal sacrifice if she could meet with Karen and put another piece of the current investigative puzzle together.

Still in her workout clothes, she plopped into a corner chair in her hotel room. She put her feet on the ottoman and checked her work messages. Sam had gone above and beyond as usual. He'd sent a file on Karen Strauss late last night while Victoria slept. She opened it now and consumed the details.

Karen Strauss was a graduate of the University of North Carolina at Charlotte and employed as a realtor with The Carolina Realty Company. She'd married Robert Green, three years her senior and an analyst with Ally Bank. They lived together in Charlotte in a house that cost more than the average. They did not have children.

Sam was thorough. He'd already checked the U.S. travel databases. Karen had not traveled to Boston recently. She had, however, flown into La Guardia airport two days before Jerome's murder.

Victoria felt a little jump in her chest as she calculated the drive time from New York to Boston. Depending on the exact locations, it could take as little as four hours.

Next, she found Karen on Facebook and scrolled through her posts. All of them related to real estate: sneak peeks of her new listings before they hit the market, and proud new homeowners celebrating their closings. Nothing personal, and none of the posts included images of Karen. Her realtor's headshot, probably filtered to perfection, told Victoria little about the real person it represented.

When Victoria's alarm went off for the second time that morning, signaling she had to get ready, she put her phone aside and pulled off her workout clothes. Her endorphins had ebbed away, but her anticipatory buzz remained. After a quick shower, she aimed the dryer at the mirror to clear the condensation, then turned it on her hair. A few swipes of deodorant, a touch of long-lasting lipstick, blush, to give her light skin some color, and a few flicks of mascara completed her routine. Out of necessity, she recycled her outfit from the previous day. Her sweaty running clothes went into a plastic bag.

Breakfast was a granola parfait with fruit and coffee from a kiosk in the hotel lobby.

Now that Victoria was on the killer's radar, she wasn't going to Karen's address alone. Sam had arranged for someone from the Charlotte FBI office to meet her there. He didn't know who. Most likely, whoever was available and willing to drop their weekend plans at a moment's notice. Since it was a Saturday morning, they had a good chance of catching Karen at home by surprise, which always worked to the FBI's advantage.

There was a bounce to Victoria's step when she left the hotel. She couldn't wait to meet Karen.

32

Karen lived in a one-story brick home near uptown Charlotte, on a street where mature trees cast shade over the sidewalks. Like many other homes in the neighborhood, Karen's looked recently remodeled. A deck with a wire railing surrounded the front porch. Small, perfectly shaped bushes and plantings sprouted up from fresh mulch.

Victoria drove past the house and parked farther down the street. She waited inside the rental car for the few minutes it took for a Jeep Grand Cherokee to pull up behind her. A tall man in a sharp navy-blue suit got out of the Jeep and introduced himself as Tim Galax from the FBI's Charlotte office. He was younger than she expected. Probably a recent recruit.

They shook hands. Her hand was missing a fingertip and now had one blackened nail bed that would fall off in a week or so. She offered no explanation. Galax must have noticed when his gaze dropped to her hand, or he wasn't much of a field agent, but his expression gave nothing away.

"Thanks for coming," she said.

"Sure. I'll just be your muscle for the day. And I've heard a lot about you. I know you don't need a bodyguard." There was something warm and calm about his smile as he paid her the compliment.

"It can't hurt to have you along. I appreciate you giving up your Saturday morning."

"Hey, there's nothing more important than learning how it's done."

He seemed sincere, respectful, and eager. She remembered being his age, enthusiastic about each new opportunity to learn and make a real difference. Her job still excited her, especially at moments like this where a break in the case felt imminent. The anticipation was almost surreal. The only thing that had changed was her age. She had at least eight years on Agent Galax. Maybe ten. And now that she thought about it, each one of those years had flown by faster than the last. Her years of service and several intense, high-profile assignments had molded her into an experienced agent.

As they walked to Karen's house, Victoria quickly grew to like Agent Galax. She appreciated his questions and his focus on how to best help her.

The wind rustled the crepe myrtles bordering the front path on Karen's property. Someone had prominently placed a security sign in a flowerbed by the porch. The door had not one, but two bolt locks. Victoria rang the camera doorbell. Her heart was beating faster than normal from sheer suspense. She was so close to getting answers. Or at least that's what she wanted to believe.

A man wearing a T-shirt and shorts with Lululemon logos opened the door. The shirt had dark sweat circles, as if he'd recently returned from a run or gotten off an exercise machine. His eyes moved from one agent to the other.

Victoria lifted her identification card and held it steady at eye-level. Agent Galax did the same. "We're here to speak with Karen Green," Victoria said.

The man scrunched his face. "Karen? Are you sure you have the right person?"

"Yes. Are you her husband?"

"Yes. Um, Robert. Robert Green." Again, he looked from one agent to the other.

"Is Karen home?" Victoria asked.

"She is. But…what's this about?"

"A murder investigation," Victoria answered.

"Murder investigation? I don't think…"

"Mr. Green, if you would, please get your wife so we can speak with her. Otherwise, I'll need her to meet with us in our Charlotte office," Victoria said.

"Hold on. I'll be right back." Robert stared a second longer, searching for information, before closing the door on them.

Enough time passed that Victoria went to ring the doorbell again, but a woman came to the door. She also wore exercise clothes—black leggings and a long-sleeved navy top made from a sweat-wicking fabric. She had red hair, smooth with streaks of gold highlights, worn pulled back in a ponytail. A light smattering of freckles crossed the bridge of her nose. Those freckles and the red hair were the only characteristics Victoria recognized from the photo. The woman's svelte figure bore little resemblance to the pudgy girl with the sunburned shoulders from twelve years ago. With the FBI on her porch, the woman's confused expression matched that of her husband, who now stood beside her.

"Are you Karen Green?" Victoria was taller than average and stood eye to eye with the woman.

"Yes," the woman answered. "Can you please tell us what this is about and why you're here?"

"Of course," Victoria said. "May we come in to discuss it?" What she had come to discuss did not make for front-porch conversation. And she could tell more about people once she was inside their homes.

"I guess so." Karen lingered in the doorway for a few more seconds before standing aside and holding the door open. "We can sit in the living room, and you can tell me what's going on and how it involves me."

"Is there anyone else in the house besides you and your husband?" Victoria asked.

"No. It's just the two of us," Robert answered for his wife.

As the agents entered, Victoria began processing everything. The inside of the Greens' home featured minimalist furniture and symmetrical designs. Which meant one or both owners clearly cherished order. Two matching porcelain mugs sat on opposite ends of the marble counter, and a tiny blue light shone on a gleaming espresso machine. All signs the agents had interrupted a post workout coffee break.

There were no water or food bowls on the ground, and no other signs of a pet, which was always something Victoria looked for. It meant the Greens could leave home without hiring someone to care for animals or having to board them if they were to take a quick trip out of town. The cities of Boston and Durham came to mind. With no children and no pets, the Greens had more flexibility than most.

A keyring lay on the kitchen island. Attached were a tiny canister of mace, a VIPERTEK stun-gun, a sleek Mercedes key fob, and a single silver key, dwarfed by the other items. Whoever owned the key set prioritized self-defense. Add that to the double bolted door and the security system, and you had a well-prepared individual. Which made Victoria wonder—well prepared for what?

Victoria followed Karen into a large room. Karen was the first to sit. Agent Galax remained standing in the open area between the kitchen and the living area. Robert Green stood behind his wife, assuming a protective stance.

Victoria took a seat on the couch. An assortment of pamphlets and papers lay across the coffee table.

Can't Conceive? Six Benefits of Adoption.
What Are My Infertility Options?
Six Family-Building Options for Infertile Couples.

Unless the materials were for a friend, the Greens had a lot going on in their personal lives already.

"My husband said you're here about a murder?" Karen asked. Her body language indicated tension. A tightness in her face. A rigidity in her back. Was she afraid, or hiding something?

"We're looking for information." Victoria took the Stone Ridge Mountain newsletter from a folder in her bag and set it on the table. "Open that to the centerfold and have a look," she said, prepared to analyze Karen's reaction.

Karen stared at Victoria's fingers, but quickly averted her eyes and picked up the newsletter. Its pages trembled ever so slightly between her hands. She looked down at the picture but said nothing.

"There are six of you in that photo," Victoria prompted. "Four of the six died recently. Someone murdered them."

Karen's mouth opened, and her free hand rose to cover it. Behind her, Robert gasped.

Victoria leaned forward. "Do you remember the people in the picture, Karen?"

"Vaguely. Jerome, of course, only because he's so famous. And the news of his death is everywhere."

"I didn't know that you knew Jerome Smith." Her husband sounded incredulous as he leaned down over his wife's shoulder to get a better look at the newsletter photo.

Karen didn't answer him. One hand still hovered in front of her face.

"Standing next to Jerome Smith is Todd Eckstrom," Victoria said. "Also from Charlotte. Also recently murdered."

"I read about that. You knew him, too?" Robert asked his wife, sounding even more shocked than before.

Karen shook her head. "No. I really don't know any of the people in the picture. I didn't know them then and I don't know them now. I barely remember this place."

"Your family owned a cabin there at one point," Victoria said.

"They did?" Robert asked. "When was that?"

"It belonged to my stepmother's family. I only went once or twice before they sold it," Karen told him.

"Lilly Fuller and her sister Cassandra are the other females. Three days ago, they were also murdered," Victoria said.

"What the hell?" Robert exclaimed. "Why? Do you know why?"

Victoria kept her focus on Karen. "That's terrible," Karen said, her voice soft. "I...I'm not sure if I ever knew their names."

"You never saw them after you were all together at Stone Ridge Mountain that weekend?" Victoria asked.

Karen shook her head.

"You never exchanged emails or texts or phone numbers?"

"No. I didn't keep in touch with any of them. I had no reason to."

Karen let the photo fall to the table. As she did, her right sleeve edged up from her wrist, just barely, but enough to expose an old scar on the underside. Long healed, but once deep. Too deep to suggest cutting. The thin, raised line crossed her pale skin on the palm side, perpendicular to the arm bones. The scar told Victoria more about Karen's mental health history than anything else in the background file Sam had sent. It indicated a past suicide attempt. At some point in her life, Karen had dealt with serious psychological pain.

Robert paced in a small circle behind his wife, clearly rattled by the information Victoria had delivered.

"What can you tell me about the male standing next to you in the picture?" Victoria asked Karen.

"Nothing. Nothing at all."

"Please try to remember something," Victoria said, frustrated that Karen hadn't given her any new information so far. "We think his name is Jeffrey. Jeffrey Markle."

Karen clasped her hands. "Oh. I met him for a few minutes at the pool that day. There was something a little dark and edgy about him, I think. But he was smart. That's all I can remember. I'm sorry. I met them all briefly. It was so long ago."

"Is he the murder suspect? This Jeffrey person?" Robert asked.

"He's someone that we need to talk to as soon as possible, and we haven't located him yet," Victoria answered before turning back to Karen. "We haven't found any connection between the four victims yet, except for Stone Ridge Mountain. Tell me what happened when you were there."

Karen clasped her hands tighter and drew them in against her chest. "I can't think of anything that would help you. I was with my father and stepmother that week. We visited Boone and Blowing Rock. Went out to dinner a few times. We hiked. That photo caption—calling us friends—that was a huge exaggeration. As I recall, we played some games that someone at the pool organized, and then a woman asked to take our picture. I wouldn't have called any of these people my friends. Not even acquaintances."

"We have reason to believe they upset someone, and that person is out for revenge."

"But you don't know who that person is? Or why they're upset?" Robert put his hand on his wife's shoulder. "Is Karen in danger now?"

"It's possible," Victoria answered. "Though less likely if she doesn't know what happened and wasn't involved. Are you aware of anyone following you, Karen? Did you pick up on any unusual or suspicious activity recently?"

"No." Karen pressed her lips together and narrowed her eyes, looking very uncomfortable with the discussion. "I can't think of anything worth mentioning. No one is following me, as far as I can tell. I think I would have noticed, right?"

"You really don't know who the other guy is from the photo? You can't find him?" Robert acted disturbed by the information they'd shared, as he should. There was also a hint of accusation to his questions.

"Not yet. But we will," Victoria answered without pulling her gaze from Karen. "Do you own a Polaroid camera?"

"You mean one of those instant ones?" Karen asked, and her voice had a slight tremor.

"Yes."

Karen met Victoria's gaze. "No. I don't have one."

"Please tell us where you were last week. Last Saturday night," Victoria said.

Karen looked up at her husband, who answered for her. "Karen wasn't in town. She was traveling for business."

"Where specifically?" Victoria asked.

Karen crossed her legs at the ankles and sat up with her shoulders back. "Upstate New York. Looking at properties for one of my clients. I don't have a real estate license there, but that's not an issue. I evaluate properties for her all over the East Coast."

"How did you get there?" Victoria already knew this from Sam's research but needed to hear what Karen would say.

"I flew into New York and rented a car. I can show you the receipts for everything. My hotel. Meals."

"What's your client's name?" Victoria asked.

"Tiffany Westview."

Victoria turned to face Robert. "And would you mind telling me where you were last week?"

"I was in Chicago for part of the week." He crossed his arms over his chest. "I don't like where your questions are heading or what you're insinuating. You're making me think we should have an attorney present."

"You're welcome to call an attorney," Victoria said. "But it's unnecessary, not to mention expensive. We're just trying to gather information. And to prevent another death, of course."

Each atonement murder flashed through Victoria's mind. Drowning. Smothering. Poisoning. As she stood to leave, she shared her dark thoughts aloud. "Whoever killed the others has a deep-seated, growing need for revenge. So, if you think of anything else about the man next to you in that picture or remember anything else about that trip to Stone Ridge Mountain, let me know right away."

Robert frowned at Victoria from his wife's side. "She will. But is it necessary to scare her like this? To scare us like this?"

Victoria set her business card on Karen's kitchen counter and answered, "I hope it isn't."

33

Karen chewed on her fingernail as she escorted the agents from her home. When she realized what she was doing, she quickly pulled her hand away. After locking her front door behind them, she poured herself a tall glass of water. She returned to the living room and sat down on the couch again, willing herself not to panic.

How had the FBI agents dug up that old photo? Where did they even find it? Karen hadn't dared to ask, though she really wanted to know. She'd never seen the photo before, didn't know it existed, though she vaguely remembered a woman taking it. And wasn't that sort of how it all began? With that one photo?

Karen gulped some water as Robert tossed their cold coffees into the sink and ran the faucet.

From across the room, concern etched her husband's face. "That was bizarre," he said. "Are you okay?"

"I'm okay. Just a little spooked." She managed a weak smile for him. "We shouldn't worry. I'm sure nothing will come of it."

"I don't know. I'd like to believe that, but I'm not so sure." Robert ran his hand through his hair as he strode into the living room to stand in front of her. "Why would an FBI agent come all the way out here from D.C. if she didn't have credible evidence that you were in danger? I mean, six people in that photo, including you, and four of them were just killed. This is…I don't even know what to say. It's unbelievable. Don't you think? It's okay if you're freaked out. Because I certainly am. I'm going to research those murders. I can't even…" He threw his hands up, at a loss for words. "You know, maybe we should hold off on everything." His gaze went to the pamphlets on the table. "Until this plays out."

Karen wished she'd cleaned off the table before the agents arrived. Having her private business on display for strangers made her feel extra vulnerable. But she hadn't expected company.

"What do you think?" Robert asked.

"When you say 'hold off on everything,' are you talking about adoption?" she asked through gritted teeth.

He didn't answer, but he met her eyes.

Her jaw shifted back and forth as she struggled to compose herself. Her hands were trembling again. She set the glass down on one of the infertility leaflets. "We're not putting a child *on hold* for anything, unless by some miracle I get pregnant on my own." And that's exactly how she would have felt about the issue before the FBI paid an unexpected visit. Now, despite her firm response, she wasn't so sure anymore. Everything had just changed.

Robert stared at her, but his expression softened. "Karen, the doctor told you that's not going to happen, right? Look, forget I mentioned it. I'm just worried about you. That's all."

Karen smoothed her hair over her head all the way back to her ponytail as she got up from the couch. She needed to get out of the house to think. There were things she had to take care of. "I have to check out a new listing for a client. Then I'll pick up ingredients for dinner. Anything special you want?"

"No, thanks. Actually, a case of that craft beer you found last time. I can't remember what it's called. You know the one, right? If they have it. Hey, I'm sorry if I upset you. I was just worried."

"It's all right." She placed her hand on his chest and took a deep breath, inhaling the scent of him. She loved him. She wasn't afraid of him. He would protect her. He'd always had her back.

"You really don't know what they were talking about?" he asked.

"No. I really don't." Karen dropped her hand and moved past him, amazed at how easy it was to lie. "I may stop at the Farmer's Market, too. Depends on how crowded it is."

"Want me to come with you?"

"No. I'll be fine. I shouldn't be too long."

"Maybe I should come."

"No," she said, with more force than she intended, before softening her voice. "I know you have things to do. But if you could get that new towel hook screwed into the wall while I'm gone, I'd appreciate it. It's in the guest bath." She smiled again as she grabbed her keys off the kitchen island.

"Yeah. Sure. I'm going to search the Internet to see what I can find out about everything," he said, already tapping his phone screen. "Because what the hell was that all about? What could have happened? It doesn't make any sense."

Karen rubbed her arms against the icy chill gathering inside her bones. She didn't have to wonder. She knew all too well what had happened. Not all the details. In fact, very few of them. But enough that she'd never forget. She hadn't wanted to see any of those people again. She'd tried so hard not to think about them.

She'd wanted the truth to stay hidden.

Or did she? She wasn't sure anymore.

34

Twelve years ago - Karen

"I wasn't much older than you when I started visiting Stone Ridge with my parents," Karen's stepmother, Meghan, said. "It's such a fun escape. Don't worry, you'll love it when we get there. Everything will be fine."

Meghan was anything but subtle. She desperately wanted them to love the community. But that's how she was, always pushing her ideas and her agenda. And Karen's father agreed with whatever Meghan decided. So, yes, Karen was worried that she was in for an uncomfortable weekend of watching her father jump through hoops to make Meghan happy. That wasn't Karen's idea of fun. Sometimes it made her sick.

When they got to the cabin, it seemed cold and musty, as if no one had been there for months. That's because they hadn't. The smell dissipated after the first day, or maybe Karen's nose just got used to it, but she still wasn't sure how she felt about the place. The terrible sense that she was trapped there with her stepmother superseded all else.

"Now that the rain stopped, we can hike or take long walks. Swim laps in the pool. Row around in a canoe on the lake," Meghan suggested. At least she wasn't suggesting they do yoga or Pilates, Meghan's two obsessions.

They were sitting around the kitchen table, a shiny piece of wood shaped like a large cross-section of a tree trunk. Karen crumpled up the plastic from her chocolate cupcake as her father tore open another one. He'd brought a large grocery bag full of snacks on the trip. *The good stuff*, he called it.

Meghan eyed them, conveying her criticism with her crinkled brow and her pursed-lip pout, a look Karen had become all too familiar with. "How about we have fruit for dessert from now on?" Meghan suggested.

Meghan's thinly veiled criticisms were becoming more frequent, and they didn't seem to come from a position of unconditional love.

"Sounds like something we could try. But after the vacation," Karen's father said. How he could muster a smile for a comment like that was beyond her.

Karen's chair scraped against the floorboards as she pushed away from the table. She smirked at her stepmother. "I'd rather eat another cupcake than have an eating disorder. They aren't the rage anymore, Meghan." Karen meant to deliver her comment with a light, snarky attitude, but it came out angrier than she intended, and she couldn't take it back now. She strode out of the kitchen and into her room without looking back.

"Karen," her father called after her.

She pretended not to hear him. She needed to get out of the cabin and away from Meghan for a few hours.

While undressing and changing into a one-piece bathing suit, Karen daydreamed about a hike where Meghan got lost in the woods and disappeared without a trace. Karen's thoughts were rarely so ghoulish, but life had been so much simpler before Meghan came into it. For years, it had been just Karen and her father. They were doing okay. They had each other. Then he met Meghan in an exercise class at the local YMCA. She'd seemed determined to become his wife, and she'd succeeded. Now, she continued to make Karen miserable with one disapproving comment after another. Karen resented her stepmother's presence almost every hour of every day. She couldn't help herself. To say they weren't close was an understatement.

Still fuming about Meghan, Karen stuck her sunglasses on her head. She grabbed a beach towel and the book all her friends were reading. When she came out of her room, her father and Meghan were still talking at the table.

"I'm going to the pool," Karen said.

Meghan's mouth twitched as if she were trying to keep it shut. Except she couldn't. "Oh, hmm, do you have a wrap you can put over that?" she asked. "If not, I've got a cute one you can borrow. It will match your suit."

Karen unrolled her towel. She wrapped it around her waist. "There. Instant wrap. Does that work for you? Does it hide enough of my body?"

Meghan let out a loud sigh. "Look, I know you don't appreciate my comments, but I'm really trying here. I just want to help guide you through an awkward stage."

Karen froze with her mouth open. Until that moment, she didn't know she was "awkward." What did that even mean? Ugly? Did her father also think that about her? Did he and Meghan talk about her "awkwardness" and what to do about it?

A flush of embarrassment and shame warmed Karen's face. She wanted to stay cool and unaffected by the comment, but her body wouldn't let her. She couldn't look at either of them.

Her father tried to soften the blow. "Karen, she didn't mean—"

Her stepmother interrupted him. "I didn't mean to hurt your feelings. I'm sorry, Karen, if I offended you. That was not my intent. Maybe I chose the wrong words. But I know what I'm talking about. You're a young lady now. And sometimes girls…young ladies…are pressured into doing things they shouldn't do. Dressing ways that really aren't best can lead to all sorts of trouble down the line."

Not the whole *you were asking for it because of how you dressed thing!* What century was Meghan from? And what was she even talking about? What things? Drugs? Sex? Karen had never had sex, not even close. And how that related to covering up her bathing suit on the way to the pool in the middle of the day, Karen wasn't sure. She lowered her sunglasses to cover her eyes, trying to maintain her dignity and confidence. "I'll be back later." She pushed the screen door open with her shoulder and let it slam shut behind her.

The path to the clubhouse wove behind other cabins, each one on over an acre and surrounded by trees. She used the ten-minute walk to calm down and forget about Meghan. Karen didn't care what her stepmother thought. She really didn't. But her father—that was a different story. Karen loved him more than anyone on the planet. She'd already lost one parent. And though she'd gotten over her mother's absence, she'd never forget the pain and shame of abandonment. Her mother had left them. She'd had enough of Karen and her father. Walked right out of their lives and never came back. Now, partly because her mother left, Karen couldn't bear to disappoint her father. She knew he loved her. He absolutely did. But Meghan had so much power over him now.

Karen entered the pool area, walking under a *25th Jubilee* banner and past a sign listing the events for the Fourth of July weekend. Games. A barbecue. Fireworks and live music. All offered the possibility of fun, if only she had a friend with her. She'd wanted to bring a friend along, but Meghan preferred she didn't. And guess who had gotten her way?

After finding an empty chair in the sun, Karen unwrapped her towel from her body, spread the towel out, and sat down. Meghan's comments rang in her ears. Karen tried to push them away, along with the uncomfortable, self-conscious feelings they generated. Propped on her elbows with her sunglasses on, she checked out her surroundings.

Most of the people were a generation older, but not everyone. Two tall and muscular teenagers, one black, one white, shouted and grunted on the nearby basketball court. They were clearly into their loud and sweaty one-on-one game, but also showing off for two bikini-clad teenaged girls on chaise lounges with a view of the court.

One of those girls was exceptionally thin. Meghan would certainly approve. And there was something magnetic about the girl's look, the self-assured way she leisurely combed her fingers through her long blonde hair and sipped from a one-liter bottle of Diet Coke. She held the drink in the air at her side, as if it was an elegant cocktail glass rather than a plastic bottle of soda.

Karen refused to buy into the whole thin-is-better thing her stepmother was selling. She'd read enough and seen enough to know that was stupid. But the confident blonde had a certain allure about her. Anyone could see she felt good about herself. She probably didn't have a stepmother telling her not to eat dessert and to cover up her body because she was "awkward."

The girl sitting beside her was also pretty, just not as noticeable. They had the same striped towels but with unique color patterns. Most likely sisters.

Only one other person at the pool looked around the same age as Karen. He sat alone under an umbrella, wearing sunglasses, and reading a book. He wore a black T-shirt over gray swim trunks. He looked up from his book when the thin blonde laughed so loud the sound carried around the pool deck despite the music and conversations. But then he went right back to reading.

Karen flexed her toes and stretched her arms overhead as she continued to people watch from behind her shades. A guy in Hawaiian trunks floated on his back in the deep end. A cute girl in a bright yellow floaty device paddled her feet underneath her like a duck. A couple leaned their heads together as if sharing a secret before both laughed. There wasn't a lot going on, so Karen lay back, closed her eyes, and let the sun's rays massage her body. She was drifting off when shouts shattered her relaxation. Thinking something terrible had happened, her eyes flew open, and she sat up. It was the two teens from the basketball court. They hooted and cannon-balled into the pool, sending a wave of water cascading over Karen's legs and book.

She jumped from her chair as the bikini blondes laughed at the commotion.

From the other side of the pool, the boy in the black T-shirt with the book scowled. Then something changed. His focus seemed to shift. His scowl disappeared. He was looking right at Karen. An understanding passed between them. A commiserating moment. She couldn't be sure, because of his sunglasses, and yet, in her heart, she knew.

35

Twelve years ago - Todd

Swimming powerful strokes underwater, Todd heard a piercing whistle blast through the air. He broke the surface and inhaled a deep breath.

"Everyone out of the water!" the lifeguard shouted, climbing down from his perch atop a large chair.

A man and a woman hurried out of the shallow-end toward the stairs. A father yanked his child from the water, letting her floaty tube slide off her body. People sat up in their lounge chairs and leaned toward the pool.

Todd swung his head around, looking for Jerome. He didn't see him. For a few panicked seconds, Todd had a brief loss of reason. He imagined his friend was in trouble, that Jerome really couldn't swim. Todd's muscles tightened with nervous energy. He shielded his eyes and swung his head around, ready to pull his friend from under the water. He spotted Jerome by a corner of the deep end, already out of the pool. Jerome was just fine. So, what was the problem?

Then Todd saw it. A brown turd floating on the surface a few feet away from him.

He leaped from the water as if jumping for a dunk shot, simultaneously shrieking, and not just once, but two shrieks in quick succession—a response so uncool and uncharacteristic that a heartbeat later, he could hardly believe it had come from inside him.

The lifeguard blew the whistle again. "Hey! Get out of the water!"

"I am. I'm going," Todd said, swimming powerful strokes to the side of the pool but keeping his head above the water. With his hands on the concrete edge, he pushed himself out effortlessly, ending up right in front of the blonde girls.

Jerome met him there, laughing. "Dude, I wish I had that on video. You should have seen yourself. You screamed like a little girl."

The hot blonde giggled.

"Shut up," Todd told Jerome, but he was laughing too.

Crawford, the guy who was working the gatehouse when they arrived, the resident handy man, was already poolside, carrying a long pole with a net on the end. Crawford had done repair work and minor renovations in Todd's grandparents' cabin, everything from hanging televisions to installing new plumbing fixtures. Apparently, when he wasn't fixing things or working the entrance gate, he also scooped rogue turds from the pool.

"What a *crap* job he's got today, huh?" Todd said. His pun elicited an appreciative laugh from one of the blonde girls.

"When can they go back in?" a woman asked, her arm wrapped around a crying toddler.

"The chemicals need an hour to work. Then everyone can go back in," Crawford announced.

A middle-aged lady with thick bangs came out of the clubhouse holding a camera with a zoom lens and shouted, "Everyone! Excuse me! While we're waiting for the chemicals to work, let's get some photos." When she spoke again, she looked directly at Todd. "All you teenagers, over here, please." She beckoned for him and Jerome to join her, then did the same to the two blondes, a girl with red hair sitting by herself, and the loner dude reading under an umbrella.

Everyone seemed to take their time deciding if they were going to get up or not. Everyone except Todd, who seized the opportunity. The long-legged blonde looked like someone who knew how to have a good time. He wanted to know her better. "Come on," he said, waving her over until she finally set her Diet Coke down and joined him.

When the six teenagers loosely surrounded the camera lady, she moved them closer together, pointing to where they should go. Todd didn't wait before edging in next to the blonde.

"This will be a nice shot of the younger generation," the camera lady said. "We need some photos of the younger crowd."

"Yeah, uh...we don't even know each other," the hot blonde responded with a coy smile, as if tempting that situation to change.

"Not yet," Todd told her, without missing a beat. "I'm Todd Eckstrom. From Charlotte."

As he expected, the others followed his lead and introduced themselves. The blondes—Lilly and her younger sister Cassandra. The guy in the black T-shirt—Jeffrey. And Todd didn't catch the name of the red-haired girl. He wasn't paying much attention to her.

Lilly turned to him and tossed her long hair to one side. He leaned toward her and caught the odor of strong alcohol on her breath. No wonder she was having such a good time.

"Okay, we're ready," the lady said. "Everyone, look at me and smile."

In a bold move, Todd threw his arm around Lilly's shoulder.

"These are for our newsletter," the lady said. "I'll take a bunch to make sure we get one where everyone has their eyes open." She held her camera to her face for a few seconds before turning it vertical, then back to horizontal. "Excellent, I got some good ones," she said, lowering her camera to her chest. "Do any of you own homes here?"

"Um, my step-mother owns a cabin," the red-haired girl said.

"What's your name, dear?"

She answered, but Todd didn't catch her name because Lilly smiled at him as she moved out from under his arm.

"I'm going to put your name in the caption with whatever else I come up with," the lady said to the red-haired girl.

"Caption it *When Someone Pooped in the Pool*," Lilly suggested. Her big smile got bigger and turned into hysterical laughter.

The camera lady's brows knitted together as she stared at Lilly. Maybe she also knew there was something more than Diet Coke in that drink.

"This is a good time to play the games we have lined up," the camera lady said. "We've got some wonderful prizes."

"Sure," Todd answered. "Always up for a good game of whatever." He punched Jerome in the arm, just for something to do. Jerome punched back harder.

"Don't go anywhere. I'll be right back." The lady walked off with her big camera against her chest.

"Well, this could be interesting...or not," Lilly said in a hushed voice. "How about we all get together later tonight and play some of our own games?" Eyes glistening, she looked at each of the teens, offering an invitation that promised fun and trouble. An offer Todd wouldn't refuse.

36

Twelve years ago - Karen

Karen wore her towel around her body like a halter dress, waiting for her turn to toss a rusty horseshoe on a spike. Cassandra, the younger, less flashy version of the blonde sisters, moved beside Karen and asked, "You're in high school?"

"Yes," Karen answered. "I'm going to be a sophomore."

"Me, too." Cassandra tucked her hair over one ear. "You ever been here before? To this place?"

"This is my first time," Karen answered.

"Same," Cassandra said. "Family vacation. My parents rented a cabin."

"You like it?" Karen asked.

"Yeah, it's okay." Cassandra looked over at her sister, who was watching Todd lean in for a throw.

The basketball boys were as competitive about horseshoes as they were with their one-on-one game. If Karen didn't know better, she'd have thought there was a big money prize at stake, rather than free ice cream bars. Despite the testosterone and swagger bursting from those two, it was Jeffrey who interested her. Especially after the look they'd shared. His intensity was entirely different. He hadn't said much to anyone, and that's what had Karen romanticizing him. He had a quiet, careful focus and kept his sunglasses on. She imagined he had big brown eyes with a deep thoughtfulness reflected in them.

She tried not to watch him too intently but couldn't help herself. With each toss, he bent his knees, swung his arm back and forth just slightly, taking his time, lining up for the shot. After, he straightened, but kept his head and shoulders focused on the target, recalculating his next move. Sure, it was only a stupid game, but she respected the way he played it. She thought he'd make a good listener. She imagined holding his hand. There was so much she had never done before, and at that moment, Jeffrey seemed the perfect guy to change all of that.

Lilly's loud laughter broke through Karen's daydreaming. Lilly had little coordination and the worst aim, but was having more fun than anyone else.

"Like what you see, Mr. Pooper Scooper?" she asked in a provocative voice when the guy who worked at the pool walked past.

The guy stammered, and his face flushed red as Lilly burst into laughter.

Todd laughed too and shook his head as if the man were stupid. "You can move along, Crawford."

"You know, you're all little sh—." Crawford held back the rest of his comment, but the meaning was clear. He stormed past them, his hands fisted by his sides.

Cassandra glared at her sister.

"Don't give me your disappointed look," Lilly said. "He was totally checking me out. He's been staring at both of us since we got here. I mean, really. He's like thirty or something. He deserves to get told off."

"I saw him scratching his crotch earlier," Jerome added. "Gross."

Karen wouldn't dream of speaking to or about an adult the way Todd, Lilly, and Jerome just had, and the quick exchange had left Karen embarrassed for everyone. Todd had laughed as if Lilly were hilarious, though he would have laughed no matter what she'd said. It was obvious he had a thing for her, the way he hung on her every word and had his hands on her arms and shoulders to "give her some pointers." At least Jeffrey hadn't said anything cruel, or that would have quickly changed Karen's feelings for him.

Every game the camera lady organized was another version of aiming and throwing something—horseshoes, corn hole, ladder toss, darts—and the two basketball players seemed to have an advantage. When they'd exhausted the novelty of the games and declared Jerome a winner yet again, Jeffrey was the first to leave, going back to his spot under the umbrella and picking up his book.

Karen said goodbye to Cassandra and returned to her chair alone. She hadn't won any ice cream. Meghan would be glad to hear it. One less thing for her to lecture about.

The basketball boys cast long shadows on the pool deck as they hovered beside the sisters' chairs. Jerome was so tall, he had to bend over to talk to them. He said something that made Lilly laugh, but the conversation didn't last long. Todd and Jerome soon walked away, gathering their towels, water bottles, shirts, and high-top shoes. Karen thought they were leaving. Instead, they ambled over to Jeffrey. He had his book open again and didn't raise his head until Todd began speaking and extended his arm, pointing to the lake.

Jeffrey mouthed a reply and their brief conversation ended almost as soon as it had begun, with Todd and Jerome heading straight toward Karen. Were they going to stop and talk to her also? She simultaneously hoped they would, because she was curious and didn't want to be left out, and also hoped that they wouldn't.

"Hey," Todd said, standing right above her. "Uh, Keri, right?"

"No, dude, it's Karen," Jerome corrected.

"Sorry," Todd said. "My bad. I was close, though. Hey, um, a few of us are going to hang out down here tonight. Lilly's idea. Maybe have a few beers or something. We're going to meet at eight thirty. There's this clearing with picnic tables on the far side of the lake." He pointed, as he'd done with Jeffrey. "If you want to come."

"Oh...maybe," she said. "Thanks for the invite."

"Okay. Well, I hope you can make it," Todd said, flashing his confident smile.

"See you later," Jerome added. He lifted a hand in a wave as the two of them sauntered off.

Karen glanced across the pool to Jeffrey. She wondered if he'd said yes to the invitation. Anticipation rippled through her. Because if he had, she wanted to go.

37

Victoria and Agent Galax headed away from Karen's brick house and back to their cars. A couple walked on the road ahead of them, accompanied by three young children—a boy on a bike, a girl on a tricycle, and the youngest child pulled in a wagon.

Victoria thought about the fertility pamphlets on the Greens' table. The couple had complicated and emotional issues to deal with. And now this, the FBI at their door asking questions and suggesting Karen might be the killer's next victim, or the killer herself. It was a lot for anyone to process.

"She seemed really shaken," Galax said when the couple and their children were far enough away. "Do you believe she doesn't remember the other victims?"

Victoria wasn't sure about Karen yet. How much did Victoria remember of her own life twelve years ago? She conjured up the milestones that anchored her past. Twelve years ago was two years after her mother's abduction. Victoria had just graduated from Georgetown and joined the FBI. She lived in her family's house in McLean. Was she dating someone? She didn't think so, just adjusting to her new life with the Bureau. What had she done on the Fourth of July? No fireworks. She knew that much because she'd always hated them for the way they terrorized the family dogs, not to mention her uncle, a veteran with PTSD triggered by the loud booms.

But if someone had shown her a picture from the Fourth of July twelve years ago, a picture with her in it...surely the memories would come rushing back to her. Especially if something unusual had occurred then. But the picture hadn't brought back any significant memories for Karen, or so she had said, with a tremor in her voice and a slight quiver in her hands.

"I think she's hiding something," Victoria answered. "But before we question her further, we need evidence that she's *not* telling the truth. So far, we have none. We've found no record of communications between any of the victims except Todd and Jerome, and those are years old."

"Do you have a plan?"

"I'm working on it. I'm going to follow up with the client she mentioned, Tiffany Westview, and make sure Karen was in New York working for Westview when Smith died."

When they reached their cars, they exchanged phone numbers and Agent Galax said, "It was an honor to meet you. Let me know if there's anything else I can do to help. I'll just be hanging out at home with my dog for the rest of the day."

"I love that. What kind of dog?" Victoria was genuinely curious and wondered if Galax might love animals as much as she did.

"A Shepherd mix. His name is Pete."

"I'm a dog person as well. I have seven greyhounds." Victoria laughed as Agent Galax's brows rose in surprise. "Anyway, thanks again and I'll be in touch if I need more help," she told him.

All six-foot three of him, if she was estimating correctly, ducked into his Jeep. He caught her watching and waved. She waved back and got into her own car.

Her flight wasn't leaving until late afternoon. She called Sam. "Any luck finding Markle?"

"No. I still can't find him. And that's not something you hear me say often. Or ever."

"Could he have changed his name?"

"Yes, but I can't find any record of this person existing ever. If you can get anything else from your source, send it along."

"I will," Victoria said. She selected Joey Lafond's contact in her phone and pressed the call button. Right from the beginning, something was off. Joey didn't seem to remember their previous conversation. With a sinking feeling in her stomach, Victoria recapped their visit. "You said he was Rita Markle's nephew, but my colleagues and I haven't found him yet. Is there anything else you can think of that might help us?"

"I said he was Rita's nephew? Really? That doesn't sound right. I wouldn't have told you that." Joey sounded irritated, almost combative. "I've known Rita Markle for years. She doesn't have any siblings. She doesn't have a nephew. Never did. Never will."

Yesterday, Joey had seemed confident and certain. Crawford had warned about Joey's memory, and it appeared he was right. Victoria felt sad for the strong, independent woman, who obviously had dementia. And now the investigation was right back to square one in the search of the unidentified man. Victoria wasn't sure what to do next.

Joey spoke again. "Now, you might have confused Rita with JoAnn Wilson. She has a nephew named Jeffrey. A very bright young man. She was always talking about him. Is that who you're looking for?"

"It might be," Victoria said, her voice gentle. "Thank you."

Shaking her head, Victoria sent Sam a message with the new name—Jeffrey Wilson—and an apology. Her confidence in Joey's ability to provide helpful information had plummeted, but she had no other options at the moment.

They needed to find the mystery man, and soon.

The FBI's Charlotte office was quiet that Saturday, the parking lot almost empty. Victoria showed her badge to the man working the security desk and waited while he made a call to verify her identity. Once he allowed her access to the building, she had her pick of desks. She chose one by a tall window, though the view wasn't much. With her laptop open in front of her, she ate the lunch she'd purchased on her way there.

With so many people working different angles of the parallel investigations, new intelligence came in fast. Yet the top suspects under investigation remained the same. Rick Haskin, Jerome Smith's former agent, and Jesse Grassman, who wanted Todd and Jerome to invest in his company. The Durham Police Department had focused on Alan Bushy, Lilly's ex-boyfriend. Each had a motive to harm one victim, two in Jesse's case. But none of the suspects had a motive to kill all four.

Sun streamed in through the glass to Victoria's right, showcasing the crumbs between the rows of her keyboard. She'd eaten far too many meals in front of her laptop. She was swiping the tiny remnants away and onto the desk with her fingertips when her phone pinged with a message from Sam.

Found him. Check your email.

Fantastic, she wrote back. *Where does he live now?*

North Carolina.

Victoria opened Sam's email and read the facts about Jeffrey Wilson. Twenty-nine-years-old. He'd earned a Ph.D. in biochemistry from Johns Hopkins and currently taught the subject as an assistant professor at North Carolina State in Raleigh. His research focused on manipulating existing molecules to develop anti-cancer agents. He'd published many articles showcasing his studies, all of them with the ultimate goal of eliminating cancer.

Sam had starred the next bullet point in his report. Jeffrey had traveled to Boston's Logan airport two weeks ago. Same timeframe as Jerome's murder.

Victoria's interest in Jeffrey skyrocketed. On her notepad, she wrote each of the many reasons. He had the intelligence required to pull off the atonement murders. As a biochemist, he had access to a lab and the knowledge to concoct the thallium sulfate that poisoned the Fuller sisters. His job also allowed him flexibility. Professors worked unusual hours and rarely had to be somewhere from nine to five. He could easily travel the twenty-five miles that separated his address in Raleigh from Lilly Fuller's rental home in Durham. And if he had a free afternoon, it would have only taken him three hours to drive to Charlotte and end Todd Eckstrom's life. And then...the big one...a trip to Boston when someone murdered Jerome.

But it wasn't that easy. The FBI's apps had cross-checked Jeffrey's digital footprint with the victims. So far, they'd found nothing to connect Jeffrey with them. Nothing aside from the photograph taken twelve years ago at Stone Ridge Mountain. But Victoria wasn't deterred. His profile, his location, his trip to Boston, and a strong gut feeling suggested he was their man. Unfortunately, they'd found zero reasons for him to kill anyone. Whatever happened in the Stone Ridge Mountain Community remained well-hidden.

Even without a motive, the photograph, combined with what they'd learned so far, offered enough circumstantial evidence to pick Jeffrey up for questioning.

Victoria called Detective Durst and gave him the information. He was on it immediately, saying he would get Jeffrey inside the Durham Police Headquarters within the hour.

Jeffrey might know something, and his life could be in danger. But that wasn't what had Victoria on the edge of her seat. He fit the killer's profile. In her mind, he'd already moved from *the next potential victim* to *the prime suspect*.

38

Victoria waited inside the Charlotte FBI field office and prepared to interview Jeffrey Wilson. The Durham authorities planned to bring him into the police headquarters and put him in a room with a video connection. She wished she had a play-by-play update on their progress. Were they still headed to the NC State campus, or already there? Her anticipation made time creep forward as she continued to study the investigation files.

With the Fuller sisters' autopsy report open on her screen, she wondered, not for the first time, why the male victims were missing dime-sized patches of hair and the women weren't. Was it related to the reason the killer had poisoned Lilly so her hair fell out, then chopped off the rest of it before killing her? What was it about hair? Souvenirs? A fetish? Was the killer bald? Jeffrey wasn't. In recent photos, he had thick dark hair.

An hour passed. Victoria got up from the desk and walked around the deserted office to stretch and use the restroom. She returned to her laptop and the Atonement Murder Case database. Sam had just added more information to the file on Karen Strauss/Green. One particular item stood out. Karen had switched high schools in Charlotte before her sophomore year. She moved from a private school—different from the one Todd and Jerome attended, or Victoria would have been doing cartwheels inside—to a public school. The switch happened twelve years ago, shortly after the teens were together at Stone Ridge Mountain. Was there any significance to the switch? Victoria thought so. She needed more details.

Another hour went by. Victoria glanced from her computer to her phone screen. She'd done that several times, making sure she hadn't missed a call from

Detective Durst. He'd promised to let her know as soon as they located Jeffrey. What was taking so long?

With mounting impatience, she focused on the school transfer issue, though it hardly seemed as promising as questioning Jeffrey Wilson. She had just typed the name of Karen's private school, the one she left, when Detective Durst called. Finally. Victoria quickly answered his call, eager for the update. "You found him?" she asked.

"No," Durst answered. "He wasn't home. And he's not at his office. That's where I am right now. The chemistry building. He's gone."

"What do you mean, he's gone?"

"He had two classes scheduled for yesterday. The first at ten o'clock, the second at two. He didn't show up to teach either. Since it's Saturday, there aren't many people around the academic buildings that we can talk to. We're waiting to get a list of Wilson's students and then we'll start calling them. From what we can tell so far, the last time anyone saw him was two days ago. Thursday afternoon on campus. He taught a biochemistry class at three p.m."

"There's no one around there who works with him?"

"One person. A chemistry professor with an office near his. She told us he was in Boston for a lecture series, so he was definitely in the area at the time of Jerome's murder. The case against this guy is strengthening by the second, though she described him as charming and brilliant, with a dark edge—whatever that means. Most of his students find him exceptionally cool. She said he can be a little hard to read, and a very private person, but everyone likes and respects him."

Most serial killers were charming. It's how they gained their victim's trust long enough to take advantage of them.

"Did anyone see him on campus the day the Fuller sisters died?" she asked.

"He taught a class that morning but didn't have one in the afternoon. He could have driven to Durham and back in a short time."

"What about his car? Are you tracking it?" Victoria asked.

"He doesn't have one. He uses a scooter."

"Seriously? Actually, that makes him easier to find. If he's on the run, he'd have to take an Uber or a bus, borrow a vehicle or rent a car. All those options leave a trail."

"I know. The same professor who told us Jeffrey doesn't have a car said he's about to get one. He ordered a fully electric SUV that cost north of a hundred grand. Told her he paid cash for it. That's a huge chunk of cash for an assistant professor."

"Yes, it is. I'll ask our financial analysts to look into his financial accounts and see if they pick up on any unusual activity," Victoria said, already typing a note to one of her colleagues. Perhaps he'd been blackmailing the victims, and they'd recently refused to pay. Though with Lilly living paycheck to paycheck, he couldn't have expected to get much from her.

"We're working on locating someone who can tell us if Wilson made thallium sulfate in this lab," Durst said. "If he did, it's pretty much all over. Cocky bastard to think we wouldn't find him. Or maybe he didn't care."

"I think we should get the public involved now," Victoria said. "Let people know we're looking for him, so he has no place to hide."

"Would you say he's a person of interest or that he's wanted for questioning?"

"I appreciate you asking my opinion. I'd frame it as if he might be in danger, so those who know him best will want to cooperate rather than protect him from the authorities."

"Okay. If he's anywhere in the area, we'll find him," Durst said.

But would they find him soon enough? The last thing Victoria wanted was another atonement murder. With the evidence against Jeffrey mounting, wariness tempered her exhilaration. With Karen's safety in mind, Victoria called Agent Galax and updated him on the situation. "I don't think we need to bring her in unless that's what she wants. But if we could keep a car outside her house until we locate Wilson, that might be best for everyone involved."

"I'm going now," Galax said. "I know where she lives, and I'm not a complete stranger to her or her husband. That should help them feel better about the situation. So, uh, does that mean you trust her now? Even though you said she was holding back earlier?"

People hiding secrets rarely told the truth when pressed. To avoid an outright lie, they skirted around an issue, offering answers that were true but not quite the entire story. Karen seemed afraid. But what motivated her fear?

"I'm not sure who to trust yet," Victoria answered.

39

Victoria headed to the Charlotte Airport with her windows rolled down, catching a breeze, but she wasn't enjoying it. Jeffrey Wilson was still out there. Unaccounted for. That did not sit well with her. And as much as she wanted to go home, she didn't want to leave North Carolina without answers.

When she stopped at a red light, her phone rang, and Agent Galax's name lit up on the screen.

"I'm at Karen's house," he said, his voice low, instantly alerting Victoria to a potential issue. "Inside with her husband, who is worried right now."

Victoria curled her fingers tight around the steering wheel. "What happened?"

"Karen left their house this morning about fifteen minutes after we did. She went to do errands." Agent Galax lowered his voice. "Robert is concerned because she hasn't come back yet, and she turned her phone off. He says that's unusual."

"Did she say anything to him after we left?" Victoria asked, wishing she was there to question Karen's husband in person.

"I asked him that same question. He said no. He doesn't have an app to track her car, but I got the make and model. It's a Mercedes SUV. GLE 350. Black. I've got the plate and I can put out a lookout for the vehicle if she doesn't come home soon."

"Do that now," Victoria said. She hoped it wasn't necessary to put authorities on alert for Karen's vehicle, but she didn't want to take a chance. "Please ask Robert for her parents' address and phone numbers and send them to me. I want to find out if they remember anything from that week at Stone Ridge Mountain. Something Karen might have forgotten. Meanwhile, can you and Robert keep calling her friends? See if she's with any of them."

"I will. And one other thing. I did not tell Robert we learned Jeffrey Wilson's identity or that he's also missing right now."

"Good call. I think that's wise until we know more. Please tell me the second Karen shows up or as soon as her husband hears from her."

Victoria's GPS chimed in with, *in a quarter mile, take a left onto the Billy Graham Parkway.* The airport was only a few miles away.

There might be an innocent reason Karen had turned her phone off. It could be a mere coincidence that both she and Jeffrey were missing. But with four of the six from the photo already murdered, likely not. At that very minute, someone else might be tracking the remaining two down, just like Victoria was.

In two hundred feet, turn left, the navigation system said.

With a loud exhale, Victoria ignored the directions and stayed straight, driving past the airport exit.

40

Twelve years ago - Lilly

Lilly ducked under a branch as she followed her younger sister on the narrow trail. They emerged from the woods into an open area on top of Stone Ridge Mountain. A few more steps and the dirt below their feet turned to the smooth rock of the much-hyped Stone Ridge Dome lookout point. Ahead of them, it jutted into the sky, forming the edge of a towering cliff. From there, the entire community was visible under a sky striped with pink and violet hues. Below the cliff, colorful cabin roofs peeked through a thick blanket of green treetops that rippled to the perimeter of the lake. The shoreline curved and turned, forming inlets and coves.

Cassandra ceased her slow, cautious steps and planted her feet in the center of the large stone surface, staying well clear of the edge. She'd always been afraid of heights.

Lilly marched past, toward the cliff. In an indentation where the smooth stone dipped into a scalloped area, someone had painted their initials. Lilly wanted to leave her mark as well, but she had nothing permanent to write with.

"What did you think of Jeffrey?" Cassandra asked.

"The guy in the black T-shirt? I don't know. Not really my type. Why? You think he's cute?"

"No." Cassandra's response was firm and immediate.

"You do, don't you? You want to hook up with him!"

"No. I didn't say that, Lilly! That's not what I was thinking."

Standing at the edge of the stone cliff, amused by her sister's frustration, Lilly turned around, wearing her most mischievous grin. "Yeah? Then why is your face turning red right now?"

Cassandra scowled. She was close to fuming, something that happened often when Lilly antagonized her. "Just because I noticed someone doesn't mean I wanted to hook up with him. He just seemed, I don't know…different."

"Yeah. I agree. Maybe he's a weirdo nerd. Or he might be hiding a deep, dark secret. You should get to know him and find out. It might be fun for you to live a little. Whatever happens here, no one ever has to know. You'll never see him again. And I won't tell," Lilly said as she reached into her purse and drew out her phone. "Anyway, I'm into Todd."

"Yeah, that's kind of obvious," Cassandra said from her spot a safe distance from the ledge.

Lilly turned around so her back was to the cliff, like a high diver preparing for a back flip. She glanced at the ground. A foot of solid rock stuck out behind her heels.

"Be careful," Cassandra called. "People die taking selfies like that."

Lilly shuffled backward a few more inches, reducing her margin of safety.

"Oh my God, PLEASE don't do that!" Cassandra yelled.

Lilly lifted her gaze back to her phone. She pressed her screen to flip the camera around.

"Move forward," Cassandra whined, sounding almost desperate. "And let me take the photo."

"It has to be a selfie, and it's supposed to look a little dangerous. That's the point," Lilly said, readjusting her smile and raising her arm higher. "This is a great shot. Come get in it with me."

"I can't. Please, just step forward a few feet," Cassandra begged. "You're too close. And you've been drinking. I know you have."

"What if I have? It's a vacation, after all. Besides, everyone has to die sometime. If this is how I go, at least I'll be famous for it. I wouldn't mind being famous. I'll text you the picture on my way down before I splatter at the bottom." Lilly laughed. "Be sure to post it everywhere for me. Do not forget! Tell everyone I was fun and brave."

Lilly blew a kiss, flirting with her phone camera.

41

Twelve years ago - Karen

Karen twirled around in front of the mirror bolted to the inside of her bedroom door, checking herself out in her new spaghetti-strap tank top. The teal top was fabulous with her red hair. But did it work on her body, or was the flesh around her upper back ruining the look?

She turned sideways to the mirror, drew her shoulders back, and stood tall as if there were a string pulling her head toward the ceiling. It worked. She smiled at her reflection before leaving her bedroom. Her sandals, which perfectly matched her top, flip-flopped against the hallway floor, signaling that she was on her way out.

Her father and stepmother sat on the couch in the center of the cabin. Gas logs crackled in the fireplace in front of them. A series they'd been watching for weeks played on the television above the mantle. They looked up at her now.

"I'm leaving," Karen announced, for her father's benefit. During dinner, she'd asked him if she could hang out with people she'd met at the pool earlier.

"You're going to be at the clubhouse?" her father asked.

Karen dipped her chin. Not really a yes or a no. She was a little nervous about hanging out with them. She didn't know them, and she wasn't sure what to expect. Cassandra seemed nice. But Jeffrey was the real reason she wanted to go. She hoped he would be there with the others.

"And they're all your age?" he asked.

"Yep," she answered.

"It's almost dark. Do you want me to drop you off?"

"No. It's not far. I can walk."

"The trail to the clubhouse has lights," Meghan said.

"Okay. Well, have a good time, and be careful," her father said. "Be home by eleven. Meghan has a headache, so I think we're going to turn in early."

"I'll be quiet when I come in. I won't wake you," Karen said. They trusted her because she'd never given them any reason not to.

Meghan gripped her husband's arm and whispered something to him.

Karen made the mistake of waiting when she should have booked out the door.

"Um, Karen, maybe you should put a sweater over that tank top," her father said, choosing his words carefully. "It gets really chilly here at night."

Karen sighed extra loud and stomped back to her room. This wasn't about the temperature. Meghan obviously didn't think Karen's top looked good. She changed into a soft pink T-shirt that fell to her hips and wrapped a sweatshirt around her waist. When she came back to the living area, she turned a small circle, stared straight at Meghan, and said, "There. Happy?" This time, she didn't wait for a response. For the second time that day, she clopped out of the cabin with hurt feelings and growing resentment for her stepmother.

"Stay at the clubhouse," her father called after her.

With the last of the daylight disappearing, Karen walked the trail that snaked behind the backyards of other cabins and houses toward the pool. The air had a chill already. The sweatshirt hadn't been such a bad idea. She'd put it on later when the temperature dropped.

At the clubhouse, she continued around the building, following a gravel trail to the lake. Ducks glided in silence across the calm water. Hidden bullfrogs croaked. Birds chirped in the trees above. A car rumbled past on the nearest road, way behind her, and her shoes crunched and slid over the gravel. But there was no one else in the woods, and she was suddenly aware of her aloneness. She gripped her elbows and shivered. The air wasn't just chilly. It was also ominously damp, as if readying for a storm.

From the lake, another trail led through the woods to the cleared area with picnic tables she'd seen earlier with her father. That's where they were meeting. She hesitated at the trailhead, stopping beside a large, impossible-to-miss sign that said, *This area closed after dark.* The lights ended there. Karen fidgeted with her hands, stared down the trail shrouded by a dense canopy of trees, then checked the time. It was already past when they were supposed to meet. Were the others waiting at the end of the shadowy path? Or had they changed their minds? She could still change hers. She could go back to the cabin and listen to music or stream a show alone in her room.

A rustling sound came from behind her. Karen folded her arms over her chest as she pivoted. Her stomach fluttered at the sight of Jeffrey coming toward her. He lifted a hand in greeting. He wore jeans and another black T-shirt with a chemistry joke. This one said, *What should you do with a dead chemist? Barium!*

"Hey," he said. "You headed down to the picnic area?"

"I was, but the trail looks a little sketchy."

"You afraid of the dark?" he asked, stepping into the glow of the last lamp.

"Sometimes. I'm Karen, by the way." She mentioned her name in case he'd forgotten it, like Todd had.

"I know. I'm Jeffrey."

His sunglasses were gone, revealing brown eyes and thick lashes. They were not the eyes she imagined. They were a bit too close together. Or maybe just unusually sharp. Something about them was not as expected, but he was still handsome.

Jeffrey slowed his pace but never stopped and, just like that, she was walking alongside him on the trail, feeling a little giddy simply because he knew her name. The night was starting out even better than she could have hoped. Beside her, Jeffrey smelled clean, perhaps it was aftershave, but a lighter, fresher scent than the one her father wore.

"So, you said you live here? At Stone Ridge Mountain?" he asked.

"No. My stepmother's family owns a cabin." She put emphasis on the word stepmother so anyone could tell Meghan wasn't Karen's favorite person. "This is my first time here. What about you?"

"My aunt lives here in the summers, and I visit every year," he answered.

She took another glance at him. His eyes didn't bother her anymore. They seemed normal already. "Does the rest of your family come with you?"

"Not this time. My family is just me and my parents. My mother has cancer. She's going through chemo. It's best for her to be alone so she can heal."

"Oh, I'm really sorry."

"Yeah. It sucks. She's been battling breast cancer for years," Jeffrey said, falling a step behind as he kicked a stone with his sneaker and sent it skittering off the trail.

Karen wasn't sure how to respond. All afternoon she'd been thinking about Jeffrey. In her head, their exchanges were clever, flirty, and sweet. She didn't expect their first conversation to get serious so fast. Should she tell him she didn't have an actual biological mother? That the real one had abandoned her?

"My parents wanted me to come," Jeffrey said. "Anyway, I usually get through all my summer reading for school when I stay here, since there's not much else to do at this place. I hike and read. That's about it."

Only the most advanced classes at Karen's school assigned summer reading, which meant Jeffrey was smart. That didn't surprise her. And she was glad they'd moved off the subject of cancer.

"Having fun yet?" he asked.

"I don't know if I'd call it that," Karen answered. "I'm with my father and stepmother. Because of the rain, we've been stuck inside together more than I'd like. We're driving to Boone tomorrow night for dinner."

"It's cool there during the school year when the college students are around. It's a fun town. I like Come Back Shack, The Local, and Lost Province Brewing Company for when we go out to eat. They're good."

"I'll ask my stepmother about them. Thanks. We're only here one more night after this. Then we head home. To Charlotte."

"Me, too," Jeffrey said. "Back to Winston-Salem, I mean. Not great timing for a visit, anyway. Supposed to rain again soon."

"Yeah. It feels like it."

The buzz of whispered conversations drifted toward them from farther down the trail, followed by the unmistakable sound of Lilly's laughter.

"I guess they're all there," Karen said, nervous again. She should have been grateful that the others were there, but she could think of worse things than being alone with Jeffrey.

They walked the rest of the way without speaking, listening to the rising sounds of conversations, until the trail ended, and they came upon the shadowy figures of four others.

"Hey, you came," Todd said as Jeffrey and Karen entered the clearing.

A light snapped on behind them.

"What the—?" In lightning-fast motion, Jerome jumped up from a weathered picnic table and flicked a beer can away from him. He stood poised to bolt.

Todd remained sitting, a casual smile on his face and a beer in his hand. Next to him sat an open duffel bag with a case of beer inside.

"No worries," Jeffrey said. "That light is on a timer. It comes on at the same time every night, even though no one is supposed to be here after dark."

"How could you possibly know that, Jeffrey? Unless you hang out here after dark. Is that your thing?" Lilly asked, her tone teasing and provocative.

Jeffrey snorted. "I just know."

The single lamp mounted on a pole cast a faint yellowish glow over the clearing and allowed Karen to check out each of the other teens.

Lilly wore an off-the-shoulder blouse and carried a purse large enough to be an overnight bag. Her cut-off shorts exposed the bottom edge of her buttocks and made her long legs seem even longer.

In a cotton dress with a denim jacket over it, Cassandra wrapped her arms protectively around her body, echoing the way Karen felt about the whole situation.

Lilly pulled the strap of her flouncy top up on her shoulder, only to have it slide right back down. "Why did you freak out?" she asked Jerome.

"I didn't freak out. I was being cautious. I can't get in trouble," he said, reclaiming his seat on top of the table in an effortless movement. "I've got scouts looking at me."

"What do you mean by scouts? Boy Scouts? Girl Scouts?"

Jerome didn't answer, but he laughed loud and hard.

"He's a top college recruit," Todd explained, handing Jerome another beer.

"Recruit for what?" Lilly asked, though she must have known. It seemed obvious.

"Basketball. Obviously," Jeffrey said, echoing Karen's exact thoughts.

"That's a little racist," Jerome said. "I'm tall and black, so you think I'm a basketball recruit, don't you?"

"I'm not racist! It has nothing to do with your skin color. I saw you on the court earlier. You're really good. You could play college ball if you wanted to."

Jerome's serious expression turned into a grin. "I'm just playing with you, dude. Basketball is totally my thing."

"Oh, right. Ha, ha," Jeffrey said, but even in the dim light, his face had flushed red, and he didn't look happy about being tricked.

"So, do you think you're going to be famous someday?" Lilly asked, moving toward Jerome.

"He already is," Todd said. "One of the top recruits in the country."

"Well, in that case..." Lilly swiveled around and sort of backed into Jerome. Pulling her hair to one side so it fell over her shoulder, she rested her head against his chest and took a selfie with him as if they were the best of friends. "Let's get this party started," she said, stepping away from Jerome. She rummaged inside her purse and pulled out a bottle of vodka.

"That's what I'm talking about," Todd said with a laugh as Lilly held the bottle out and did a cute little happy dance.

Karen had consumed alcohol before with friends. But not much. Less than half a can of light beer once or twice. But never hard liquor.

Lilly twisted off the top, took several gulps, and said, "Who's next?"

"Did you bring a chaser?" Jerome asked.

Lilly sneered. "No. Didn't think you'd need one big fella." She held her taunting stare on Jerome, then thrust the bottle at her sister.

Cassandra hesitated before taking a single sip. She was quick to deliver the bottle to Todd, who consumed a generous swallow.

Jerome drank next, then got off the table and handed the bottle to Karen. With all eyes on her, she took a gulp, quickly placing her hand over her mouth to cover her initial surprise. Smiling outwardly but cringing inside as the liquid burned its way down her esophagus, she passed the bottle to Jeffrey.

"So, where are you all from?" Lilly asked, again in that teasing voice she seemed to have perfected. She pushed her hair aside, making what might have been a careless gesture look enticing. "I'm from Durham and I'm going to be a senior at North Durham High School. One more year and I'm a free woman."

They each shared some information. Cassandra and Karen were the youngsters of the group. The three guys were all heading into their junior year of high school, but Todd and Jerome were a full year older than Jeffrey because their parents had started them in school a year late. A strategy intended to improve their chances of being sports standouts. Though Todd and Jerome were the oldest and largest, Lilly had assumed the role of the group's leader.

The vodka moved around in a rhythm. After a few more rounds, Jerome stood near the table with his hands in his jean pockets. Lilly and Todd sat close together on the tabletop, hips and legs touching. Cassandra had one bench to herself, and Karen and Jeffrey had the other. Jeffrey seemed to grow quieter as the others became louder. He'd shared little since they arrived in the clearing, and certainly nothing personal since they were alone on the path, which made Karen more interested in peeling back his mysterious layers. She wanted to know more about him.

The liquor's sting lessened the more Karen drank. Her head spun, just a little, and in a pleasant, fun way. She felt good. As she inched closer to Jeffrey on the bench, no longer noticing the chilly temperature, she wished she'd kept her cute new tank top on rather than letting Meghan influence her decisions.

"You smell nice," she told Jeffrey.

"Thanks, it's cologne," he answered. Always so serious.

Remembering his sick mother, Karen wanted to cheer him up. "I like it. What's it called?"

"Dark Night. My mom gave it to me." Jeffrey reached for something she couldn't see behind him. When he righted himself, the space between them had grown. She hoped it wasn't intentional, that he wasn't trying to inch away from her, but she wasn't sure.

The next time the bottle reached her, it was almost full. She stared at it in bewilderment. "How did this happen?" she asked, her voice coming out louder than planned. "I thought we were drinking a lot of this stuff? Shouldn't it be almost gone by now?"

"It's a second bottle. And if you can't figure that out, you might want to slow down a little." Jeffrey raised his brows in a way that made him look bemused, despite his serious demeanor.

Karen only laughed. She didn't feel like being cautious. Not tonight. She took a big gulp, not minding the taste or the burn at all anymore. She felt great. And she didn't want to waste the feeling. Something spectacularly memorable needed to happen.

That's when Lilly stood from the table and threw her arms wide open. "Let's play a game," she said, her eyes lighting up with mischief. "Truth or dare." She grinned as if she knew exactly how the game would play out.

"I'm in," Karen said, grinning right back at Lilly.

42

Twelve years ago - Lilly

Todd wanted her. That was obvious. And Lilly was looking forward to getting to know that body of his, the one he'd been showing off all day on the court and then in the pool, his muscles rippling under smooth, tan skin. He shared the same confident swagger as her ex. Though she didn't want to think about him and how he'd dumped her—all because she'd gotten a little wild one night and made out with his best friend. But Todd...well, he didn't go to her school or live anywhere near her. Whatever they did together wouldn't get back to anyone. Perfect. Just perfect.

She got up from the table, mostly to mess with Todd's head and play a little hard to get, to make him think she wasn't a sure thing. He'd appreciate her that much more for it later.

In the dim light, surrounded by lurking shadows and pitch-black trees, their current location seemed the perfect setting for a horror movie. Lilly imagined hot girls and their jock boyfriends running through the woods screaming as someone chased them with a chain saw. Not a nice thought. Seeing as she was the only hot girl there, she'd be the first to go. She tossed her head back and laughed out loud to regain her party mood, but the skin on the back of her neck prickled.

Standing a few feet away from the group, she congratulated herself for being incredibly generous with her limited supply of liquor. Wouldn't it be interesting if her sister stumbled back to the cabin staggering drunk tonight? That might show their parents Cassandra wasn't as perfect as they thought. Not that she'd done anything to disappoint them yet, nothing Lilly knew of. But Cassandra was young. That could all change tonight.

So far, it was Karen who had surprised Lilly. She had pegged the girl for a prude, but maybe not. Karen was making moves on Jeffrey in a big way. Though he didn't seem interested. Maybe he'd rather be with Cassandra?

Karen held the vodka bottle with two hands and gulped, making her pale skin bulge at the neck. "Chug, chug, chug, chug," Lilly shouted.

"Shh," Jeffrey hissed at her. "Someone's going to hear us."

"Shh," Lilly mimicked, mocking Jeffrey. "No one is going to hear us way out here."

When Karen lowered the bottle, droplets of clear liquid streamed down her chin. She wiped the back of her wrist over her mouth and laughed a loud, throaty laugh. Not so bad after all.

Sitting on the bench, Jeffrey leaned one arm against the top of the picnic table, carving something into the soft wood with a pocketknife. He hadn't drank much, which meant more for the rest of them, yet it bothered Lilly. She sauntered over to him. "Your shirt is a little morbid, don't you think?" She plucked a bit of the fabric away from his chest, then pivoted away without waiting for a response. "Anyway—" she said, twirling in front of the table with her arms overhead to grab everyone's attention. "—the game is truth or dare."

"Dare," Jeffrey shot back.

Lilly challenged him with a hard stare as she handed him the vodka. "Five big chugs."

Jeffrey met her gaze. "You want everyone to catch up to you, huh? You had a big head start, didn't you?" Jeffrey's lips curled into a half-smile, but Lilly sensed something cold behind his eyes. Did he dare to judge her? Did he think he was better than she?

Lilly tossed her hair back and let out a laugh she knew guys loved. But his comment had bothered her. In fact, how dare he? Suddenly, everything about Jeffrey bothered her. She couldn't pinpoint her discomfort with him, but it was there. She wanted him to leave.

43

Twelve years ago - Karen

Karen now understood the phrase *liquid courage*. She was having a great time. Much better than she'd expected. She hadn't played a game of truth or dare since a sleepover in her elementary school days. That game hadn't involved vodka and an intriguing boy with dark hair and long lashes. She was so grateful Jeffrey had come along when he did, so glad she hadn't turned around and gone back to her stepmother's cabin.

She'd answered two questions so far. "Have you ever stolen anything?" which came from Cassandra. And "How many times have you had sex?" which came from Todd, predictable because he'd asked everyone the same question. When Jerome grinned and gave her the option of truth or dare, she chose dare. She hoped it would involve kissing Jeffrey, something she couldn't stop thinking about. He seemed so nice. So sweet. How cool would it be to start the school year off with an older boyfriend? Her first actual boyfriend. She couldn't wait to tell her friends about him. Or maybe she wouldn't tell. Maybe he'd be her special secret. But she was getting ahead of herself. They hadn't even kissed yet. And what if he already had a girlfriend? That's what she'd ask him when it was her turn again.

Jerome paced in a small circle, thinking up Karen's dare. "I got one," he finally said, coming to a standstill and pointing at Karen. "Lift up your shirt, take a selfie, and then send it to a group chat on your phone."

"That's one, two, three dares," Karen said, holding up her fingers as she counted. She was marginally aware that the liquor was taking over her personality, and that her body was tingling. "That's okay. I've got this." She pressed her phone on and flipped the camera around. After turning her back to the group, she grabbed hold of the bottom of her T-shirt and hiked it up to her neck, pulling her bra up with it. She aimed her camera at her chest and pressed the round button on her phone screen.

"Let me see, so we know you aren't faking," Jerome said over her shoulder.

Karen leaned back against his chest as Lilly had done. She found a group message with two of her good friends and attached the photo. "Sending it now," she said, "Going, going..."

"Wait, don't," Cassandra yelled as Karen pressed the arrow.

"Gone!" Karen shouted.

"You shouldn't have," Cassandra said.

Karen giggled as she slid her phone into her back pocket. "What? It's just my friends."

"It probably won't send, anyway," Jerome said. "Not if your phone service is anything like mine at this place."

Karen didn't care if it did. She wanted to do something crazy. Triumphant, she held her phone up, showing off the thin blue line moving in slow motion across the screen.

She sat next to Jeffrey again and drank more vodka. There were more questions, followed by coy answers. Todd and Lilly wanted to know everything about each other's sexual histories, so the rest of them got to hear all of that as well. And boy, did Karen have a lot to learn. The bottle came around again. Karen took a smaller sip but didn't stop.

"Truth or dare," Todd said, facing her.

"Dare," Karen answered, letting her body slide to the left until she was leaning heavily against Jeffrey's shoulder.

"Okay," Todd said. "Here's one. You ready?"

She nodded.

"Take off your clothes, all of your clothes, and jump in the lake."

Karen realized that one hour ago, she would never have accepted that dare. But the Karen of the moment was up for any challenge. She wasn't afraid. Or shy. And not one bit awkward.

"Here I go," she said. In her mind, she copied Lilly's languid movements and sauntered a few feet away from the table. Her legs twisted together as she moved, tripping her up. In a fit of giggles, she righted herself and balanced with a hand on the edge of the picnic table. She pulled her sandals off and flung them away.

The others hooted and hollered, egging her on, adding to the fun and excitement, except for Jeffrey. He shook his head and muttered, "I don't know about this. She's really drunk."

Karen's smile felt lopsided as she faced Jeffrey and pointed to her chest. "Who? Me? I don't think so. I feel fine." She pulled her sweatshirt from around her waist and let it fall. She unbuttoned her shorts, slid them down her legs, and flung them at Jeffrey. He ducked to the side, and they hit the table with a thunk because she'd left her phone in her back pocket.

"She's got to go all the way under," Todd said, talking as if Karen wasn't there. "When she comes back, I'm going to make sure she has wet hair."

Lilly started chanting, "All the way in. All the way in. All the way in." Other voices joined hers.

Karen took a bow before stumbling toward the lake, taking a direct route through the forest. Her lips moved silently to the chant continuing behind her. *All the way in. All the way in.* She was going to do it. Her face tightened with determination, then gave way to a silly grin.

It's not like I'm about to climb Mount Everest here.

But her excitement was genuine.

It was a little disappointing that Jeffrey didn't follow her as she made her way through the trees, the earth cold under her bare feet. No one did. They trusted her to go in, and the proof would come when she came back soaking wet.

A branch slapped her face. She extended her hands, waving them through the darkness in front of her so it wouldn't happen again. The chorus behind her grew fainter as voices dropped out. The lake was farther away from the clearing than she'd thought. She stubbed her toe on a tree root, cursed, but kept going.

Karen emerged from the forest, her skin tingling with anticipation. A solar light reflected its glow on the surface of the lake. Almost there. A few feet from the water's edge, she yanked off her T-shirt and tossed it away, then did the same with her bra. She felt brave, happy, and very much alive, though her balance was off. Pulling one leg through her underwear, she teetered before toppling over, which sent her into a laughing fit. Still giggling, she pushed herself to her feet and brushed debris from her legs and bottom.

The lake rippled before her. "I'm doing it!" she shouted at the top of her lungs. She ran and plunged into the water, her feet sinking in thick muck. She shrieked and belly flopped to free her feet.

"Hey! Hey! What are you doing?"

The sudden shout startled her. A male voice. It wasn't near the water. It had come from the picnic area, where the faintest glow of light reached her through the trees. Shouts and wild laughter echoed through the cool night air.

Karen stood stock still and listened, suddenly alert. Her chest heaved as water streamed down her naked body.

"Hey! Get back here!" the male voice bellowed. "Get back here!"

The thick slime below her squelched with each step as she hurried to get out of the water. She climbed up the embankment, slipped on the slight incline, and fell on the dirt ground.

A shattering noise erupted beyond the woods, and the dim light disappeared.

What was happening?

The forest was pitch black now. More yells, slapping footsteps, soft grunts, and rustling came from far away. Were those her friends disappearing into the darkness? How quickly the fun had ended, replaced by fear and vulnerability.

With her hands wrapped around her body, she lurched over tufts of grass and rocks, wincing when a sharp rock stabbed into her sole. Another step and her foot landed on soft fabric. Her shirt. *Thank God.* She scooped it up and thrust her neck through a hole. It wouldn't fit. She yanked it off, twisted it around, and tried again. The material ripped apart as she rushed to pull it over her wet body.

Have to find the rest of my clothes. My underwear. Back at the picnic table?

She wobbled forward and straight into the sharp branches of a bush. Hissing slurred curses, she turned herself around and tried to get her bearings. She crouched, hovering just above the ground, and ran her hands over the dirt, grass, and exposed roots.

Where are my clothes?

She patted the ground for what seemed a very long time before she stood and pulled the hem of her ripped T-shirt down to cover her bare bottom. It was a futile effort. The shirt stretched no further than her hip. Barely dressed, she moved in the general direction from which she'd come, or so she thought, taking slow, unsteady steps in the darkness with her arms stretched out in front. She no longer heard chanting, laughing, or the sounds of the others running away. Branches and leaves scraped against each other in the wind. The trilling insects grew freakishly loud. Her body shivered and her legs shook. Yet one concern emerged from the haze of her frantic thoughts and made her moan. Her father and stepmother must not know she was out there alone, drunk, and practically naked. The mere thought of them finding out catapulted a spike of horror through her body. But it didn't last long. Her body had a more pressing problem.

With little warning, vomit rose from her stomach and spewed out in a torrent that wrenched her throat, tore at her abdomen, and felt like it burst vessels in her eyes. When it was over, she remained leaning over with her hands on her thighs. Swaying on her feet, she gasped for breath.

Sounds came from the woods. A creature larger than a forest animal moving toward her.

She tried to stand up and walk, but something was very wrong with her body. Her head was spinning, and the cold made her shiver violently.

Thank God, someone had come back to help her.

44

The temperature in Charlotte crept up during the day. By the time Victoria reached the home of Karen's parents, it was too warm for a jacket. She left hers in the rental car, exposing the gun in her holster. Karen's stepmother, Meghan Strauss, couldn't seem to take her eyes off the weapon as Victoria stood on the doorstep introducing herself. When Meghan finally averted her gaze from the gun, she glanced up and down the street and toward her neighbor's front porch. There was no one around, and Meghan invited Victoria inside the two-story brick house.

As Victoria listened for signs of anyone else inside, she took in the country farmhouse décor, yellow walls, and flowered curtain valances. Crosses hung on several windows. Short on time, she skipped pleasantries and began asking questions immediately. "I'm here about your stepdaughter, Karen. Have you heard from her today?"

"No," Meghan answered, clearly confused. "Why would she be here? What's going on? Has something happened to her?"

"She's missing. It hasn't been long. But we believe she might be in danger."

"Danger? Why? What has Karen done?"

Interesting that she went straight there.

"I don't know what she's done. I'm hoping you can tell me. Did Karen ever mention anything about Jerome Smith, the NBA player, when she was younger?"

"The one who just died? No. Karen doesn't even follow basketball, as far as I know. Why would she say anything about him?"

"She never mentioned meeting him when she was younger? At Stone Ridge Mountain?"

"Stone Ridge Mountain?" Deep lines formed around Meghan's mouth as she pursed her lips. "Why are you asking me about Stone Ridge Mountain?"

"Something happened there. Twelve years ago. It might have involved Karen. Are you aware of anything?"

Meghan shook her head. "Karen didn't like Stone Ridge Mountain. She never wanted to go."

Victoria wasn't convinced. "Why did she switch schools before her sophomore year of high school?"

"I don't see what that has got to do with anything."

"Please, Mrs. Strauss. If you could just answer the question."

"All right," Meghan answered, intertwining her fingers then clasping her hands. "Karen had a bit of trouble years ago and...it was something that happened at Stone Ridge Mountain, as a matter of fact, but I just don't understand why it would matter now."

"It might relate to the cases we're investigating."

"The cases?" Meghan's frown deepened. "I really don't think...."

"Please, tell me what happened," Victoria said, biting into her lower lip to remain patient.

"It was nothing, really. A private matter. If it happened today, with what young people do these days on social media...It was simply a terrible lapse in judgment and character on Karen's part."

"What did she do?"

"She took an inappropriate photo of herself and sent it to two of her friends. And when I say inappropriate, believe me, it was nothing compared to stories I've heard about. Anyhow, her friends forwarded it to other friends, and so on, until it made its way to the school administration, or perhaps a parent sent it to them. I'm not condoning what Karen did. We were mortified. For Karen, I mean. But certainly no one got hurt, except for her. You have no idea the depression she endured. She even tried to...well, never mind. The embarrassment alone should have been punishment enough. Unfortunately, her school thought otherwise. They expelled her. We had to enroll her in public school."

"And she was at Stone Ridge Mountain when she sent the photo?"

"Yes."

"When?"

"In the summer. I believe it was a Fourth of July weekend. The only time Karen ever went to the cabin with us. She was at the community clubhouse with some other teenagers she'd just met. It was a dare. There was alcohol involved. She'd never touched alcohol before. Obviously, the others were terrible influences. We shouldn't have let her meet with them."

"Did you find out who she was with?"

"No. She never told us their names. She only knew their first names, anyway."

"What about the people from her former school who shared Karen's photo again and again? What was their punishment?" Victoria asked, trying to determine if the expulsion had anything to do with the murders.

Anger flashed in Meghan's eyes. "That's a good question, isn't it? And one I asked the school administrators several times when we were discussing the incident. Nothing happened to any of them. Nothing at all. I suppose they would have had to expel the entirety of their student body if they'd taken any action. Anyway, all of that is thankfully far behind us." Meghan swished her hands together. "Karen's had her share of struggles recently, but she's in a good place now."

"By struggles, are you referring to her difficulties trying to conceive a child?" Victoria asked.

"She shared that information with you?"

"I'm aware of the situation," Victoria said.

"Yes. That was challenging for her. She and Robert want children. It devastated her to learn she couldn't have them. And for no reason. Just one of those things. But eventually she came to terms with it. She accepted that conception wasn't God's plan for her. She and Robert are considering adoption. And once she moved on, once she accepted God's will, that's when things really turned around for her. I saw it with my own eyes. My stepdaughter went from deeply sad to hopeful. What a beautiful difference to see. God works in mysterious ways. What seemed like misfortune to my stepdaughter might just turn out to be the greatest blessing for an innocent, unwanted child. That's what I tell Karen. And she's definitely embraced the concept." Meghan smiled, seeming to forget the FBI had paid her a visit and her stepdaughter was missing. Victoria let her keep talking.

"She's in a good place now," Meghan said. "In fact, I don't think I've ever seen her so happy before. She may have made mistakes when she was younger, but not anymore. She's atoned for her sins."

Meghan's choice of words sent a chill down Victoria's back. No one outside of law enforcement and the victims' immediate family members knew about the message the killer left behind at the crime scenes. How odd that Meghan chose that word.

Meghan's face suddenly clouded. "Should I be worried? Should we call her friends?"

"Robert is calling them now. How often do you see your stepdaughter?"

"We try to have brunch on Sundays. Though she's been traveling a lot lately for that big client of hers. Tiffany. My stepdaughter travels for her, checking out properties and often purchasing them."

"Anything in the Raleigh or Durham area?"

"Well, yes actually. She sent me pictures from a property there earlier in the week. I think she met up with a friend in the area."

"Do you know the friend's name?"

"No, I don't. And she doesn't post anything on social media about her personal life. Unlike most people her age. She's very private. Her posts all pertain to her job. I suppose she learned her lesson the hard way, after what happened when she was younger."

"What about Boston? Has she visited Boston for her client? Or any other client? Or for any reason?" Victoria asked, in case Karen hadn't been truthful.

"No. Not that I know of."

"What about Karen's father? Would he know where she is right now?"

"I doubt it. He's golfing for a few more hours." Meghan shifted her weight and placed a hand over her chest. "You said she's missing?"

"She might be," Victoria corrected.

"Have you checked her listings? She has one house out in the boondocks that's been on the market for a year or longer. It just won't sell. She's invested a lot of time trying to make it more presentable. She doesn't have cell service when she's there, so sometimes she's out of reach for hours. Robert should have mentioned that. That's probably where she is. Check that place before assuming whatever it is you're worried about."

"Thank you. I will."

45

Instead of starting the car and driving off, Victoria stared through her windshield, thinking. Something kept tugging at her conscience. She didn't feel right about leaving the area. Not until they located Karen.

She checked her messages and found an update from the FBI's financial arm. They'd already looked into Jeffrey Wilson's accounts. His mother had died of cancer almost ten years ago. His father passed earlier in the year. It was the recent sale of his family's home and liquidation of other assets that padded his bank accounts and allowed him to purchase an expensive SUV. Which meant blackmail and extortion were off the table for now.

Though Detective Durst hadn't left her any messages, she called him and asked, "Have you located Jeffrey?"

"Not yet." He sighed. "If he's been on the run since yesterday, he could be long gone. Possibly out of the country."

Victoria wanted to help with the search, but it would take a few hours for her to get to the area. And like the detective said, Jeffrey might be long gone.

"Does he have a partner?" she asked. "Does he own any other residences?"

"No, and no. He has the one condo near the campus."

"What about his aunt's cabin at Stone Ridge Mountain? Did someone check there?"

"She sold the cabin six years ago. Jeffrey has no siblings. No immediate family."

"I know," Victoria said with a sigh. "NC State has a huge campus. He could be hiding in one of the buildings."

"We're searching them. But it's going to take some time."

Victoria bit into her bottom lip as she tapped her steering wheel. "Okay. Let me know when you locate him. I've got a tip I'm going to follow in Charlotte to find Karen."

"Before Jeffrey does, right?" the detective said. "If it's not too late for that."

"Right," Victoria answered. She had a hunch Karen might have disappeared on her own accord, but no evidence to back up that feeling.

After ten minutes on the Internet browsing a local real estate site, Victoria had the information she needed. Karen Green had two active property listings in the area. One had gone on the market last week. It was a million-dollar home, built ten years ago, on a third of an acre. The other also listed for slightly over a million, but that's where the similarities ended. Built in 1950, the old home included fifteen acres. After ten months on the market, it was still available, and from the looks of it, that wouldn't change.

Victoria read over the property description, presumably written by Karen.

So much potential! Historic, large, three-bedroom, one-bathroom home on fifteen acres, with a large barn. Great opportunity for privacy and land and only forty-five minutes away from Charlotte. The property needs some work, but with a little vision and some remodeling skills, this gem of a fixer-upper could be a wonderful forever home or a farm. No restrictions! Home being sold as-is. Sellers will not make any repairs.

The listing included thirty pictures of the property. The current owners had done little to nothing in property maintenance, and it looked as if they had abandoned the home years ago. The first ten photos showcased the outside from various angles. Overgrown bushes. A field of tall weeds where the front yard should be. A rusting propane tank. Then came the exterior of the dilapidated barn and the home—faded cedar shingles, plenty of them missing—which didn't bode well for the condition of the interior. The next pictures confirmed Victoria's suspicions. Old furniture and belongings filled the dark rooms. Piles of indistinguishable items lay on tabletops, curio shelves, and side tables. A hoarder's paradise.

Meghan Strauss claimed Karen had worked to make the property more presentable. Did that mean it was previously in worse condition? Hard to believe.

Nothing except filling multiple dumpsters and then gutting and rebuilding the interior could render the home desirable. It would be easier to tear it down. Victoria couldn't imagine anyone driving out into "the boondocks" to see it at the current price. She might be one of the first.

With the address, 414 Old Mill Road, entered in her phone's navigation system, she headed out, calling Ned on the way.

"Hey, where are you?" he said, sounding cheerful.

"I'm so sorry. I can't even believe I'm saying this."

"You're not coming home today?" He didn't sound angry, but the upbeat tone had left his voice.

"I think we're close to something with our current suspect," she told him.

"I know how huge this case is. Do what you need to do. I'm here. The dogs are great. Exercised. Teeth brushed. Fed and happy."

His understanding meant the world to her, and she wondered what she'd ever done to deserve such a kind and supportive partner.

"All I ask is that you promise me one thing," he added.

"And what might that one thing be?" she asked in a teasing, suggestive way, though she knew he was serious.

"That you take care of yourself. Don't do anything risky that you don't have to do."

"I will take care of myself. I promise."

They'd had a similar exchange recently, during her last case, and she'd made that same promise. Then she'd gotten shot and almost drowned in the Gulf of Mexico. Not her proudest moment, though the events proved critical to the investigation. But she wouldn't make that mistake again. Trust no one. Expect the worst at all times. That's what she'd learned.

"Do you want to talk about the case?" he asked, same as he had yesterday, because he always asked.

Ned was a great listener. Intuitive and intelligent. She wanted to lay out all the different pieces and hash them out with him, to see if they could make sense of things together. But she preferred to keep her work life separate from her personal life. She wanted her home life to remain a peaceful escape. As if the ugly world outside didn't exist when she was talking to Ned or at home with him and her animals.

"I'd rather talk about what you're doing," she said.

"Okay. I'm putting the last of my things in the closet and drawers. Breaking down some boxes so it won't be a mess when you get back. And right before you called, I got a message from my friend David. The one you met at the wedding."

"David from college. I know who he is."

"He says congratulations on our engagement. He and Maria are going to be in D.C. next week. He has meetings, and she's coming with him. They're going to stay for the weekend. They want to know if we can get together for dinner. If you're in town."

"Yes. Absolutely. But if I'm not there, please go without me. I'm sure they want to see you."

"They want to see both of us."

David and his wife, Maria, were good people. Victoria and Ned would have a nice evening with them. Despite those facts, she'd rather spend the night at home with Ned watching a movie and hanging out with the dogs. But if she and Ned were going to be a solid team, she had to be a team player.

"What about the meeting you had with Bob?" she asked. "Do you want to tell me about it now, or do you still want to wait until I'm back?"

His answer didn't come right away, but when it did, he said, "Okay. We better talk about it now."

We better? Suddenly, her nerves were on alert. Her face tightened.

"I told you I've been covering for Bob a lot lately, with little warning. But he never told me why. That's what he wanted to talk about. Turns out he has some health issues."

"Oh, no. Something serious?"

"He didn't say, and I didn't ask. I figured he'd tell me if he wanted me to know. He can be a very private person. But he's in his sixties, so he's decided to retire and sell the veterinary practice. He's giving me first right of refusal. I can probably keep working there under a different owner, along with the vet techs, or—"

"Or you could buy it from him and own it?" she blurted out, excitement stirring inside her.

"Yes."

"What did you tell him?"

"I told him I was interested. Very interested. But I had to think about it and discuss it with my fiancée."

"Do you want to own it? I mean, it comes with a lot of management headaches you don't have to deal with currently."

"It's a good, established practice. I think owning it is worth the headaches of running it."

Victoria's smile spread. "Then you should buy it."

"We haven't really talked about this yet, but I still have loans to pay from vet school and buying this business will mean taking out a pretty large business loan. Bob didn't mention a sales price, but with the building, the equipment, and the client base, it has got to be at least a few hundred grand."

"Ned...we have the money. We. It's our money. And you said it yourself, the clinic has an excellent reputation. The location is great. It sounds like a solid investment. I'm all for it."

"I don't know if I feel comfortable about taking your money for this when I could—"

She cut him off before he could finish. "Our money, Ned. What would it take for you to get comfortable with the idea? Because if you want this, it's happening. I love the idea. I love it for you and for us."

"Let's talk about it when you get back," he said, and though there was some hesitance, she could hear the smile in his voice.

The GPS broke into their conversation. *In half a mile, turn right onto Old Mill Road.*

"Hey, Ned. I'm getting close to my destination. I'll call you back later, okay?"

"Okay. Love you."

"I love you, too. I'm really excited about this. It's awesome news."

Ned's exciting opportunity left her questioning her decision to stay in Charlotte. What if she'd been chasing false leads for days and neither Karen nor

Jeffrey were involved? What if the real killer was somewhere far away, rubbing his hands with glee while he planned his next kill? Maybe he already had Karen *and* Jeffrey captive. Maybe they were already dead. No. She couldn't let those fatalistic thoughts creep into her head. She never knew for certain where a clue might lead or if it mattered until she pursued it.

In five hundred feet, make a right turn, the GPS said.

Ned was taking care of their animals and didn't seem to resent her absence. They could discuss the veterinary practice as soon as she got home. Right now, this was where she needed to be. She'd set the ball in motion by following the clues to the Stone Ridge Mountain Community. Karen and Jeffrey were missing now. They might be in danger.

Victoria could feel it—a heightened sense that she was getting close to understanding why someone had recently murdered four people who hadn't seen each other in twelve years.

As she turned right onto Old Mill Road, she wondered who else besides the stepmother knew Karen occasionally came out to this secluded property all alone.

46

Ned took a few steps back from the fence and admired his work. He'd secured the railings good as new.

"There you go. You aren't getting out on my watch, guys," he said to the donkeys, who were keeping their distance. Before repairing the fence, he'd given them de-worming medicine, and they were wary of him now.

He picked up his toolbox, one he'd had since doing construction work in college and grad school to help pay the bills, and headed back to the house. Myrtle, the alpha of the hounds, ran up to him and rubbed her head against his leg as he walked. He leaned to the side and patted her. Since Victoria wasn't coming home, Ned considered inviting friends over to play cards or watch a movie. It would be the first time he had people over without Victoria there, as if it was his place. Something about that seemed strange. He had to get used to living as if this was his place, too, or the arrangement wouldn't work.

Still contemplating the idea, he placed his toolbox on a shelf in the garage, where it looked a little lonely. Storage space was plentiful in Victoria's spacious home. She'd purchased the property for its amazing yard, perfect for her adopted greyhounds and foster dogs. The inside was clean, thanks to a crew that came out weekly, but in the past few years, she'd done little to decorate it. Several rooms were empty. Ned's move wouldn't change that much. He'd left his furniture back at his condo. Most of it was from IKEA and didn't seem right in the large house.

He felt pretty good after telling Victoria about Bob and the vet clinic, and glad he hadn't waited any longer to share the news. She seemed really excited about the opportunity. He appreciated her enthusiasm but wasn't sure about borrowing her money. Everything was happening pretty fast now. They still had a lot to discuss related to being a couple. A wedding. Family. Children. Their expenses. He assumed she'd paid for her house in full, but he wasn't sure. Ned still had vet school loans. Selling his condo would take care of a sizeable chunk of them. Would Victoria want a prenup? Should he offer to sign one even if she didn't bring it up?

After grabbing a drink from the fridge, he went outside to the patio. Two dogs trotted through the back door beside him. The others went through the dog door. In Victoria's absence, they followed him everywhere. He sat in one of the cushy chairs with his phone and typed a reply to his friend. *Not sure if Victoria will be in town, but I am. Let's definitely get together.*

He hoped Victoria could join them. Dave and Maria had already met her at the wedding not too long ago. Victoria had impressed them by taking charge of the investigation into their missing friend. Rather than thinking of her only as an FBI agent, Ned wanted them to get to know a more personal side of his fiancée. David and Victoria had work travel in common, though unlike Ned, Maria didn't have to worry about her partner getting shot or knifed during his workday.

A career with the FBI usually involved a lot of boring bureaucratic paperwork and politics, and Victoria claimed hers did. Yet it sure seemed she had experienced more than her share of danger.

Ned grabbed the remote and turned on the television hanging over the outdoor fireplace. Time for the game, something he probably wouldn't be watching if Victoria were home. On the large screen, everyone in the stadium stood with heads bowed. *In memory of Jerome Smith* ran across the bottom of the program. Even weeks after Jerome's death, they were kicking off the game with thirty seconds of silence in his honor. And Victoria was busy tracking down his killer.

Her dedication made him proud, and her unpredictable travel schedule wasn't a problem. He'd always been a flexible, go-with-the-flow sort of guy. Being apart so much, he and Victoria rarely took each other's presence for granted. But he couldn't help the uneasy feelings that lingered around when she was away. And because he loved her, that probably wasn't going to change. She didn't need his protection, and yet he wished he could provide it. He took a gulp of his beer. At least he could take excellent care of the animals she adored, so she had no worries on this end.

In the paddock to his right, a donkey brayed.

"It's not mealtime yet, Bud," Ned called out.

For an animal lover, or almost anyone, the property was an absolute paradise in every respect. But right now, it was missing the best part of it all—Victoria.

Ned shuddered involuntarily as he stared out at the mountain views beyond the steel gate surrounding the property. He hoped Victoria was safe.

47

Victoria drove a quarter mile down Old Mill Road without passing a single house, only woods. The pavement changed to dirt with a sparse layer of gravel, and the road narrowed to one winding lane. The car's left tires thudded into a rut she couldn't avoid. Crawling vines strangled tall trees. They obscured what lay ahead until she rounded a bend and the secluded property from the listing came into view. The road dead ended right in front of it.

Karen's black Mercedes wasn't there. There were no vehicles in sight. Victoria let out a heavy sigh as she stopped the car in front of the barn. She'd used up a lot of time driving out there, and now she had to live with her decision.

She shut off the engine and checked the top corner of her phone. Five full bars. Yet Karen had led her stepmother to believe she didn't have cell service there. Strange, but there were explanations. Perhaps cell service depended on the phone carrier, as it had at Stone Ridge Mountain.

Victoria got out of the car for a quick walk to stretch her legs before driving back. That's when she discovered she wasn't alone after all. Near the barn, a large doe stared back at her with wide eyes. When Victoria shut the car door, the deer bolted. It sailed over a sagging fence, and its white-tailed bottom disappeared into the woods.

Victoria turned to the house. The website pictures had been kind. Disrepair, peeling paint, and mildew were more pronounced in real life, and the place looked a lot worse than it had online.

A *pop, pop, pop* erupted from somewhere off in the distance. Not too close, but loud and clear, ringing out through the woods.

Gunshots.

Victoria stood still and listened. The popping sounds continued. Were people hunting nearby? She pulled up a map of the area on her phone. Mostly woods surrounded the property. But that wasn't all. The Caldwell Shooting Range was located approximately one mile away.

For obvious reasons, Karen had left that information out of the home's description. Listening to constant gunfire did not lend itself to a peaceful environment, though that wasn't the worst of the obstacles the property would have to overcome for someone to shell out over a million dollars for it.

As Victoria looked up from her phone, something caught her eye—dark splotches on the gravel. Dark like blood spatter. Was it Karen's?

Victoria crouched for a better look at one, knees hovering above the earth. The mark was fresh, with no accumulation of dust or debris over it. She lifted her gaze and scanned the ground. A trail of similar dark patches led toward the barn and stopped short of the doors.

Perhaps it wasn't anything serious or sinister. Karen might have come out to work on fixing up the house. She could have cut herself before leaving. Maybe Victoria had just missed her. Or perhaps the trail came from an injured animal in need of help. But unless Victoria investigated further, she couldn't know for sure. Two people were missing and might need help.

Victoria took her ring off and placed it inside her backpack again, then grabbed her standard bag of supplies from the rental car. She slung it over her shoulder and returned to the dark splotch, where she took gloves from her bag. She pulled the gloves on and placed three pieces of the stained gravel into an evidence bag. Maybe it was animal blood, but maybe not. Next, heeding Ned's words and taking the utmost precaution, she dictated a message to Agent Galax.

"It's Victoria Heslin. I'm at one of Karen's property listings. 414 Old Mill Road. I'm about to enter the barn. I'll check back with you in an hour. If you don't hear from me by then, this is where someone should look first. Thank you."

With the steady sound of gunshots resonating in the air, she headed to the old barn. The mottled trail ended a few yards from the rickety door, which was partway open.

"This is the FBI. Is anyone in there?" Victoria called from the doorway, though not in the authoritative voice she normally used for approaching a known crime scene. Instead, her voice was firm but gentle. If an injured animal had crept inside to die, she didn't want to terrify it more than necessary. Its last interaction with another lifeform should bear kindness.

Hearing nothing, she put covers over her shoes and continued inside as a long and fast succession of gunshots boomed in the background.

Rays of light beamed across the interior from the open doorway, showcasing streams of floating dust particles in a space packed with piles of discarded items. A layer of grime covered everything, years or decades of dust and dead bugs.

"Hello?" Victoria called, sweeping the room with her gaze.

Again, no response.

To her left, someone had moved objects aside, disturbing old cobwebs and creating a narrow path through the mess. Victoria moved along the path, passing an old push mower, an axe, rusting shovels, stacks of planting pots, weathered barrels, and rotting work boots. She sneezed once, twice, and finally, a third time, as dust rose and settled around her. In the barn's corner, four black plastic containers were corralled together, separated from the rest of the junk. Victoria turned on her flashlight and moved its beam slowly over one of the quart-sized receptacles. Without picking it up, she nudged it so the front faced her. On the remnants of a peeling label, under bird and insect droppings, she recognized a faded image. A skull and crossbones. Victoria turned the next container around. She squinted at the faded image, bits of it long gone, until her brain filled in the missing components. A snarling rat with a long tail.

Rat poison.

And the primary ingredient in rat poison was thallium sulfate.

Finding the poison had left Victoria's senses tingling, though she would not jump to conclusions. Thallium sulfate killed the Fuller sisters, but it wasn't a shocker that the old barn contained the poison to control unwanted pests. And yet someone had recently moved those containers away from the rest of the junk. And this wasn't just any old barn. It was part of Karen's listing.

After taking pictures of the containers, Victoria resumed her search. Close to the rat poison, a gray tarp covered an object with squared edges. A splotch of dark liquid gleamed from one corner. She hurried to move the tarp aside and uncovered an antique wooden chest. A chest large enough to hold a body. The rusty hinges creaked out a pitiful grating sound in the quiet barn as she threw the top open.

There was no body inside. The chest appeared to be empty except for a moth-eaten plaid blanket spread over the bottom. But the blanket wasn't entirely flat. Victoria moved the material to the right, revealing several items beneath it.

She tucked the flashlight under her arm and lifted out a book that looked to be a writing journal. The word *Thoughts* was centered on the otherwise blank white cover. Positioning her body so she had a view of the barn's only entrance, she opened the journal. Tucked between the cover and the front page was a blank envelope with a DNA helix logo in the corner. Victoria recognized the logo. It was from Ancestry Answers, a consumer DNA testing company. Last December, she'd briefly considered buying kits from Ancestry Answers as Christmas presents. Something for her father, who already had every material possession he needed or wanted.

Without actually reading the journal, Victoria skimmed through the pages, all the while knowing that she shouldn't be touching it. But what if it led her straight to the perpetrator before he killed again?

The first pages of the journal contained bullet-pointed lists in black ink. Someone had perfectly formed each letter, containing them neatly between the rows. Then the writing grew messier, turning into a mixture of print and scrawled script. Some words stayed within the lines. Some took up the space of three rows and filled the margins. The black ink became red, and the pen's depressions ran deep, indenting the paper.

Then something jumped out at her. One word in large capital letters scrawled across the center of a page. JEFFREY. Someone had underlined and circled the word several times.

Victoria closed the journal and set it back down. She quickly moved the plaid blanket to the right and scanned the rest of the chest's contents. A bright pink fabric filled a gallon-sized, filmy plastic bag. Two smaller plastic bags next to it looked newer, the plastic less opaque. They appeared to be empty. The last object, tucked in the chest's corner, was a thick and ornate men's ring.

Victoria lifted the larger bag from the chest. She didn't open the sealed Ziplock top, but turned the bag around. As best she could tell, the item inside was a pink shirt with ripped stitching along an underarm seam. A square patch of fabric the size of a man's wallet was missing from the material. Someone had cut the patch out with scissors, leaving straight edges in the remaining fabric.

The two smaller bags were sandwich sized. On closer inspection, they weren't empty after all. Each contained a few slender fibers approximately an inch in length. The fibers looked like human hair. She turned the bags over and made out their labels. A black J on one. A black T on the other. J for Jerome? And T for Todd?

She held up the ring. Saw the *NCAA Champion* engraving. Couldn't be too many of those out there. She knew it was Jerome's missing ring.

Victoria placed everything back and called Detective Lambert. She gave him the address and said, "I spotted a trail of blood, or what looks like blood, which gave me probable cause to enter and look around. I need backup, a warrant, and an evidence team out here."

48

Victoria had at least another twenty minutes before backup arrived and someone secured a warrant to search the property. She wanted to continue reading the journal, but without the warrant, the evidence was off limits to law enforcement. Any information she gained from reading it would be inadmissible. The blood trail had given her probable cause to search the barn, but a defense attorney could argue that opening the journal was a breach of privacy. Victoria would not be the reason that critical information became inadmissible and destroyed the case.

A long lull occurred between muffled gun shots and a scratching sound came from somewhere close to the barn. She grabbed her gun. The sound might have been branches dipping in the wind and scraping against the old walls, but she wasn't sure.

The gunshots resumed as she crept around the barn with her back pressed against the exterior wall and peered around the corner.

A clattering sound startled her and sent her heart rate soaring. She aimed her weapon and shouted, "FBI!"

A feral cat leaped from a rusting riding mower and ran off into the brambles.

Victoria lowered her gun. As her gaze moved away from the cat, she spotted more splotches of dark liquid in the grass and dirt. Probable cause to continue her search. With her weapon raised, she followed the spots toward the house. The trail disappeared in the thick grass. She kept walking toward the front porch. There were no traces of blood on the stairs or in front of the door, where a lock mechanism for realtors hung from the handle. Victoria retraced her steps through the patchy yard, the covers on her shoes now filthy, until she picked up the trail again on the side of the house. It led to a cellar door entrance in the back. Two wide doors in the ground reminded her of the Wizard of Oz and the storm cellar where Dorothy's family had hidden from the tornado. A small splatter of ruby red on the door's peeling paint erased any doubt about the nature of the trail she'd followed.

Three large stones lay atop the cellar door. One by one, she rolled them off, and they hit the ground with an echoing thud. She stood still and listened, but heard only the constant gunshots from the shooting range. She continued to scan the area as she dictated a message to Detective Lambert. "It's Victoria again. I'm following that same trail of droplets—definitely blood—into a basement through cellar doors behind the main house. Going in now."

Lambert was on his way with the evidence team and other officers. It shouldn't be too much longer until he arrived. Meanwhile, a life might be at stake. Victoria gripped the cellar door's handle and heaved one heavy side open. From where she stood outside, she saw only five rickety stairs and the darkness below.

Carrying her weapon, she looked around once more before slowly descending into the underground space. The first stair groaned under the pressure of her step. The second felt soft and rotten. Worried the wood might cave in and leave her sprawled on the ground with broken bones, she tested the remaining planks with a light touch of her toe before placing her full weight on them.

The cellar smelled dank and musty. There were no windows. The only light came from the daylight above. She turned on her flashlight and took cautious steps. Another smell wafted to her from deeper inside. Something foul and sick.

Just like in the barn, a path several feet in diameter wove through stacks of abandoned items. Someone had cleared the path haphazardly, with boxes and rusting tools and things she couldn't make out piled on top of each other to the sides. As she headed away from the door, the offensive odor grew stronger. About three quarters of the way in, she made out a large, lumpy form on the ground. Less than a foot high, but several feet long, and without the sharp angles defining most of the other objects littering the space. A little closer and she recognized what she was seeing. A body curled into a fetal position. Male, from the size and build. Unmoving.

Victoria crept to the body. Zip ties secured the man's hands in front of him and also bound his feet. Blood covered his upper lip and chin. A thick stream of it had run into his hair and congealed like glue. A pool of vomit surrounded him. The smell told her he'd vomited within the past few hours.

Victoria pressed two fingers against his carotid artery, but kept her gaze roaming the room. She felt relief at the pulse thumping under her plastic gloves. He was alive. But for how much longer?

In a hurry now, she swung her light from corner to corner, around the menacing dark piles of furniture and junk, then across the walls. Water had trickled down the cement, leaving stains and darkened patches. But there were no messages there. No words about atonement.

When she finished circling the entire space, making sure no one was hiding in the corners or behind the larger piles of junk, she crouched beside the stranger. She shook his shoulder, gently at first, then with more force. "Can you hear me?"

He still hadn't moved.

Keeping her eyes and gun trained on the cellar door entrance, Victoria took out her phone, and dialed 911. While waiting for an operator to answer, she checked the man's pants pockets for a wallet or other identification. She found none.

The call connected. Thank God.

"My name is Victoria Heslin. I'm a federal agent. I'm requesting emergency medical aid at 414 Old Mill Road."

"Did you say you were with the FBI?"

"Yes." As Victoria spoke, she heard something moving near the cellar entrance. She tucked her phone between her chin and shoulder. With both hands on her gun, she moved along one wall toward the door.

"What is the nature of your emergency?" the dispatcher asked.

"I found a male in his early thirties. No identification. He's alive, but unresponsive. No visible external injuries except a broken nose. I suspect severe internal injuries...or poisoning. I also need local PD to help clear the location, secure the scene, and search the property."

She'd reached the cellar entrance and saw nothing. She climbed the steps as she asked. "How long until the ambulance gets here? I'm not from the area. I don't know where the nearest fire station or hospital is. I think we're a long way out."

"Hold on, ma'am. I'll have an ETA for you soon."

There was no one in sight around the entrance, and Victoria attributed the sounds she'd heard to another wild animal. She hurried back down the stairs and to the man.

His eyes fluttered open. He moaned.

"I think he's gaining consciousness," Victoria told the dispatcher.

"See if you can get him to talk to you."

"I'm with the FBI," she told the man. "Can you tell me who did this to you? What happened? Who tied you up?"

The man didn't respond, but the 911 operator said, "An ambulance should arrive in twenty minutes."

Twenty minutes could seem like a lifetime in certain situations, and this was one of them. "Just hold on," Victoria told the man. "Help is coming."

Victoria left his hands bound. He certainly appeared to be a helpless victim, but she didn't know who he was, what he'd done, or what he was capable of doing. She was cutting the ties from his feet when he turned his head on the floor.

"An ambulance is on the way," she said again. She refrained from telling him he was going to be okay. She didn't know that and didn't want him to think he could wait and tell her what happened later. There might not be a later.

He blinked several times, then seemed to focus on her. He lifted his head a few inches off the floor, hovering there as he opened his mouth. Instead of speaking, he gasped, clamped his teeth down, and curled into an even tighter ball.

Victoria could tell he was in terrible pain. She prayed he wouldn't die. And while she waited, she could do nothing to help him. Witnessing his suffering, unable to provide the care he needed, sent her stress level soaring. She gritted her teeth in frustration and felt veins in her forehead constrict. What if the ambulance didn't arrive soon enough? Or didn't make it to the hospital in time to save him?

She stepped back and blew out a giant puff of breath before settling down against the nearest damp concrete wall. She kept her gun in her hand and her eyes trained on the door. *Come on. Come on. Hurry,* she thought to herself. "They're coming. They'll be here any minute," she said aloud, just as much to calm her own nerves as to reassure the man on the ground.

He stirred again, pressing his bound hands against his abdomen.

"Can you tell me your name?" she asked, not expecting an answer.

His eyes remained shut, but his lips moved.

She jumped up and moved closer to him. "I didn't hear you. Say it again."

He whispered through clenched teeth, and this time she heard him say, "Jeffrey Wilson."

49

After telling Victoria his name, Jeffrey moaned, squeezed his eyes shut, and blacked out again. Mercifully for him, but not for Victoria. She urged him to hold on as she frantically dictated a group message to Detective Durst in Durham, Agent Galax and Detective Lambert in Charlotte, Lt. Detective Suarez in Boston, Sam, and her boss.

Jeffrey Wilson is in the basement of Karen's property listing. He's unresponsive. All I got was his name. No other details. Ambulance and backup are on the way.

A flurried exchange of questions and information ensued, and Detective Lambert said he'd escalate the search for Karen Green with more Charlotte PD officers.

The ambulance still had not arrived, and Victoria continued to wait. Recalling the killer's strange obsession with hair, she moved her flashlight over Jeffrey's head. Dried blood had crusted in his thick hair. But she still saw it. A bleeding patch of scalp on the top of his head where someone had pulled his hair out from the roots. Just like someone had done to Todd and Jerome.

"Can you tell me who put you here? And why?" she asked again, in case Jeffrey had another bout of consciousness.

He gave no response.

She sat against the wall, irritated that all she could do was hope he didn't die. The dank, moldy basement seemed to close in on her, sealing Jeffrey's fate and the answers she so desperately wanted. She checked the time on her phone again and again, willing the ambulance to move faster.

Finally, a siren wailed in the distance. Some of the tension released from her shoulders as she jumped to her feet.

"They're here. I'll be right back. Hang in there!" She ran through the cellar, knocking over a ceramic flowerpot on her way. As it shattered, she slowed and eased up the rotten stairs. Once outside, she gulped fresh air as she raced to the front of the property, where she waved her arms to get the driver's attention. Every second might matter.

The driver pulled up next to Victoria's rental car. The ambulance's rear doors swung open. Two young men who looked like weightlifters, one with a shaved head and tattoos swirling on the side of his neck and arms, and one with a short buzz cut, climbed out carrying a stretcher with equipment between them.

"He's back here. This way," she said, beckoning them to follow her as she ran. When they caught up to her at the back of the house, she pointed through the cellar door opening. "He's down there. On the floor. Be careful on the stairs."

They left the stretcher outside and carried a backboard. Victoria led them to Jeffrey, and held her flashlight up to give them as much light as possible. Jeffrey didn't stir as they rolled him onto the backboard and carried it across the basement. The medics grunted and muscles bulged in their arms as they transported their patient up the stairs. Shaved-head was at the foot of the backboard. On the second step, the rotten wood gave in under him. His leg plummeted down, and he lost his grip on the heavy load.

Victoria gasped as one end of the backboard dropped.

"Grab him!" Shaved-head shouted.

She'd already leaped to catch the end just in time, holding it up near her shoulders as Shaved-head struggled to get up to the next step and back under the board. They were all panting when they emerged outside.

Victoria jogged alongside them back to the driveway, carrying her gun and keeping her eyes peeled for any sign of a threat. The stretcher's wheels got stuck in the thick weeds twice, then bumped over gravel until they reached the waiting emergency vehicle and hoisted Jeffrey inside. The medic with the buzz-cut sliced the zip ties from Jeffrey's wrists and began prepping his arm for an IV.

"He might have been poisoned with thallium sulfate. It's rat poison," Victoria said. "Or an overdose of ketamine."

"We'll let the attending doctor know," the medic with the shaved head answered.

As the ambulance doors closed, Victoria added, "I'll head to the hospital soon. I need to speak with him once he's conscious and stable." She spoke as if his recovery was a foregone conclusion now. She needed him to be okay. The investigation hinged on it.

The ambulance sped off on the rutted road. A cloud of dust rose behind it, and Victoria sighed. The evidence team and additional officers shouldn't be much longer. But whoever had put Jeffrey in the cellar might return. The thought of it gave her another shot of adrenaline. She couldn't relax yet. She needed to be ready.

With the ambulance out of sight, Victoria turned toward the barn. Her gaze passed over her rental car. Something didn't look right. She stopped and stared, stuck her hands on her hips, and swore.

Someone had slashed all four of her tires.

50

Victoria pulled her eyes from her completely flat tires and looked around. There was no sign of anyone else. The sun was going down; it had almost disappeared behind the tree line. The gunshot sounds had ceased. She could still hear the faint rumbling of the ambulance traveling over the gravel road. The driver hadn't turned on the sirens yet. She grabbed her jacket from the passenger seat and slipped it on as she called Agent Galax.

"What's going on there now?" he asked.

"The ambulance just left with Jeffrey. And I discovered that someone came out here while I was in the basement and slashed my tires. Whoever did it is probably long gone by now."

"Jeez. Are you still alone there?"

"I won't be for long. Detective Lambert is on his way with an evidence team and back up. I'll get a ride back to Charlotte with someone. Any sign of Karen?"

"Not yet. Her husband and I contacted her friends, her colleagues, and her current clients. She's not with any of them and they don't know where she is. Neither does her father. Robert is anxious. He's sure someone kidnapped her. He keeps asking if we've located the other person from the photo. Obviously, he doesn't know what you've found out there in the basement of her listing. I don't think he's involved."

"If Robert really is worried, rather than putting on an act, he's going to be in for a real shock soon," Victoria said. "Did you contact Tiffany Westview? The property investor Karen works for?"

"No. We've only been contacting people in the Charlotte area that she might have been with."

"Can you find out if anyone else around the age of twenty-nine is missing in North Carolina? Or anywhere. I don't know who else might be involved, but just in case. I don't want to find out there's another person dying in an abandoned house, and we didn't get there soon enough."

"Will do," Agent Galax said.

After agreeing to keep each other posted, Victoria ended her conversation with Galax. Though she'd told him that whoever slashed her tires was gone, she was on full alert until other law enforcement arrived. Carrying her weapon, she walked the perimeter of the house and the barn, again examining the places where someone could hide. The house remained locked and there was no way to secure the padlock on the front door from the inside.

Satisfied she was alone at the property, Victoria called Sam. "I need information on Tiffany Westview. I was told Karen works closely with her. She scopes out potential investment properties that Westview either flips or rents. I want to know if any of those properties are in the Boston area. Or maybe in Charlotte. That could be where Karen is right now. Can you look into that and meanwhile, get me a phone number for Westview?"

In the time it took for Victoria to get back to the Hyundai and get a pen and paper, Sam was ready with Westview's phone number. Victoria called it right away. The call went to voicemail. Victoria left a message.

Her next step was to deal with her car because it wasn't moving anywhere without four new tires. She pulled the rental agreement out of the glove compartment and spoke with the agency. She was finishing up with them when she heard gravel crunching, the first indication a vehicle was approaching the property.

"I have to go," she said, cutting off the call. In a heartbeat, she'd slid her phone into her pocket and pulled out her gun.

Through the trees, she couldn't see whoever was coming, only hear their steady approach. She used the rental car to shield her body, keeping her gun raised and her finger poised near the trigger.

A black sedan appeared around the final bend, driving straight toward her.

Victoria had a second to think about Ned before zeroing in on the approaching car with every speck of her concentration. Her heart pounded, blood pulsing at her temples and resounding in her ears. She kept her gun aimed until she recognized Detective Lambert behind the wheel. Lowering her weapon, she let out the breath she'd been holding, relieved she wasn't about to have a showdown with anyone.

Lambert got out of the sedan. "Hey. I got a warrant. Not on site, but a judge signed off on it. A few cruisers and an evidence team are right behind me," he said, staring at her weapon and giving Victoria a questioning look.

She pointed to her car. "I didn't see or hear anyone. I was in the cellar when it happened."

He walked around the Hyundai, taking in the completely deflated tires. He stopped by the back bumper and scanned the area. "Someone came back for Wilson, huh? Maybe to finish the job?"

"I don't know. Did you get a guard positioned at the hospital?"

"Yes. I've got an officer there. The hospital staff has already registered Wilson as a John Doe for now. They're taking care of him. He should make it. As soon as he's able to talk, we can head back there. Guess you'll need a ride."

She nodded. "The rental car agency will tow this one. I'm supposed to leave it here. I'm just going to grab my suitcase and put it in your car." She headed to the Hyundai's trunk, grateful that with everything going on, she hadn't forgotten about her belongings and left without them. Now that they had a warrant, she was eager to get back to the journal. It might tell them if anyone else was next. But before she got the chance, two more vehicles ambled along the road and into the driveway. The forensics team had arrived. Four of them. Two men and two women. Close behind them were two marked police cars with armed officers to help protect the scene and the forensic techs.

Victoria brought them up to speed on the case and what she'd found. After the officers cleared the area, two of the analysts headed to the basement with their supplies and two went into the barn. Not wanting to disturb the evidence any more than she already had, Victoria pointed out the location of the rat poison and the chest, then stayed back, giving the techs room to set up their lights.

"I'd like to take the journal once you've logged it as evidence and photographed the pages," she said minutes later to the woman who was taking photos of the chest.

"What journal?" the woman asked.

A sinking feeling erupted inside Victoria, growing stronger as she hurried to the chest and peered inside. Only the blanket remained. Everything else was missing.

Victoria dropped her head into her hands. She'd left the chest open. Whoever came back knew she'd found it. The journal and other evidence were gone. But there was little time to dwell on the matter. Lambert beckoned from the barn's entrance. "Agent Heslin! I just heard from our officer at the hospital. Jeffrey is conscious. He wants to talk to us right away. Let's go."

51

Trees obscured the moonlight and the vehicle's headlamps provided the only lights on the road as Victoria left the abandoned property in Detective Lambert's car. Lambert spoke with someone who was obviously his spouse or partner. He told the person not to expect him home for dinner and not to wait up for him. "I'll send you an update when I know more. Love you," he said before placing his phone on the seat between his legs. "You know how it is," he said with a glance toward Victoria.

"Yeah, I do." She rested her head against the cool glass window and thought about Ned. What was he doing without her? Probably watching a game.

"Good detective work, by the way." He smiled. "I meant to tell you that already."

"Thank you," she answered, though all she could think about was the lost journal, the hair fibers, and the other items from the chest.

They'd reached the crossroad and her phone rang. "It's Sam," she said upon seeing his name. "Let's see what he has to say."

"Hey," Sam started off. "Did you get in touch with the property investor yet? Westview?"

"Not yet. I'm with Hugh Lambert, the lead on the Eckstrom case from the Charlotte PD," she added, in case Sam didn't recognize his name. "We're on our way to interview Jeffrey at the hospital. I'm putting you on speaker, okay?"

"Sure. Hello, Detective," Sam said. "Victoria is on to something with Westview. Not that I ever doubted her instinct, but…anyway, I tracked Westview's digital footprint for the last few weeks and found a few interesting things."

"You think Westview has something to do with the murders?" Lambert asked.

"Only indirectly," Sam answered. "Westview is a successful influencer. She's twenty-six years old. Makes millions every year. Investing in real estate is now her hobby. She buys properties, has teams fix them up, then turns them into Airbnb rentals. She chronicles the renovation processes. They all end up looking pretty special, if you ask me. Anyway, according to her credit card, Westview stayed in a Boston hotel for two nights, the day before and after Jerome's murder. She paid for the hotel, food, and gas. However, Westview shares almost every day of her life with the public. The day before and after Jerome's murder, she posted videos of herself in Belize."

"How do you know she didn't record the videos weeks ago and post them at a later date?" Lambert asked.

"I don't, but we can find out if necessary. And I've requested video camera footage from the gas station where someone used her credit card. But that's not all we found. Westview was in the Durham area before Jerome got murdered. She purchased gas about forty miles outside the city."

"Let's see what Westview says when she gets back to me," Victoria said. "But it looks as if someone else was using her credit card in Boston. That's one way to get around a city without leaving your own digital footprint." Then something else occurred to her. "Does Westview own any properties in Charlotte?"

"She owns six through a trust holding company. They're all vacation rentals."

"Karen would know exactly where they are if she helped purchase them. She might be hiding inside one of them right now. Can you send the addresses?"

"I already sent them to you and Detective Lambert."

"Thank you, Sam. You're way ahead of us," Victoria told him.

"I'll get officers to each of them within the next few hours," Lambert said.

Victoria rode silently for the next twenty minutes, listening to Lambert speaking to his superiors and getting updates regarding the search for Karen.

They weren't far from the hospital when Victoria's phone rang again. It was a number she didn't recognize.

"This is Tiffany Westview," the caller said over music playing in the background. "I got your message. What's this all about?" Westview sounded serious. "Are you really the FBI?"

After convincing Tiffany that Victoria was indeed the FBI, she asked, "Were you in Boston for business two weeks ago?"

"No. I haven't been to Boston this year," Westview said.

"What about Durham?"

"North Carolina? No. I've been to Charlotte this year, and Kiawah, South Carolina, but nowhere else in the Carolinas. Why?"

"Because someone used your credit card in Boston for a hotel, gas, and food. And gas outside Durham."

"It was *not* me. Why does it matter? Is this a credit card theft thing? I didn't report it."

"No. We're investigating crimes that happened in those areas around the time you were there."

"I wasn't there. Someone must have stolen my credit card. Oh, wait. There's someone you can check with. Karen Green. Karen works for me. She's used my credit card before when she misplaced hers. She might have used it if she was checking out a property for me, though she wasn't supposed to be in Boston. I'll just send her a message and find out. If it was her, it's perfectly okay."

"No," Victoria said. "Do not call her. Do not message her. Not unless you want an obstruction of justice charge. And we'll find out if you do. We need to speak with her first."

"Uh, did she do something?"

"This is an ongoing investigation," Victoria said. "We'll get back to you."

The evidence against Karen was building to an impenetrable concrete wall. But the question remained—why was she killing people? What was her motive?

Victoria hoped Jeffrey would have all the answers.

52

Twelve years ago - Karen

Karen woke up shivering on a rough, splintery floor. Her head pounded. The bitter taste of vodka lingered in her dry mouth. She didn't know where she was.

Shards of dull gray light came through cracks in the walls and formed skinny vertical lines around a door. Shovels, a ladder, and edging machines rested against a wall. On the opposite side hung inner tubes for floating in the lake.

A storage shed? What am I doing in here?

She was naked except for her T-shirt, inside out, with the tag pricking against her arm.

She moaned and dropped her head, dry heaving the remaining contents of her stomach onto the dusty floor. Only bile came up, pulling and stretching her abdominal muscles with every heave. Taking ragged breaths, she wiped her mouth with the back of her hand. Parts of the night came back to her. The vodka. She wouldn't forget that as long as she lived and vowed to never touch it again. What else did she remember? The dares. Sending a shirtless photo. Jumping in the lake. The others leaving her alone. She couldn't find her clothes.

Then what? She racked her throbbing brain to remember but couldn't. She must have blacked out. A sickening feeling told her she was better off not knowing.

Her feet were numb with cold, and her back ached from sleeping on the hard floor. She pushed herself up, banging her head on a shelf as she stood. She ran her dirty hand gently over her scalp to soothe the fresh and biting pain there, though the throbbing inside her skull was worse. Her first hangover and she hated every second of it.

As she moved toward the door, a sharp sting between her legs made her wonder why her body hurt in so many places. She pulled the door handle. It didn't open. A surface bolt crossed the space between the door and its frame. She shook the door, thinking if there was only one bolt, she might dislodge the screws and get out. The walls rattled, but the bolt persisted. She pummeled her fists against the wood and yelled for help. Just as suddenly, she stopped. The thin beam of light coming from around the door hit her shirt. There was something there. A crusty filmy substance over the pink fabric. What was it? Her gaze moved down. She spotted dark smudges between her legs, high on the skin of her inner thighs. Blood. And it wasn't time for her period.

Oh, God. No!

First came the shock. An out-of-body experience like none she had ever known. Then disgust. It hit her like a freight train and consumed her. She prayed she was having a nightmare. Any second, she would wake up in her own bed, stretch and roll over, her vague memories nothing more than bad dreams. Meghan would have fruit and egg-white omelets waiting. Yet she knew that wasn't going to happen. Her discomfort was too sharp, too real, too painful.

Who had done this to her? Todd? Jerome? Jeffrey? It had to be one of them.

She rubbed the blood off her legs. That's when she noticed the purple bruises around her wrists.

What would her father and stepmother think if they knew? If they saw her now? She couldn't let them or anyone else find her this way. She had to escape the shed, find something to cover herself in, and get back to the cabin before anyone saw her. She would shower and scrub every ounce of her body, erasing her shame so that no one, including herself, would ever know what happened.

Brush rustled nearby. Someone was coming.

Karen froze.

The clop, clop of heavy footsteps came closer.

She held her breath.

The footsteps stopped right outside the shed. Just on the other side of the door. The person coughed several times, a deep, rattling sound that pierced her nerves. The coughing stopped and the bolt on the door scraped to one side.

She crouched in the corner, wrapping her arms around her knees, covering herself as best she could. If there was another lock, one requiring a key, then whoever opened it might have done this to her.

The door opened without the click or scrape of a second lock turning. Light from a gray sky entered, exposing her. She shielded her face with her hand, willing herself to be invisible. Finally, she had the courage to peer up. She saw muddy boots first. In the doorway stood the man who had cleaned the pool yesterday. He held a shovel over one shoulder and stared down at her. "Uh, you okay?" he asked.

Looking at her feet, she shook her head. Tears rolled from her eyes.

"Why are you in here?" he asked in a menacing voice that struck terror inside her.

She didn't respond.

"What happened to you?" he asked next, sounding angry rather than concerned.

"Nothing," she answered, so filled with shame she couldn't even lift her head. Not for a single second did she consider telling him someone had assaulted her and bolted the door to the shed.

She heard the man cough up phlegm and spit. Then silence. He was still standing there, as if waiting for a good explanation.

"I was with some friends," she said. "We were just playing a game. And then...I don't know. I got lost." She choked on the words before pulling her legs in tighter against her body.

"That's what happened?" he asked, still standing there in the doorway. "And uh, you also lost your clothes?"

She nodded but couldn't speak.

"Hold on. I'm gonna get you something to cover up with. Don't go anywhere." His voice had softened some since he first opened the door to the shed. He closed it then, leaving her alone again in the dark.

Yesterday, she'd felt sorry for the man whose job was to scoop poop out of the pool. She was embarrassed for him when Lilly and Todd made jokes at his expense. But that was then. Before she knew the true meaning of shame.

It felt like an hour, but it was probably only minutes before he came back and tapped on the door. "You still in there?" he asked from outside.

She sniffled. "Yes."

"You sure you're okay, though? Nothing happened to you?"

"I'm okay," she said, without meeting his eyes. "Nothing happened."

"If you're sure, then. I'm gonna put a towel out here for ya' to wrap yourself up. Okay? I'm going now."

Karen waited until she no longer heard his boots clopping away. She opened the door, grabbed the big green beach towel, and wrapped it around her body. "Wait," she cried.

The man was pretty far away but heard her. He turned around and trudged back toward the shed. "What is it? You need something else?"

Tears streamed down her face. "You can't tell anyone about this, okay? About finding me here. Don't tell anyone. Please. Please."

She was about to plead with him again before he agreed with a slow nod. "I don't know what you did, but I won't tell anyone about seeing you. Your secret is safe with me. I won't tell a soul."

"Thank you," she said, feeling guilty, disgusting, and more alone than she'd ever felt before in her life.

She waited inside the shed for a few more minutes, summoning the strength to leave and face her father and stepmother, if it came to that. She couldn't hide in there forever. But what would she say to them? Not the truth. She couldn't tell them she'd gotten so drunk that she'd passed out and someone had done something terrible to her. Her father would be angry no matter what story she came up with. He must be worried sick that she hadn't come home, but she'd gladly take his anger over his disgust any day.

She swallowed and tried to think. Decided she'd tell her parents that she stayed at one of the other girls' cabins. She'd tried to call and send a text. But with the terrible reception there, it must not have gone through.

Feeling so heavy, and yet totally empty inside, as if her soul had left her body, she finally left the shed. Outside, clouds hung low in the sky. Twigs and debris littered the ground. During the night, rain had fallen, bringing with it a dampness that had penetrated her bones. She couldn't imagine that deep coldness ever leaving her body.

She stared up at the stone cliff across the lake. Just two days ago, when she arrived, she'd stood up there with her father and Meghan, looking down at this very spot. She'd viewed the lake, the clubhouse, and the clearing with a mild disinterest. No fear. Back then, she hadn't a clue about what the place had in store for her.

Do not think about it again. Nothing happened. Nothing happened.

Wiping tears from her eyes, she turned and trudged across the muddy ground. In her ripped T-shirt and the towel around her bottom half, she searched for the rest of her clothes.

Her shorts were on the picnic table in the clearing. The rain had soaked them, and they went on cold and heavy, exacerbating her chill. Her phone was still in the back pocket. It wouldn't turn on. Either the battery had died or water had destroyed it. If her parents had sent a dozen frantic messages, she didn't know it yet.

She found one sandal and then the other, but not her bra.

Wearing the towel around her shoulders like a cloak, she plodded down the puddle-strewn path to the clubhouse, eyes on her filthy feet and her stained sandals, terrified about what awaited her.

Thank God her family was leaving tomorrow. She'd stay inside the cabin until then. She couldn't bear to run into any of the teens from last night. It was a small blessing that she'd never have to see them again. Todd. Jerome. Jeffrey. One of them had hurt her. But maybe, if she tried hard enough, she could convince herself she'd never even met them, and nothing terrible had happened to her.

53

Twelve years ago - Todd

Lilly was definitely into him. She kept touching him, his back, his neck, his leg. She'd scooted closer on the picnic table until she was practically sitting on his lap, her hand wrapped around his inner thigh. He could feel the heat of her against him, and his heartbeat quickened in anticipation of what they would do later. When he'd left the pool, he'd found her on social media. He'd checked out her posts and followed her. There was no question Lilly liked to party. And he was going to show her an incredible time. He didn't want to get so drunk that he couldn't remember it. He'd stopped drinking the hard stuff after a few sips, though he still pretended for a few more rounds until he switched to nursing a beer with one arm draped over Lilly's shoulder.

"All the way in. All the way in," he chanted as the freckled girl plodded into the woods to jump into the lake. He chose that dare, thinking everyone would go with her, leaving him and Lilly alone. That didn't happen. They seemed content to stay where they were. Maybe they'd all had too much to drink.

"Some of you should go after her. Make sure she really does it," he suggested.

"Make sure she doesn't drown, you mean?" Jeffrey asked.

"Yeah. That, too," Todd answered.

Jeffrey stood up and looked toward the woods. "I'll go after her. Anyone else coming?"

"I'm staying right here," Lilly said. She pressed her soft lips against Todd's neck and a thrill coursed through him.

"You guys should all go check on her," Todd said, urging Jerome and Cassandra to leave.

"You're the one who dared her to go in the lake," Cassandra answered, glaring at him and her sister.

But Jerome cooperated. "Come on." Smiling, he gestured to Cassandra. He was carrying the bottle with the last of the vodka and already heading after Jeffrey.

"Hey! What are you doing?" The sudden, angry shout came from the direction of the trail. A man's voice. His presence was so unexpected it made Todd jump up from the table at the same time Lilly tightened her grip on his arm, digging her fingernails into his flesh, and Cassandra screamed.

"Can't you read?" the man yelled as he took giant strides into the clearing. "There's no one allowed out here after dark!" He wore a hoodie with the hood pulled over his head, obscuring his features and making him seem extra creepy.

Everything happened in a blur of instinctive responses. Cassandra yanked Lilly away from Todd. Jerome hurled the vodka bottle, but with too much force. It smashed the only lamp, shattering the bulb and plunging the clearing into an inky blankness as he sprinted into the woods.

"You broke the damn light! You spoiled little—" the man shouted. "Get back here!"

Cassandra and Lilly ran off. Todd figured they would head back to the clubhouse if they could find the trail in the dark and not end up lost deep in the woods. He quickly zipped his duffel around the remaining beers and hightailed it after the sisters, following the sound of their footfalls and Lilly's giggling.

The man's shouts rang out behind them. "I want your names!"

"Sorry, dude!" Todd hollered back as he sprinted off. He hoped the guy hadn't gotten a good look at them. Though what was the big deal, anyway? Why were they racing away as if they'd killed someone? They hadn't done anything wrong, really. The only damage was a broken light bulb and some littering. Nothing that couldn't get fixed in minutes. But what if the guy was a huge prick and wanted to teach them a lesson? If Jerome got a drinking citation, or a vandalism charge, that could mess up all his college prospects.

But that wasn't likely. The man was probably someone's father out for a night walk. One of those people who was obsessed with preventing litter. Or maybe it was creepy Crawford out patrolling the place. He was just a maintenance worker. Not the police. Not a security guard.

The man shouted again from faraway, probably still in the clearing. He wasn't following them. Lilly's laughter trickled through the trees ahead. From behind came grunts and the swift and solid sound of Jerome running. Good. They were all going to be fine.

With the beer sloshing in his bag, Todd slowed to a jog. Light reached the trail as he neared the end on the other side of the lake. When he got to the clubhouse, Lilly and her sister waited together under a streetlamp. Todd collected himself, walking now, ready to take up where he and Lilly had left off. They could grab a few towels from the pool to use as blankets. Go to the tennis courts and sit on the benches or lie down on the tables there.

Lilly tossed her thick hair back and smiled. Her eyes beamed and her tan skin glowed. God, she was gorgeous.

He was only yards away from her when a déjà vu sensation hit him, as if he'd experienced the exact moment before. The entire scene played out in his mind. He saw himself emerging from the woods carrying a case of beer in his duffel. Two blonde sisters watched him approach. Jerome was somewhere behind him, calling his name. "Todd! Hey!"

Had it already happened? No. That was impossible.

A strong smell filled his nostrils. His mouth, too. A skunk? Weed? A wave of nausea followed, and with it, more confusion. He hadn't drunk near enough to make him sick. Something else was happening. His heart raced and sweat dripped down his face. A wave of fear rose inside his chest. He couldn't catch his breath. He gripped the handle of his bag tighter. His arm went numb and started jerking.

"Todd?" Jerome asked.

Todd felt himself fading. He stumbled toward Lilly.

She jumped away and stared at him, wide-eyed. "What's wrong with you? What are you doing?"

He could only shake his head, though his whole body trembled involuntarily. The ground rose to meet him, or maybe he was falling. As he smacked the pavement, his bladder let go, hot liquid spread over his groin, and the world went black.

54

Twelve years ago - Jerome

Todd's body jerked and spasmed on the pavement. His hands scrunched into claws.

"Why is he doing that?" Lilly screamed. "What the hell is wrong with him?"

Jerome recoiled, a guttural reaction to what he saw, but quickly pulled himself together and pushed past the girls to get to Todd.

"Should we call an ambulance?" Cassandra asked, her voice a frantic pitch.

"No! We can't. You're drunk, you're all drunk," Lilly said.

"That's your fault," Cassandra spit back. "You're the one who made everyone drink so much. That's totally on you! He's dying! We have to call an ambulance."

Jerome shut out their screaming and tried to recall the information he'd researched before the trip. Bits of it came to him, but he wasn't entirely sure of what he remembered. "We don't have to call an ambulance. He's not dying. I think we only call 911 if he doesn't, you know, go back to normal in a few minutes."

"You think?" Lilly shrieked. "Or you know? And what's wrong with him?"

"It hasn't been a few minutes yet, I don't think," Cassandra said. "I don't know."

Jerome placed his hand behind Todd's head to keep it from banging against the road. "You okay, Todd? You gonna come out of this?"

He remembered something about keeping the person from biting his tongue. Was he supposed to hold it? Put his hand right in Todd's mouth and hold his tongue down?

"Where's Jeffrey? Maybe he'll know what to do. Where is he? Where did he go?" Lilly said. She wasn't screaming anymore, but her voice had lost its sultry rasp and sounded desperate.

"Shut up and calm down!" Jerome shouted to her. "I know what to do." He took a deep breath. "You're okay, Todd. You're going to be okay, right? This stuff happens and then you're okay. Right?"

The tremors had stopped, but Todd remained unconscious. He wasn't moving at all.

Jerome pointed at Lilly. "Give me your phone."

"Why my phone?" Lilly asked.

"I need to call Todd's grandfather! My phone doesn't work here."

Cassandra stepped forward. She tapped her phone, presumably entering her password, and handed the device to Jerome.

Jerome just stared at it.

"What are you waiting for?" Lilly shouted, bouncing on her toes.

"I don't know his phone number." Jerome handed the phone back to Cassandra. The number would be in Todd's phone, but Jerome didn't know Todd's passcode. "Stay here with him. I'm going to his grandparents' cabin. Don't leave him!"

"Wait. What if...what are we supposed to do..." Lilly said at the same time her sister said, "We'll stay. We won't go anywhere." Then she shouted, "Go. Hurry!"

Jerome had already taken off running.

It was only by pure chance that Jerome knew about Todd's medical condition. And thank God he did, or he would be freaking out right now, not knowing what had just happened to his friend. Six months ago, Jerome had seen one of Todd's medical forms before a tournament. He hadn't meant to. He was carrying the team's paperwork for Coach P and dropped the whole folder. The forms spilled out on the gym floor. When he picked them up, he saw the notation. Todd had epilepsy and took medication for it. Jerome had heard of epilepsy. He'd thought it was pretty scary stuff, though it couldn't have been all that terrible or Todd wouldn't be such an excellent athlete.

Riding the bus on the way home from that tournament, Jerome did some research. Epilepsy was a neurological condition resulting from abnormal brain activity. The scariest part about epilepsy was its unpredictability. Seizures came on suddenly and without warning. Based on what Jerome had read, he thought

Todd's friends should know about the epilepsy in case of a seizure. But Todd was all about being strong and invincible, turning weaknesses into strengths, not accepting them.

Build up your weaknesses until they become your strong points. That was a quote from Knute Rockne on Todd's math notebook. Similar inspirational quotes were on posters in his room. He admired strength and despised weakness, and that's probably why he didn't want anyone to know about his condition. And as pig-headed as Todd's attitude might be, Jerome hadn't said a word about Todd's epilepsy to anyone else.

Jerome thanked God for Lilly and Cassandra. They would look after Todd for a few minutes, and he didn't have to be alone. It wouldn't take long to reach the cabin. Jerome was fast as hell. Fast enough that the top basketball programs all wanted him.

Except...he slowed to a jog and looked around. Was this even the right way? Shouldn't he have been there by now? He gulped in breaths and started to panic. It didn't matter how fast he could run if he ran in the wrong direction. The trails all looked the same. Fear and adrenaline had his heart pounding. Cursing on the balls of his feet, he turned in a small circle and squinted in the dark, trying to recognize something around him. When nothing looked familiar, he forced himself to choose a trail. He sprinted down it, praying he'd chosen correctly.

Finally, he saw The Eagle's Nest sign. He picked up the pace, flying down the driveway, and burst into the cabin without knocking. He was gasping but still shouted, "I need help. Todd had a seizure. Help!"

Todd's grandfather padded into the living room immediately, wearing pajamas. "Where is he?"

"He's at the clubhouse."

Mr. Eckstrom grabbed a coat and car keys, stuffed his feet into shoes by the door, and hurried outside. On the way, he called Todd's parents.

55

Twelve years ago - Todd

Todd woke up on the ground with a headache so terrible it felt as if his brain might explode. He was exhausted and could barely move. Liquid drenched the front of his pants. He thought a car might have run him over.

Jerome stood to one side, and Todd's grandfather on the other, lifting Todd from the ground. It was just the three of them. No one else was around.

"Steady there, Todd. We're moving you into the car and taking you back to the cabin," his grandfather said.

Todd tried to ask what happened to him, but he couldn't form the right sounds and get the words out.

Later, when the fog cleared from his brain, and he'd listened to Jerome describing the seizure, Todd's physical pain paled compared to his mental anguish. He hadn't cared to hear the details, but Jerome had spared none. Apparently, Todd had stared at them like a complete psycho before he started shaking. Then he fell. He'd convulsed on the ground. His hands had curled up like a dead person's. He'd pissed his pants. He'd freaked out everyone around him. Todd didn't remember any of it, but the rest of them weren't likely to forget any of it. His face flushed now with the heat of his shame.

"Don't tell my parents about this," he told Jerome. "I don't want them to know. If they find out, I'll have my license taken away. I won't be able to drive anymore."

"Uh, don't worry about that right now," Jerome said, and that's when Todd knew it was already too late.

"You told them?" he asked, praying it wasn't true.

"Your grandfather called them."

Todd swore and hung his head. "That's never happened before. The seizure. Not like that. And it's never going to happen again."

"How do you know?" Jerome asked.

"I just know," he lied. "Don't tell anyone. Okay? Promise me you won't tell anyone. Not a single soul."

"I won't," Jerome said. "No one will ever have to know what happened tonight, if you want it kept secret. It was just me and the two sisters who saw you."

"What about the other two?"

"I don't know what happened to Jeffrey or Karen. I guess they hightailed it out of the area when that guy came. But dude, seriously, it's not your fault or anything. There's no reason to be, you know, embarrassed about it. It's not like something you decided to do. It's a medical condition. I looked it up before tonight. It's not even a rare or uncommon disease. I mean, I don't know anyone else who has it, but lots of people do."

Todd walked away. He locked himself in the bathroom and took a long shower.

After midnight, he was wide awake on his bed. His soiled clothes were in the washing machine. Jerome snored in the twin bed across the room, emitting soft snorts every six seconds like clockwork. Todd went to the social media sites he used and unfollowed Lilly. He focused on the little boxes he needed to uncheck and avoided looking at her photos. He couldn't bear to. He was so grateful they were leaving Stone Ridge Mountain soon and he'd never have to see her again.

The chant from earlier that evening popped uninvited into his head. *All the way in. All the way in.* He remembered the dare he'd given the red-haired girl. For an instant, he wondered if she had gone in. Jerome didn't know what happened to her or Jeffrey, only that they weren't around when Todd had the seizure.

Todd wanted to forget about the entire evening, the entire trip, and everyone he'd met there.

56

Victoria leaned against the wall outside Jeffrey Wilson's hospital room and brushed thick gray dust off the pants she'd worn the last two days. Exploring the barn and basement had left her filthy. She sneezed and blew her nose with a tissue to clear out some of the dust.

An officer from the Charlotte PD stood outside Jeffrey's room with some serious muscle and a gun. With him on guard, Jeffrey was safe. He also couldn't escape.

Lambert was nearby with his phone to his ear, getting updates from the officers who were searching for Karen Green at Westview's Airbnbs.

The door to Jeffrey's room opened. His doctor looked out into the hallway. She had dark hair pulled back into a bun and a mask that matched her purple scrubs.

Lambert lowered his phone and strode toward the doctor, asking, "Can we see him now?"

"Yes," the doctor answered. "He's awake and stabilized. You can go in. He's not out of the woods just yet, but he wants to talk to you. He's been asking if you apprehended the woman who did this to him." The doctor stared at Lambert, then Victoria, waiting for an answer.

"We're working on it," Lambert said.

"I guess you'll have to tell him that," the doctor said, moving into the hall. "You have twenty minutes. No more. He has a long road ahead of him and needs to rest."

"Thank you, Doctor," Victoria said. She and Lambert entered the room, and the doctor left.

Jeffrey seemed larger and taller now that he wasn't curled into a ball. A bandage covered his nose, and the skin around his eyes had bruised to a deep purple. The rest of his face was unusually pale and tinged with green. Tubes traveled from his arms and chest and disappeared under the bed around the far side of his body.

Lambert introduced himself, followed by Victoria. "I found you unconscious in a basement," she said.

"I remember. Barely," he mumbled, his voice raspy. "Thank you. I don't want to think about what could have happened if you hadn't found me."

"How are you holding up?" Victoria asked, though their twenty minutes were ticking away.

A shiver shook Jeffrey's body. "Can't say I'm feeling good about my prognosis. I'm facing the possibility of permanent neurological issues, among other things. But I'm alive."

"We're glad you are," Victoria said. "We have some questions for you."

"I know. First, I have some of my own," Jeffrey answered. "Where is she? Have you arrested her?"

"When you say, her? Can you be more specific?"

"The one who did this to me. The lady with the red hair. Karen. If that's even her real name. I think it is."

"Is this the woman?" Victoria asked, showing him Karen Green's headshot, the one from her realty company's website page.

"Yes. That's her. Good. So you've got her. She's in jail? Prison? Whatever you call it."

"We're looking for her," Lambert answered.

"Looking for her?" Jeffrey's eyes widened. "That doesn't make me feel too good about being stuck in here." Jeffrey wrapped an arm around his torso, pulling the attached tubes taut. "If she told the truth, and I believe her, she already murdered four people and wanted me to be her number five."

"Karen told you she killed four other people?"

"She told me all sorts of psychotic stuff. She's insane. Deranged."

"Did she tell you why she killed them?" Lambert asked.

Jeffrey nodded, then winced. "She told me she was on a quest for revenge. She didn't say that right away, not when she was acting all normal, but once I was tied up at that old house, then she told me everything."

"Let's start from the beginning," Victoria said. "How well did you know Karen?"

"I didn't know her at all."

"You met twelve years ago at Stone Ridge Mountain." Victoria removed the newsletter with the photo of the six teens from her bag and gave it to Jeffrey.

Jeffrey studied the picture.

"Wow. These are the other people she killed, aren't they?"

"You tell me," Victoria said.

"Well, are they dead?"

"All except for you and Karen," Victoria answered, still unsure of who was telling the truth.

Jeffrey's eyes remained glued to the photo. "That's Karen on the end. But she doesn't look anything like that now. Even if I had remembered her, I wouldn't have recognized her."

"Recognized her when?" Lambert asked. "When did you see her again?"

"Two nights ago," Jeffrey answered, dropping the newsletter onto the bed. "I was alone in my office grading lab reports when she knocked on my door. I figured she might be a graduate student or an assistant professor."

"What did she want from you?" Victoria asked.

"Help. That's what she said, anyway, before she abducted me."

"How did she manage that?" Lambert asked. "Did she have a gun?"

"No." Jeffrey closed his eyes for a few seconds before resuming. "When she came to my office, she acted calm. Professional. I had no reason not to trust her. No reason at all. Then she totally rattled me, caught me off guard, with the reason she was there."

"And how did she do that?" Victoria asked.

"She flat out announced that she'd been raped and that I might know who did it."

"Did you suggest she go to the police?" Lambert asked.

"Yes, of course I did. Several times. But she persisted. She said she had reason to believe her rapist was one of my students. She seemed sincere. She convinced me she didn't want to make a mistake by implicating the wrong person." Jeffrey closed his eyes again and pressed his lips together, taking longer this time before he continued.

"I walked to her car, a black Mercedes SUV, and got in with her. She wanted me to look at some photos. It sounds stupid and unsafe to hear me say it now, considering what happened, but it didn't seem like a death wish then. There were people around. It was still light outside. It wasn't as if I ducked into a dark, secluded alleyway with someone who looked like a lunatic psychopath. She seemed...normal. She handed me a file with Polaroid photographs. But they weren't photos of students. They were just...body parts. A black male. While I was looking at them, she needle-spiked me in the leg."

Jeffrey took a deep breath and pressed his hand over his chest. He shook his head before reaching for the cup on his bedside table and taking a drink. He had trouble swallowing.

"Then what?" Lambert asked.

Jeffrey placed the cup down. "I woke up as she was dragging me out of her car. My hands and feet were tied. When I struggled, she kicked me in the face. She was an entirely different person. Totally unhinged. She had another syringe and threatened to kill me right there if I didn't cooperate."

"Cooperate in what way?" Lambert asked.

"She wanted to know what I remembered about a night from over twelve years ago. The night after this photo was taken." He tapped the photo still on top of his hospital sheet.

"And what did you remember?" Victoria asked.

A strangled sound came from Jeffrey's throat. Victoria thought it was a laugh at first, but his face clouded. He gripped his throat and squinted, but kept talking, his voice growing raspier with each word. "We were teenagers. I was visiting my aunt like I did every summer. I remember there were two high school jocks. One of them was Jerome Smith. And there was a girl who was sort of in charge, someone who really enjoyed her alcohol, if you know what I mean. We were all drinking together that night."

"Who is the *we*?"

"Everyone in that photo, I think."

"There wasn't anyone else with you?"

"No, not that I recall. We were the only people around the same age at the pool. That's how we got thrown together for that photo and maybe some games. I can't remember."

"And then what?"

"We drank beer and some hard stuff, playing some stupid game, and then the little party got broken up when some guy showed up yelling that we weren't supposed to be there. Everyone took off, including me. I'd had enough of their fun and games for that night, anyway. I wasn't drunk like the rest of them. I went back to my aunt's place. Never saw or thought about any of them again. Until Karen appeared at my office and tried to kill me. She said she ended up all alone in the woods, and someone raped her that night. If you believe her, that is."

"Why wouldn't it be true?" Victoria asked.

"Uh, because she's deranged." Jeffrey tipped his head and stared at Victoria as if she were the crazy one.

"She didn't see her assailant?" Lambert asked.

"No," Jeffrey answered. "She said she was completely unconscious when it happened. Blacked out. Didn't remember any of it happening. So, who is to say it happened at all? But she'd suspected Todd or Jerome. And I wouldn't put it past them at the time. They were pretty jacked up on their own testosterone, if you know what I mean."

"I thought you didn't remember them?" Victoria asked.

"I remember that much. I had no choice but to think about it while my life flashed before my eyes yesterday. Some of it came back to me."

"There were three males drinking that night with her, but she only suspected two of them," Victoria said. "Why didn't she suspect you?"

"Because she thought I was a nice guy. And I am. She didn't think I would hurt anyone. That's what she said yesterday when she was kicking me in the face, ironically." Jeffrey snorted. "She didn't suspect me until after she tested DNA from the other guys."

"How did she test their DNA?" Victoria asked. "What was she matching it to?" As soon as the question was out, Victoria realized Karen must have had a child. But where was it now?

"She told me she had evidence," Jeffrey said with a slight roll of his eyes. "Semen on the T-shirt she'd been wearing that night. Twelve years ago."

Victoria thought about what she'd found in the barn. The pink T-shirt with the patch cut out of it.

Jeffrey gave a slight shake of his head and scoffed. "She'd found a lab that processed that evidence into a DNA sample. I'm not surprised they were willing to take her money. It probably cost her a few thousand dollars. But as someone with a doctorate in science, let me tell you that no lab would have much confidence in a DNA sample that old. It had to be damaged at the least."

"But she collected DNA from Todd and Jerome before she killed them?" Lambert asked.

"She pulled their hair out from the roots. Did the same to me." Jeffrey touched his fingers to the top of his head. "She also took their toothbrushes and swabbed their mouths for saliva, thinking that might get her better results than the hair."

All the items in the chest made sense now. The plastic bags with hair samples torn from the male victims' scalps. The envelope from the DNA testing company.

"She created three DNA kits," Jeffrey continued. "One from the evidence of her rape, one from Jerome, and one from Todd. She sent the samples to a DNA company and expected to get a match with one of them. I mean, like I said, I don't know how good any of her samples were, especially the old one. It's no surprise she didn't get a match. Very doubtful they had a usable DNA profile. She said the results came back inconclusive, so don't ask me why she ruled them out. Not that it mattered by then." Jeffrey's shoulders quivered. "She'd already murdered them."

Victoria and Lambert were both quiet, processing the information until the detective asked, "She killed the men because she thought one of them raped her, but did she tell you why she killed the women?"

"Yeah. She went on and on about it. She blamed all of us for her assault. Especially the girl who brought the liquor and made sure everyone got drunk."

"So, if it wasn't Todd or Jerome who raped her, who was it?" Victoria asked, narrowing her eyes at Jeffrey. "What will we find when we test your DNA against the assault sample?"

Color flooded Jeffrey's pale skin as he tried to sit up straighter. "Didn't you hear me? No way those tests could be accurate with that old sample, if it even existed." He could barely croak the words out, but kept right on going. "I've never raped anyone. And why are you asking me that question when she killed four people? She's gloating about it, and you haven't even arrested her yet?" That was all he could say before he gripped his neck again. Alarming wheezing sounds rose from his throat.

Victoria thought about calling for the doctor, but Jeffrey seemed to recover. His eyes flashed with anger as he faced them.

"We found a Polaroid camera in your desk drawer," the detective said.

"I don't have a Polaroid camera." Jeffrey shook his head, then let it fall back against his pillow and closed his eyes.

The doctor knocked once and opened the door almost immediately. One look at Jeffrey and deep frown lines appeared on her face. "That's it for now. He needs to rest. You can come back tomorrow, if it's okay with him, but call first to make sure."

Victoria and Lambert left their business cards on Jeffrey's bedside table in case he thought of anything else.

There were a few things Victoria still didn't know, and they were important.

Was Jeffrey telling the truth?

57

Detective Lambert dropped Victoria off at the airport. After completing some paperwork at the rental car agency, they gave her another car.

She took her damp workout clothes out of the suitcase and spread them over the back seat so they could dry a little. If it weren't so late, she'd find a store and buy a new, clean outfit and underwear. But it was almost eleven at night. All the stores were closed.

She hoped the FBI or the Charlotte PD would locate Karen Green any minute. Karen knew the FBI and police were looking for Jeffrey. Did she think she'd get away with abducting him and holding him hostage? Victoria couldn't wait to hear what the woman had to say for herself.

Victoria headed to the hotel closest to the airport, the one that didn't have room for her a few nights ago. Maybe she'd get lucky there tonight. If so, she'd wash her clothes and take a shower. But none of that happened because Agent Galax called with an update.

"I think we found her! In one of Westview's rental homes. There's someone in the house, even though it doesn't show as rented in the Airbnb system. Neighbors saw a woman go in. There's a garage with no windows, so we can't see if her SUV is in there. They've already got a warrant for her arrest and to search the place and any vehicles on the premises."

"What's the address?" she asked.

He gave it to her, and she entered it into her GPS.

"Great. I'm only five miles away. I'm coming." After hanging up with Galax, Victoria followed her navigation system's directions. She hoped that by the time she arrived, Karen would be in handcuffs. The evidence screamed that Karen was the killer. And the information Jeffrey shared shed light on Karen's motive. But why now? Why had she waited twelve years and then turned into a disturbed vigilante? Victoria needed to hear the entire story.

When Galax called back a few minutes later, she said, "I'm two miles away. What's going on there? Is it her?"

"They think so. But the subject is barricaded, potentially armed and dangerous. They've got a SWAT team surrounding the place."

Victoria reached the Airbnb address and saw over a dozen police cruisers parked there. From inside her car, she took in the scene. Officers surrounded a cute bungalow with white trim and a welcoming wraparound porch. It seemed the least likely place for harboring a murderer.

An officer with a PA system crossed the neighboring lawns, telling people to stay inside and shelter in the lowest areas of their homes.

Victoria got out of her car, and both Agent Galax and Detective Lambert rushed to meet her. Lambert carried a Kevlar vest. "Glad you're here," he said. "We've confirmed it's Karen. She's alone."

"Did you arrest her?" Victoria asked, already aware something unusual had occurred.

"No. She won't come out. She's made some threats about harming herself and says there's more we don't know yet. We called in a negotiator. Meanwhile, she wants to speak with you."

"With me? Did she say why?" Victoria asked.

"No. Just that she'll only talk to you," Lambert answered.

"She must realize we found Jeffrey, but she probably doesn't know he's alive," Victoria said. "Maybe she wants to feel out how much we know."

"We've got so much evidence now. She can't possibly think she'll talk her way out of the situation," Lambert said, handing Victoria the vest. "You should wear this. No record of her owning a gun, but that doesn't mean she doesn't have one."

"Right. Thank you." Victoria agreed with his logic. There was no previous record of Karen drowning, smothering, or poisoning anyone, but the evidence strongly suggested she'd recently committed those crimes. A shooting might be next on her agenda.

"Let's get this done," Lambert said. "Get her cuffed. Then we'll make sure she hasn't kidnapped anyone else."

"No recent reports of missing persons in the area. Not yet, at least. I've been checking," Galax said.

"That's good," Victoria answered as she put on the heavy bulletproof vest. With the weight of her Glock against her hip, she mentally prepared for what might happen next. She had the training and experience for this. She'd negotiated with criminals who would rather die than face the consequences of their actions. And now that she understood the motivation for the killings, she had an angle to work. Yet still, Victoria was nervous. She would not underestimate Karen, who carried a VIPERTEK stun gun and mace on her keychain. Though she didn't look the part, Karen was highly unstable. She'd also subdued and incapacitated three grown men and two women.

Victoria had faced similar risks in other cases, but not since she got engaged. Never did she have so much to lose.

"We've got your back," Lambert said.

Victoria wanted to call Ned and tell him she loved him, but he would be sound asleep now. She'd only scare him. Besides, he knew she loved him. She pushed her dark thoughts away and summoned her strength. This was her job.

She planned to leave the rental house with Karen cuffed and no one harmed. But Karen might have something very different in mind.

58

Victoria walked up to the Airbnb with her jaw set and a fluttery feeling in her chest. Somewhere down the road, a car with a loud muffler slowed to a crawl before an officer turned it away. Despite the number of officers surrounding the property, all else was quiet, as if everyone was waiting with bated breath.

A curtain panel moved behind the front window, and a hand disappeared to one side. Victoria was about ten yards from the porch when the front door cracked open. Karen peered out. Victoria could see wisps of red hair and part of a shoulder, nothing more.

"Stop right there," Karen said.

Victoria stopped with her hand on the top of her gun. "You wanted to talk to me?"

"Yes. Why are there so many police here?" Karen asked, sounding remarkably calm and reasonable considering what she'd done and the number of law enforcement members surrounding her. "I thought I was the one in danger."

"I thought you might be, too, this morning," Victoria answered, sounding just as calm, which only made the scene seem surreal. "Then I went looking for you and found Jeffrey Wilson."

"Jeffrey Wilson? Who is that? I don't know a Jeffrey Wilson."

"Yes, Karen. You do," Victoria said. "You came back and slashed my tires and took your journal."

"No. I didn't."

"Then there's a big mix-up, and we really need to get it sorted out. Please show me your hands and come outside so we can talk."

Karen stayed where she was.

"Jeffrey is alive. I talked to him."

Victoria expected Karen to slam the door and make the arrest difficult. Or, at the least, to say something about waiting for her attorney to arrive. But she didn't. The door opened wider. Karen stepped onto the porch wearing the same black leggings and navy top from earlier in the day. With the door open behind her, she held her keychain and a metal thermos, the kind people used for hiking and workouts. The top of the thermos was already off. Victoria had an ominous feeling about what was inside.

"You want to talk? Okay, let's talk." Karen sounded different from earlier that morning and from even a few seconds ago. Bold. Angry. Confident. As if she'd just thrown all pretenses to the wind.

Victoria lifted an arm behind her, signaling for the law enforcement officers to stay back. "Please don't make this more difficult than it has to be, Karen. I don't want anyone else to hurt you."

There was a flash of understanding, maybe empathy, in Karen's eyes, but it was gone as quickly as it came, replaced with a haughty stare. "You're a clever one, Agent Heslin. I hadn't decided how this was all going to end exactly. I was still working out the best strategy. A good one, actually. And then you show up. First at Jerome Smith's house. Yeah, I saw you there. A minor celebrity sighting of sorts. I knew who you were. I thought it was neat that you were part of the investigation. Did you find the picture I took of you?"

Victoria nodded.

"But then you found out about Stone Ridge Mountain. *That* I was not expecting." Karen smiled with tightly closed lips. The effect was unnerving. "And then you drove all the way to my listing, the one no one cares about, and found Jeffrey. I know because I heard you on the phone with the police when I went back there. Didn't think he would make it, though. He deserved to die." Karen tossed her head. "So here we are. You've got me. And I'm forced to go with Plan B."

"No, you're not. Let me help you. I found out a lot of things in the past few days," Victoria said. "I know about the rape. I understand why you had to do what you did."

Karen's mouth dropped open. A range of emotions crossed her face. Surprise. Anger. And then she laughed. "You don't know everything. But Jeffrey told you that? He finally confessed? I guess the guilt got to him."

"He didn't confess. He swears he didn't rape you."

Karen laughed. "That's what they all said."

"Please put the thermos down and come with me. There's a lot to talk about."

Karen went on as if she hadn't heard Victoria. "I was so careful. I'm always careful. Ever since that day twelve years ago, I've been excruciatingly careful every minute of my life. I never wanted to be a victim again. But now...I'm not sure what I am, standing here with you, my little hideout surrounded by the police. Am I a victim again? Because I feel a little helpless." She gave the thermos a few shakes and her eyes lit up. "I'm not though. I still have options."

"You're not a victim. You're a survivor." Victoria took two steps forward. She had to get that thermos out of Karen's hands.

"Don't come any closer or you won't get any of the answers you're looking for," Karen shouted, lifting the thermos until it was just under her chin.

Victoria held her ground. "We can still get justice for what happened at Stone Ridge Mountain. Not revenge, but justice. Don't you want that?"

Karen's face tightened. Her free hand balled into a fist. "I already got my own justice. Not with Jeffrey, though, if he's still alive. Not yet." She held Victoria's gaze. "I'm waiting on one more DNA test. When the results come, then you'll have the proof you need."

Victoria took another step forward as she spoke. "I know. We'll find out who did it. It wasn't your fault."

"I said don't come any closer!" Karen screamed. Her false front from earlier had completely crumbled, and her emotions poured forth. "I know it wasn't my fault! Of course I know that now!" She took a deep breath and lowered her voice. "As an adult, that's obvious. But by the time I reached that point of understanding, it was too late. I was fifteen! I was too ashamed to tell my parents. What would they think of me? My stepmother already despised me. And then, I got kicked out of school. Everyone in the city had a picture of my naked chest. They—Todd,

Jerome, Jeffrey, Lilly—they hurt me in so many ways. You have no idea! They were the worst people I've ever met."

"I'm sorry they hurt you," Victoria said. She still didn't understand what had set Karen off so many years later. Why had she held on to the resentment for so long only to have it explode? But now wasn't the time to delve into that. They needed Karen to calm down before anyone else got hurt.

Karen's eyes shone, and she shifted her weight, moving slightly forward and back on her toes, every muscle spring-loaded inside her. "They deserved what they got, all right. Every one of them. They ruined me!"

Victoria was quick, but from where she stood, she'd never make the distance to the porch before Karen went back inside. Victoria took a small step. Just a few more and she could lunge for the thermos.

Karen thrust a palm out and shook her head. "Stay where you are!"

"I want to help you," Victoria said. "We'll open an investigation and finish the testing process. Just put the thermos down and put your hands up."

"I don't think so. I've done what I needed to do, and I don't intend to spend the rest of my life in prison." Karen braced one hand on the porch railing, closed her eyes, and brought the container toward her mouth. "Make Jeffrey pay for doing this to me. He ruined my life."

"Karen, wait, no!" Victoria shouted.

Karen tipped her head back and took greedy gulps and swallows.

Victoria dove up the stairs and tackled Karen, knocking her over. Both women crashed onto their sides. The thermos fell from Karen's grip and rolled down the porch steps.

Karen clutched at her abdomen with one hand and clawed at her throat with the other. A white foam oozed from her mouth.

Victoria grabbed Karen from behind and wrenched her off the ground. With her arms grasped tightly around Karen's abdomen, Victoria thrust upward with her fists. Karen choked and sputtered, but she didn't vomit. Victoria repeated the action again and again.

Officers crowded the porch. They shouted and scrambled to help, but none of their efforts worked.

Victoria cradled Karen's head as her eyes rolled back.

59

Two months ago - Karen

Karen sat on the edge of her chair beside the examination table with her arms crossed and her hands under her armpits. Even with a sweater on, she was shaking. Her teeth chattered as if the room were freezing. She wanted to flee, in case the news was bad, but what if it wasn't? Everything seemed to ride on this moment and the news her fertility doctor would deliver when she walked in any moment now.

A soft knock on the door preceded the doctor's voice. "Hello. It's Doctor Baxter."

"Hi," Karen said, dropping her hands and gripping the sides of the chair, her stomach now rock hard. "Come in."

Dr. Baxter entered wearing a white doctor's coat and carrying a paper chart in a folder. "Hello, Karen. How are you?"

"Fine, thank you." Karen released one hand from the chair and pressed it down on her leg to stop it from bobbing.

"Good. It's nice to see you again." Dr. Baxter settled herself on the swivel stool across from Karen and smiled. "Your husband isn't with you today?"

"No. It's just me."

"That works out well because I want to ask you about something in your medical history. First, let's have a look at your scans together, and I can explain what's going on inside you, why you're having such a hard time conceiving, despite the fertility treatments." She pivoted on the stool to face the computer monitor and pulled up Karen's test results. "This is your hysterosalpingogram. Your HSG x-ray."

A black and white, mostly gray image of her uterus and fallopian tubes appeared on the screen. A stain had made some areas darker than others.

Karen sat ramrod straight and peered at the image. Was it normal or not? She felt light-headed. Her hands were clammy and now both legs trembled. She tried to quell her emotions and pretend they were discussing someone else's reproductive dysfunction.

"You can see the scar tissue there." Dr. Baxter pointed to the image. "And there. Both fallopian tubes. It's extensive."

Karen gulped as her doctor continued with the bad news.

"Usually that's the result of chronic inflammation over an extended period. Most often from an untreated infection. But there's no mention of it in the medical history forms you filled out. You've never had a sexually transmitted disease or other pelvic-area infection that you're aware of?"

Dr. Baxter posed her question in a neutral tone. Maybe a concerned tone. Definitely not a judgmental one. She probably dealt with sexually transmitted diseases every day. And yet, Karen still couldn't admit the truth, not even to a medical professional.

It was no longer about shame. She regretted the way she'd handled the event, as if it was all her fault, as if a passed-out fifteen-year-old girl was to blame. But she remembered how she felt then, remembered her relationship with her father and Meghan, how when she most needed her friends, they were busy sharing her topless photo with the entire school, and she understood why she'd kept everything to herself, why she'd hidden her awful secret from everyone, including the husband she loved. After the rape, she was terrified of being pregnant. A week after the assault, she got her period. She didn't have to worry for long. But then came the discomfort, which progressed to pain. She'd known something was wrong. How could she not? But she'd kept it inside. She silently dealt with physical pain and mental anguish from the callous betrayal of her friends and classmates, the ones who had shared her photo. Coping with that pain strengthened her. As the years passed, she believed she'd won. Her body had taken care of the STD on its own and everything was behind her. How wrong she'd been. The repercussions of that awful night had returned, haunting her like an evil demon that just wouldn't die. And this was the grandaddy consequence of them all.

She swallowed again and answered, "No. No sexually transmitted diseases. Not that I'm aware of."

"I see," Dr. Baxter said, though she looked skeptical. Her understanding gaze lingered on Karen's face, as if trying to uncover the truth there. "Well, some women don't even realize they have an infection. The symptoms might have been mild, though there would have been pain and discomfort in your pelvic region. Painful urination. You don't recall anything like that?"

"No, nothing like that," Karen reiterated, her teeth clamping together, her fury building inside. "So, that's why I can't get pregnant? And there's nothing I can do about it? And surgery can't fix it?"

"Unfortunately, no. Barring a miracle, a very unlikely event, I don't believe you can get pregnant and carry a child to term. But there are many other options you can explore." Dr. Baxter offered a slight smile, then spun on her chair again to face a wall of brochures and pamphlets. She gathered some and handed them to Karen. "Take these home and read through them. We can talk again when you're ready for the next steps, if you want to take any."

Tears blurred Karen's eyes as she focused with all her might, trying to keep it together. Her hands fisted so tightly she could feel her nails cutting into her palms. "Thank you," she said.

On her way out, Dr. Baxter smiled again, an apologetic smile, an I-feel-your-pain smile, and said, "I'm sorry. That wasn't the news I wanted to give you."

Karen felt empty. As if her insides had been ripped out of her body. Only once before in her life had she felt so desperate and deflated that she wanted to give up. Twelve years ago. Emerging from the shed cold, alone, terrified, and empty. The incident that had led her to exactly this moment and permanently destroyed her dreams of having her own biological children.

She left the exam room and plodded through the lobby with her shoulders slumped forward. At eye-level on the wall across from her, a muted television broadcast sports news. The image changed in a flash, and Jerome Smith's gloating face stared straight at her. He held his hand to the camera, showing off a fat ring representing a recent sports success.

The words on the bottom of the screen blurred with Karen's vision.

A vein throbbed in her temple as she gritted her teeth.

60

Two months ago - Karen

Karen smacked her fist against the desktop in the Carolina Realty Office. She'd made another mistake with her latest contract. Now she had to redo the whole thing. She could barely focus. Her thoughts kept returning to her fertility issue and her scarred ovaries. Like kindling to a fire, her fixation nurtured her anger, and her obsession grew. New neurological pathways had formed in her brain, funneling her train of thought back to that night again and again, no matter where they began. Bitterness pumped through her veins now, a constant companion.

She closed her eyes and drew in a deep breath before calling Westview. "Okay, we're going with seven hundred thousand for the two units. A ten thousand due diligence. It's very low, even with the work they need, but worth a shot. I'll put the contract together and send it for your electronic signatures."

"I'm about to hop on a flight," Westview said. "You can sign for me and get them out. Negotiate up to another thirty grand on each, but that's as high as I'm going."

"Got it," Karen said, knowing her client enjoyed the thrill of getting a deal as much as she enjoyed acquiring the properties.

"I'll be in the area on Tuesday. I want to see them. If I don't approve, we'll pull the offer, but I'm sure I'll be fine with them. You haven't steered me wrong yet. And I'd prefer not to lose the ten grand. What else? Oh, can you reserve a room for me in the same hotel as last time? That resort? Or any decent place with a spa if there's another closer to the property. No, never mind. I liked the place I stayed last time. You've got my credit card information."

"Yes. No problem." Karen sometimes felt like Westview's personal assistant, but considering her wealthy client's penchant for real estate, Karen wasn't about to complain.

She was redoing the paperwork when a whiff of strong perfume signaled her colleague, Michelle, was in the vicinity. Sure enough, Michelle sidled up to Karen's desk, interrupting her work.

"I just listed a condo for sale in uptown Charlotte," Michelle said. "I'm loading the pics now. Place is fantastic. Take a quick look. Oh, and the owner is your age, gorgeous, successful, already moving on to something even better, or so he says. Not buying quite yet. Too bad you're already married. If only I were a decade younger." Michelle ran her tongue over her lip and grinned.

Karen forced a smile because she just wasn't in the mood for a real one, hadn't been in days. Her disappointment and anger weighed too heavily. She'd gotten good at faking a decent attitude, because no one wanted to work with a miserable realtor. "I don't have any clients looking for a condo right now," she said, turning back to her laptop.

"You never know what tomorrow might bring. Always be prepared," Michelle said, before leaving the paper on Karen's desk and walking away.

After signing Westview's initials and sending the new contracts, Karen successfully negotiated with the selling agent, came up with an agreed upon price, and redid the contracts yet again. It was late when she finished. When she finally closed her laptop, ready to leave the office, she glanced at the paper with Michelle's 'fabulous' new listing. The name written across the top of the document snapped Karen awake like a bolt of electricity. Todd Eckstrom.

Michelle's description of Todd replayed in a mocking loop. Gorgeous—successful—already moving on to something better. Her stomach tightened and the corners of her mouth twitched. She got up from her desk and paced the empty office.

For so many years, not knowing who had raped her brought some comfort. The nameless, faceless person made the act seem less real. Not anymore. That comfort had dissolved, giving way to a fierce and gnawing need to confront the people who ruined her life. She had to know who was responsible.

Her memories from that night existed in a haze. Possibly she'd filled in the blanks with what she believed had happened, rather than the truth. But some memories had engraved themselves on her brain, despite her efforts to erase them forever. They haunted her now. Lilly's teasing voice chanting, "drink, drink," and later, "all the way in, all the way in." Lilly was the main reason Karen had done things she never would have considered under normal circumstances.

There was Jerome's dare with the picture. The one that got her expelled from school, subjecting her to relentless bullying and ridicule, so much that she'd attempted to end her life before turning sixteen. Since then, she'd endured years of seeing Jerome's smiling face on the television and in magazines. Every time she turned around, there he was, basking in his success with people praising him to the high heavens for being so great at stuffing a damn ball into a net, for God's sake! It made her sick!

Then there was Jeffrey, whom she thought was so sweet, whom she'd daydreamed about holding hands with and kissing…he'd let her go off alone. He'd done nothing to help her.

And then, of course, there was Todd. The one who dared her to strip and jump in the lake. He'd separated her from the others. Was it on purpose? At the pool that day, and later in the woods, he'd barely looked at her. He obviously didn't find her attractive like Lilly. In his mind, she'd hardly existed. She didn't matter. Which meant he'd have no issue with harming her. And that's why Karen believed Todd was most likely the one who had raped her. The one who had irrevocably destroyed her life. It was him.

Despite an avalanche of hardships exploding from that one night, Karen had pulled her life together and done well for herself. Success was supposedly the best revenge. She'd gotten a lucky break working with Westview. Karen's income helped her and Robert afford a wonderful home, furnish it just the way they wanted, and still have money socked away. She could stay home and be a full-time mother if that's what she wanted. And she did. She dreamed of being the kindest, most supportive and devoted parent to her children. Not overly critical and constantly sneering her disapproval like her stepmother. And a world apart from her own mother, who had abandoned her family. Karen had learned from their misdeeds. She longed to show herself, Robert, and the world what a wonderful mother she could be. Except she couldn't. Not with her own biological children.

When Dr. Baxter clarified Karen would never conceive, she no longer thought of herself as successful. That night at Stone Ridge Mountain, they had hurt her in a permanent way. And they'd gotten away with it. That had to change. The pain. The shame. They needed to feel it, too. She would finally take control. Once and for all, it was time for them to pay.

But she still didn't know what she would do or how to do it. Not until she arrived at Todd's condo, and he told her the last thing she had expected to hear.

After cautious preparation, Karen visited Todd the next night, the element of surprise on her side. She had ketamine in her purse, after finding it in the barn at the Old Mill Road property. The former owners must have used it to sedate their farm animals. The drug was a decade old, and perhaps not as effective as it once had been, but according to her research, she had enough to sedate a horse and then some. With the syringes she'd purchased at a drugstore, she was prepared for anything. If Todd wouldn't admit to what he or Jerome had done, she'd show him what it felt like to be helpless, just as she'd been that night. And if he attacked her again, she'd be ready for him.

Michelle was right. The condo looked great. And so did Todd. As fit and confident as ever, which only fueled her anger. He didn't recognize her. She told him her name. Still no recognition. He thought her visit had something to do with Carolina Realty Company. She could have played along, but she didn't waste any time tricking him. She told him exactly why she was there—because of what happened July 4th weekend, twelve years ago, at Stone Ridge Mountain.

Instead of a confession, instead of dropping to his knees on the floor and begging for forgiveness, he said, "Because of what happened to me?"

What was he talking about?

"What? You? No. Because of what *you* did to me?"

"Look, I don't even remember you, but I know I didn't do anything to you. You must have me confused with someone else."

She told him she knew he'd raped her.

"Whoa. No. No way. I don't know anything about that. You're way off."

"You don't remember the drinking? It was vodka. The sight of it still makes me sick. You don't remember daring me to take my clothes off and jump in the lake?"

He shook his head. The look he gave her wasn't apologetic. More like she was pitiful and delusional and for those reasons, he felt sorry for her. "I remember that weekend," he said. "While we were there, I spent too much time outside sweating in the sun. Drank too much alcohol and not enough water. Something like that. Who knows? Anyway, I had an epileptic seizure, and because of it, I wasn't allowed to drive for the next five years. I haven't had a seizure since. Apparently, I've outgrown it, although I can never be sure. But that one incident really screwed things up for me. My license got taken away for my senior year of high school and throughout college. *And* I had to abstain from alcohol. Still do, mostly. I always have to worry it could happen again with no warning. Anytime. Anyplace. Can you imagine what that's like, hanging over your head when you're a teenager supposed to be having the time of your life?"

She didn't know if she believed him or not, but the more he went on complaining about how much he'd had to give up and how much he'd suffered because of what happened to him that night, the angrier she got.

That night had tormented her for twelve years. And the only thing Todd remembered was how it had affected him. If she had to pinpoint the exact moment she snapped, it was right there, looking out the floor-to-ceiling windows at the vibrant colors lighting up Charlotte's skyscrapers. But it didn't feel as if anything had broken. Instead, everything had come together. An act of divine inspiration, perhaps, as if what she did next was always destined to happen.

61

In the quaint neighborhood surrounding Tiffany Westview's Airbnb, Victoria stood almost in a state of shock with Agent Galax, Detective Lambert, and other officers from Charlotte's Police Department, watching yet another emergency vehicle screech away, this one with Karen inside.

It was early morning, but the neighbors were peering out their windows despite the officers' previous warnings to shelter inside. The ambulance's blaring siren had drawn their attention. One of them came onto his porch with a rake in his hand, though it was the wee hours of the morning.

"Show's over!" Detective Lambert said with a scowl, waving the man back inside his home.

Victoria didn't know what to do next. Follow the ambulance to the hospital? Find a hotel and crash for a few hours until the sun rose? Put on the smelly clothes draped over the new rental car's back seat and go for a hard run, trying to feel normal again? She was exhausted, emotionally drained, but too wired to sleep. The urgency of the situation had passed, leaving her with an adrenaline high. Normally that represented an excellent, feel-good, accomplished moment in an investigation. But not this time.

Still wearing the Kevlar vest, she shivered. Visons crept into her mind, images of Karen convulsing on the ground and foaming at the mouth. Victoria could only hope she'd slapped the thermos away before Karen had consumed too much of whatever was inside.

"The hospital is close," Lambert said, startling her as he walked past. "They'll be there within minutes."

Jeffrey's recovery gave Victoria hope. When she found him in that cellar, he had looked near death, and yet he had survived.

"We're going to search the bungalow now," Lambert told her. "If you want to stick around."

Victoria nodded. She returned to the porch. The thermos lay in a flower bed near the bottom of the stairs. Some of the liquid had spilled out on the floorboards. Victoria kneeled for a better look. In the small puddle, the paint peeled and curled, as if an acidic substance was eating it away.

Karen's keys were on the ground. Victoria scooped them up. She entered the house, walked through the kitchen, and out a door that led to the garage. The Mercedes SUV filled one side. Victoria unlocked the car and opened the passenger door. The car was clean. No debris on the all-weather floor mats. No dust on the console. She opened the back and found a shovel. Had Karen planned to bury Jeffrey somewhere in the woods behind Old Mill Road?

Victoria went to the driver's side. Tucked underneath the front seat was a plastic bag. She took photographs of her find before pulling it out and looking inside, breathing a sigh of relief when she saw the contents. Everything from the chest was there, including the journal. Taking the bag with her, she went to find Detective Lambert.

He was in the kitchen, surrounded by several Charlotte PD officers, suggesting most of them should go home. When Karen recovered enough for an interrogation, they'd have plenty more work ahead of them.

As the officers dispersed, Victoria made eye contact with Lambert. Just then, his phone buzzed. He held up a finger for her to hold on for a minute as he answered the call.

She waited, covering her mouth as she yawned.

It didn't take long before he met her eyes again. When he shook his head, her blood ran cold, though she hoped she was wrong.

"Karen died in the emergency room," he said.

"Did they...?" Victoria asked, not bothering to finish when Lambert added, "They couldn't do anything else to save her."

The investigation wasn't over, but the Atonement Killer was gone. The news felt like a major blow, and she shouldered some blame for Karen's death.

Lambert said nothing, and it took a few seconds for Victoria to remember what she held in the plastic bag. She told the detective what she'd found.

Lambert pulled two chairs together, and they sat down at the kitchen table. Victoria opened the journal. Hoping for the answers they still needed, they began reading.

62

Days later, Victoria settled into a swivel chair behind a desk in the Washington, D.C. FBI office. She'd just finished the tedious process of filling in and checking dozens of boxes on her case report. She still had to write a detailed narrative on the Atonement Task Force's efforts and submit it to her boss for approval.

The Charlotte PD had scanned the pages of Karen's journal and uploaded the files into the Atonement Killer Database. Victoria had read over every page on the night of Karen's death, and again every day since then. It was all there, almost everything law enforcement needed to know about Karen's motive and her evolving state of mind.

Her journey into a mental breakdown began with her struggle to get pregnant. Robert was angry and blamed himself, until he underwent testing, and they learned his body was not the problem. Then came the fertility treatments and the drugs that went with them. The failed attempts. The journal pages from that time period contained self-help advice and quotes—snippets about faith and hope. Breathing exercises. Karen had tried to cope.

Her anguish intensified when she learned she'd never conceive, and then, at her lowest point, she saw Jerome Smith gloating from the television at her doctor's office. After that, she wanted answers and revenge. She'd tracked the victims' habits, routines, and schedules with meticulous detail. She'd planned to confront them, to show up by surprise, and make them see what they'd done. For twelve years she'd kept the stained T-shirt in a box under her bed, knowing it might yield the power to reveal her assailant. The time had come to learn who raped her.

The visit with Todd went very wrong. Karen claimed she hadn't intended to kill him, only to confront him, and perhaps sedate him so he felt helpless. When he denied the rape, she came up with a plan to test his DNA herself. And then something happened, something Victoria could not explain. Karen seemed to snap. She'd drugged Todd. It was no easy feat for a woman to undress an unconscious man and drag and roll his body into the bathtub. But that's what Karen did. With adrenaline flooding her system, she'd filled the tub with enough water to submerge Todd's head until he died. Then used her Flirty Red lip color to write the atonement message.

After killing Todd, Karen felt better. In her own written words—*as if someone had finally lifted a weight from my aching shoulders. Murdering them is the antidote for my pain.*

That line sent chills through Victoria's body every time she read it.

Karen focused on Lilly next, though she didn't kill her right away. The rat poison from Old Mill Road was just what she needed, the perfect revenge for the person who got her so drunk that she passed out. Karen wore a blonde wig when she visited Durham and broke into Lilly's apartment. Lilly's liquor stash was the ideal place to hide the tasteless thallium sulfate poison. But Karen hadn't paid attention to every single detail. She must have flicked the lights off when she left Lilly's apartment. Lilly wasn't imagining things when she called her ex and told him someone had broken into her place while she was working.

Not long after Karen contaminated Lilly's alcohol, a trip to New York to check out properties for her client gave Karen an excellent opportunity to get to Jerome. Thanks to Westview's credit cards, Karen rented a car in NY, and drove to Boston. Wearing the blonde wig again, she pretended to be a party guest, looking every bit as if she belonged, and left no trace of herself behind. She took pictures of Jerome's genitals to humiliate him, as he had done to her. Karen even stuck around an extra day to witness the commotion she caused and shot a picture of Victoria from the crowd.

A few days after killing Jerome, Karen drove back to Durham. The poison in Lilly's liquor stash might have permanently sickened her, but that wasn't satisfying enough. Karen needed Lilly to know why she was suffering. But Karen wasn't expecting Lilly's sister to be there. Cassandra had shown up at the wrong time. There wasn't a single mention of her in the journal. Whatever role she had played at Stone Ridge Mountain, Karen didn't hold her responsible, yet felt she had no choice but to silence her.

And Jeffrey...Karen didn't think he'd raped her. Not until after she killed the Fuller sisters. That's when she received the results from Todd and Jerome's DNA tests and learned, in a shocking surprise, that neither of them had assaulted her. The test results, though, were inconclusive, so why was she so quick to rule them out? Perhaps someone who recently murdered four people couldn't make rational decisions. In any case, in her mind, the process of elimination left her with Jeffrey as her assailant. And that's when she decided that not only would she kill him, but she would make him disappear and frame him for the other murders. While Jeffrey was unconscious in her car at NC State, she'd returned to his office and planted her Polaroid camera there.

If Victoria hadn't gone out to Old Mill Road when she did, Karen might have succeeded in burying him. Would law enforcement believe the Atonement Killer got away? That he was hiding somewhere? Evading them? Probably. Because if Victoria hadn't found Jeffrey, they might not have found the journal either.

Chilled by all Karen had done and what she'd almost gotten away with, Victoria sat back in her chair and let it all sink in. According to the journal, the only people involved were the six teens in the photograph. There was no one else.

Todd had dared Karen to undress and jump in the lake.

Jerome had dared her to send the topless photo.

Lilly supplied the vodka and encouraged everyone to drink. Each victim died in a way that reflected their roles in what happened to Karen that night. Though twelve years had passed, she hadn't forgotten.

Someone approached Victoria's desk and stopped next to it. She looked up from the journal pages on her laptop screen.

Murphy stared down at her. "Tim Galax put in a transfer to the D.C. office. You recommend him?"

"Yes," Victoria said. "He's great."

"He likes dogs or something?" Murphy asked, joking.

Victoria smiled. "He's a good agent. I'd be happy to work with him again." She turned back to her emails, thinking about shutting down her laptop and heading out before rush hour traffic.

"Are you working on that report?"

"Not yet. I was reading over the journal again. It's mind blowing, the resentment she harbored. It made her sicker and sicker inside, twisted her mind until she believed murder was the only antidote to her pain. She actually wrote that. The journal will definitely become a new case study at Quantico. Something every FBI Agent in training will learn from. It's very tragic and poignant, don't you think?"

Murphy pursed his lips and gave her a look that said he'd finished discussing it further. "You back at Georgetown writing a psychology paper for your favorite professor, or are you writing an FBI case report?"

Victoria smiled even though her boss wasn't joking. "I'm almost ready to start it."

Murphy tapped his knuckles against her desktop. "I'm glad we can close the case. Congratulations on finding the killer."

They'd only found the killer after five people died, including Karen. It didn't seem like anything to brag about. But no one seemed to hold Victoria responsible for Karen's death. Instead, she'd received an outpouring of congratulations for her work on the case.

"One less monster out there," Murphy said. "They come in all shapes and sizes, don't they?"

She shrugged.

"Why are you being so hard on yourself, Heslin? You get the credit for this. And you rescued Jeffrey before he died."

"Maybe he'll develop a cure for cancer with his lab work. It's the least he can do, considering he might have been responsible for the events that led up to Karen's whole murderous rampage. Anyway, we should find out if his DNA matches soon enough." She'd wanted to delve into Jeffrey's medical records and find out if he'd ever been treated for an STD, but the law didn't allow it.

"If he's the guy, don't hold your breath that anyone will prosecute him. There's no statute of limitations in North Carolina, but he was a minor. They all were.

And they were drinking. Plus, it's her journal against his word that it wasn't consensual. That she killed four people and attempted to kill him sort of ruined her case. So, back to my original question. You think you'll have the report finished tonight?"

"Yes. I'm on it." Victoria picked up her latte and remembered it was empty. She let out a loud puff of breath as she scooted her chair closer to her laptop and started typing.

63

On a Saturday morning, Victoria sat in her home office behind a handcrafted desk. Light streamed in through the enormous bay windows. She was thinking about the power of unexpected events. A single occurrence could change someone forever. She wondered about the realtor who found Todd's body in his bathtub, and the cleaning crew who came across Jerome's corpse in a guest room. But mostly she thought about the fifteen-year-old girl on a family vacation who accidentally drank too much and crossed paths with a rapist. Victoria had no sympathy for Karen the adult, a cold-blooded killer with the charm and accomplishments to hide behind. But Karen the teenager with fresh scars around her wrists, that was a different story. She was a victim and a survivor who had Victoria's full sympathy.

A large framed photograph hung over Victoria's office mantel. A gift from her parents almost seventeen years ago. In the photo, a middle-school aged Victoria and her horse, Rodney, sailed over a fence during a show. Victoria wore her black velvet helmet, a navy jacket, tan jodhpurs, and a crisp white shirt with her polished leather riding boots. She was a year younger than Karen had been at Stone Ridge Mountain. Victoria's world was horses then, and though she had friends from school and from the barn, Rodney was pretty much her best friend. At that point in her life, a rape was unimaginable. It would have rocked her world, the same way her mother's abduction and death had ten years later. That crime had changed just about everything in Victoria's life, including her future. It was the reason she joined the FBI.

If Victoria had been in Karen's situation at fifteen, would she have told her parents? It was impossible to know. She could think of many reasons a person that age or any age would keep the ordeal as her own terrible secret.

As Murphy had said, the twelve-year-old rape of a confessed serial killer was not a top priority for anyone. But Victoria didn't want to let it go.

She heard Ned's footsteps on the hardwood floors, dogs' nails tapping alongside him, and she pivoted in her chair to greet him.

Looking irresistibly handsome in faded jeans and a T-shirt, he smiled down at her. The two dogs with him nudged their noses into her lap.

"Working?" Ned asked. He placed his hand on her shoulder, leaned down, and kissed her.

"No. I'm just thinking," she answered, staring into his sky-blue eyes.

"About what?" His hand remained, warming her shoulder.

"You never know what other people are going through."

"Are you talking about Bob?"

She'd been thinking about Karen, but the same went for Bob.

"He has surgery scheduled at the end of the month," Ned told her. "Then he starts chemo. I feel sorry for him, but he seems very grateful that we're going to buy the practice. He's been telling all the clients."

"He knows the business he built will be in excellent hands. I hope he gets better so he can enjoy his retirement."

"Me too," Ned said. "You going to be in here long?"

"I'm just waiting for Fenton to send a digital copy of the papers for me to sign."

"Your attorney approved the purchase?"

Victoria laughed. "He doesn't have to *approve* it. Not really. But my trust isn't like a savings account. Anything coming out of it goes through our family attorney. It's just the way my grandfather set it up. It hasn't been a problem yet." She smiled and put her hand over Ned's. "I'm excited."

"Me too."

They kissed again. He pulled her from the chair, and she melted into his arms. When she wasn't thinking or worrying about the world outside her little bubble, life was mostly wonderful.

After a few minutes, Ned pulled away. "Let me know when you're done in here. I'll be waiting." He raised his brows suggestively, then pressed his lips to her neck again before backing out of her office.

"Just a few more minutes."

What Ned didn't know was that she wasn't only waiting on the approval for the vet practice funding. She'd also reworked her will and switched her life insurance beneficiary to him. Everyone faced risks. The possibility of freak accidents. But Victoria had more brushes with mortality than she cared for lately. She had to prepare. They weren't married yet, but that didn't matter to her. The wedding wasn't happening anytime soon. The date still had to be determined. Anything could happen between now and then. And if it did, she needed to make sure Ned was legally in charge of her estate.

She turned back to her computer and scanned her personal messages but didn't see what she was looking for. Out of habit, she logged into her work email. She didn't have to right then. Probably shouldn't have, since Ned was waiting for her. But constantly checking her inbox to keep ahead of information and delete unnecessary messages always gave her a small sense of satisfaction. And now, it was about to deliver a big one.

She'd previously submitted the DNA from Karen's assault into CODIS, the FBI's database of DNA profiles. The software continuously searched its existing DNA profiles against new ones and would show a match if the rapist's DNA was already in the system. The profiles came from other unknown criminal cases, and from felons convicted of assaults, homicides, and burglaries.

A new message from the CODIS system awaited her. Victoria opened it. "Oh, no way," she whispered aloud. The software had found a match.

But that couldn't be. Because it meant the sample didn't match Todd, Jerome, or Jeffrey. They'd never been arrested. Their DNA wasn't in the system. Unless...what if Karen wasn't the only female they'd raped? That seemed to be the only explanation. One of them was a repeat offender and that's why his DNA was in the database. And why did that surprise Victoria? It shouldn't have.

Too excited and upset to remain sitting, she got up from her chair and continued reading.

Surprise number two came fast. The DNA that matched Karen's assailant wasn't from another forensic unknown. It matched a convicted felon. Six years ago, authorities in North Carolina had arrested a man for failing to pay his property taxes. During his arrest, he had to submit a DNA swab.

Victoria gaped at the info on her screen.

That man's name was Crawford Naught.

It took Victoria less than two seconds to place him. The tall maintenance worker. *Mr. Fix It.* When Victoria was at Stone Ridge Mountain, Mabel had referenced the incident that led to Crawford's arrest.

Victoria recalled his reaction when she showed him the picture. His mention of entitled brats. Crawford was forty-two years old now, making him thirty when the rape occurred. His reprehensible action had set in motion a terrible chain of events leading to four murders and a suicide.

Victoria knew exactly where to find him. She opened her browser and began searching for a law enforcement contact in western North Carolina.

It wasn't necessarily a happy ending, but sometimes in her work, even a little closure brought satisfaction. For now, she would take it and do all she could to get the state of North Carolina to pursue justice. That was the least she could do for fifteen-year-old Karen.

EXCERPT - THE ONES THEY BURIED

Phoebe Watson was a rising star in the fitness industry. Then she disappeared.

The mystery captivates the nation, and the investigation **takes a dark turn** when her body is discovered a year later, **buried deep in a remote, wooded area.**

Only **one person seems to know something** about those remains—multi-millionaire Catherine Bower, one of Phoebe's former clients. Soon after Phoebe disappeared, Catherine suffered a life-altering accident. FBI Special Agent Victoria Heslin believes there's a connection between Phoebe's murder and Catherine's accident.

As Victoria digs deeper, she uncovers **a thick web of secrets and lies**, and every thread she untangles points toward **a shocking truth.**

If you liked *Flicker in the Dark* and *The Housemaid*, you'll love The Ones They Buried.

Keep reading for the first few chapters of Agent Victoria's next investigation.

Chapter 1

One year ago
Phoebe

Phoebe Watson's social media posts went viral, reaching millions of views within a matter of days. The surge would have thrilled her, if only she'd been alive to see it.

Hours before her death, she was counting down seconds on her watch. The gym reverberated with the music she'd chosen. The beats and her encouragement drove the participants to push their limits. Floor-to-ceiling mirrors lined one wall, reflecting determined faces and bodies glistening with sweat.

Phoebe moved with strength and grace, performing each movement with precision as men and women gasped and grunted around her.

"And...done!" she finally said on the last repetition, clapping her hands. "Excellent work, everyone!"

A man in the front row shouted, "You tried to kill us, didn't you?" which might have been morbidly ironic, though no one, not even her killer, knew what would soon unfold.

Phoebe only laughed with appreciation as she kneeled to roll up her mat.

From the back of the room, a man weaved around bodies to reach her. Appearing to be in his mid-thirties, he sported closely cropped black hair and a tanned complexion. Phoebe had noticed him earlier. He wasn't one of her regulars, though something about him seemed familiar.

"Your class was hard," he said.

"I take that as a compliment," Phoebe responded with a grin. Among her group of participants, hard and good were synonymous when it came to their workouts. She'd designed her routines for the dedicated fitness enthusiasts who pushed themselves until they were drenched in sweat, gasping for breath, and feeling the fire in their muscles. The man standing before her wasn't one of those people. Throughout the routine, he'd found it difficult to keep up.

"Was this your first time taking one of my classes?" she asked.

"First time, yes. I haven't joined the gym yet. I got a guest pass to try it out."

"Oh, that's great. Welcome." Phoebe stood with her rolled-up mat tucked under her arm and pressed an errant strand of red hair behind her ear.

He smiled and said, "I've seen you at Mrs. Catherine's house. I didn't know you worked here, too."

Catherine was one of Phoebe's personal training clients and perhaps the wealthiest, based on her luxurious home and lifestyle. Phoebe drove to the estate three times a week to give private sessions whenever Catherine was in town. Last Christmas, she rewarded Phoebe with a generous bonus, and the gold barbell pendant that never left Phoebe's neck. Catherine Bower was a dream client. How did this man fit in with her life?

"I take care of her yard, and her house," he said, as if he'd read Phoebe's thoughts. "My name is George."

"Oh, right." Often, on her way to and from her car, Phoebe noticed George at Catherine's place. Perhaps if he'd worn the cap he usually wore, she would have recognized him right away. He'd always seemed nice enough. Phoebe smiled at him now and said, "You're the reason her yard always looks amazing."

George's eyes lit up. "Thank you. I certainly try. It's an honor to take care of a special property like Catherine's."

"I bet. I enjoy being her trainer. Well, glad you came." Phoebe gave a little wave before turning away. She unplugged her phone from the stereo system and took a quick peek at her messages.

We need to talk.

It was from her ex.

No, we don't, she thought, without answering the message. He'd been trying to speak to her ever since she ended their brief relationship. He couldn't seem to accept that she wasn't interested. The more he texted and called, the less she wanted to have anything to do with him.

She glanced toward the doorway, worried he was waiting for her. He was a fanatic about going to the gym most nights. Fortunately, she didn't see him. She pulled on her hoodie and left the studio, reminding herself never to date anyone from the gym again. Her busy schedule centered around work, leaving little opportunity to meet people elsewhere. That's why she had accepted an invitation to have a drink later that evening with a new guy. He'd intrigued her with his charm and confidence. She hoped her decision wouldn't lead to regret.

Darkness had descended during her class, but the parking lot was well lit. Phoebe hurried to her little Toyota waiting in a space designated for staff. She was reaching for her door handle when a man's voice startled her.

"Good night, Ms. Phoebe."

George stood two spaces away, in front of a familiar blue pickup truck. The door of the truck proudly displayed a magnetized sign that read *George's Landscaping*.

Phoebe waved. "I hope to see you again in one of my classes."

"Yes. You'll definitely see me again soon," George answered.

Chapter 2

Present Day
Deja

On her first day of work with the agency, Deja Torres stood by the reception area at Atrium Gardens, an assisted living facility inside a gated country club community. Fidgeting with nervous energy, she absentmindedly chipped away at her gel polish, ruining a nail before realizing what she'd done.

It's just the uncertainty of it all. Meeting your first client, she reminded herself, stuffing her hands into the deep pockets of her white uniform. *You've got this.* And she did. There was no way her new job could demand as much from her as her previous gig with a large online retailer. Package delivery work entailed long shifts with no bathroom breaks and carrying heavy items onto front porches. Furniture crammed into boxes weighed more than she'd ever imagined. She still had the muscles to prove it. Thankfully, her delivery days were behind her. She hoped her new position would prove more satisfying and less strenuous.

A young-looking twenty-three-year-old, Deja frequently received compliments on her stunning appearance. She had shiny hair, smooth dark skin, a slender frame, and big brown eyes accentuated by false lashes. People told her she could be a model. Her beloved grandmother, a significant influence in Deja's life, had discouraged her from modeling. Deja had immense respect for her grandmother's wisdom and values. Gran believed Deja's true beauty didn't reside in her outward appearance, instead with an internal gift possessed by too few people—the gift of compassion. "Nurtured properly, it flourishes with life's experiences, and never fades away," Gran said.

Guided by her Gran's insight, Deja had recently completed a course for certification as a caregiver. Soon after, the Senior Specialty Concierge Agency hired her. Deja's first assignment was with a wealthy client in a very fancy place. Obviously, the agency didn't say those things, not in so many words, but the signs were unmistakable. A one-month stay at Atrium Gardens cost more money than Deja would make in a year.

As she followed Jasmine, one of the nurses' aides, through the long, carpeted hallway, Deja marveled at her surroundings. They passed a glass-enclosed space containing small, colorful birds. A sitting area had plush couches gathered around an impressive stone fireplace. A formal dining room featured elegant, upholstered chairs and neatly folded cloth napkins. The vacant rooms made Deja think of a luxury hotel preparing for a grand unveiling.

They rounded a corner and arrived at a central desk area. The luxury-hotel ambiance faded away, and reality set in. The smell of disinfectant permeated the air. A few residents sat around the desk in their wheelchairs. They seemed disconnected from the world around them, offering no acknowledgment as Jasmine greeted them with friendly hellos.

Jasmine turned down one of the many hallways branching from the central area. Room 104 was near the end of the corridor, two rooms away from the emergency exit. A copper plaque on the door announced the name of Deja's client. *Mrs. Catherine Bower.*

While most of Atrium Gardens' residents were elderly, Catherine was not. One year ago, she'd suffered a terrible accident. Deja didn't know what happened exactly. She understood the accident had led to an anoxic brain injury—a trauma caused by lack of oxygen to the brain, similar to a massive stroke. Catherine couldn't walk, get dressed, or feed herself. At only forty-nine, she depended on caregivers for even the most basic functions.

Jasmine tapped her knuckles against Catherine's door, not bothering to wait for a response before entering. Deja trailed behind her, stepping into the private room. Sunlight flooded the space, casting a glow on exquisite furnishing and tasteful décor, though several items provided clear reminders of the room's purpose and the occupant's vulnerability: grab-bars and a sturdy shower chair in the bathroom, and safety rails on the full-sized bed.

In the center of the room, Catherine sat in a high-tech wheelchair, facing a television, her back to the door.

"Just talk to her as if she understands you. They probably told you, right?" Jasmine said. "Come on, I'll introduce you and then I have to get home and take care of my kids."

Jasmine stepped in front of the wheelchair. "Catherine? You awake? Your new caregiver is here. Her name is Deja. She's here just for you. Aren't you lucky to have someone to take care of whatever you need?"

Deja moved to Jasmine's side and could barely contain her surprise when she saw Catherine for the first time. She looked so put together, her black hair styled in a sleek bob, not a strand out of place. A hint of blush swept across her pale cheeks.

"She's so beautiful," Deja blurted, embarrassed as she immediately realized she'd spoken as if Catherine wasn't there.

"She just got back from the beauty shop," Jasmine said.

With a smile, Deja introduced herself to Catherine.

Catherine's expression remained neutral. She gave no sign she'd understood what anyone had said.

"Sometimes she says things or tries to. None of it makes sense as far as I can tell," Jasmine said. "Don't worry. She has a way of letting you know when she's unhappy or uncomfortable. She'll twitch and frown, things like that."

"Is there a list of things she likes or doesn't like?" Deja asked.

"No. You'll figure it out. Just talk to her about whatever comes into your head. Feed her. Keep her clean. Let her watch television. Okay? Well, good luck. I have to go. You'll be fine," Jasmine added, perhaps noticing the way Deja twisted the edge of her uniform between her fingers.

Jasmine left the room, and Deja was alone with Catherine.

"It's nice to meet you," Deja said. "I'm glad to be here. I hope I can help make things more comfortable for you. If you can be patient with me while I work it all out, I think we'll be good. I promise you'll get to do a lot more than just watch television when I'm around."

Deja placed her hand on Catherine's shoulder. Not something she would normally do with someone she'd just met. Yet if Catherine couldn't understand her words, a gentle, firm touch, a universal form of communication, seemed important. Deja had to start somewhere.

She looked out the window at the manicured lawn, and bird feeders hanging from tree branches just outside the window. "We could go for a walk since it's a nice day. Would you like that?" To her own ears, Deja's cheerfulness sounded forced. Adjusting to one-way conversations would take some practice. Catherine didn't appear to be paying attention, anyway. With her gaze fixed on the television, her eyes widened and her perfect eyebrows lifted.

Deja turned to see what had caused Catherine's response.

A flashing red ribbon emblazoned with *Breaking News* scrolled across the bottom of the screen. The camera swept out, revealing a dense expanse of woods. Stark yellow crime scene tape crisscrossed from tree to tree, forming a perimeter.

The reporter announced, "Just a few hours ago, authorities in Rutherford County discovered the body of a woman in the remote area you see behind me. I'm told local residents refer to the area as Madison Creek Woods. At this time, law enforcement is not releasing information about the discovery, and the victim has yet to be identified. We will keep you informed as further developments emerge."

Deja felt an immediate surge of compassion. She understood the profound sorrow that would consume the woman's family.

"Want me to change the channel?" Deja asked. "The news can be so depressing."

Catherine jerked her head, which surprised Deja. She'd asked a question, and Catherine seemed to have responded with a definitive, non-verbal answer. Deja couldn't say if the response was a yes or a no, but it was something. Maybe Jasmine and the agency were wrong about Catherine. Maybe she understood people and could communicate in her own way.

Still staring at the television, Catherine croaked out the sounds, "Ee-bee."

"What's that?" Deja asked, leaning closer.

When Catherine repeated the sounds, Deja focused on the first consonant and heard it clearly. "Phoebe."

"Phoebe?" Deja asked. "Is that what you said?"

"Phoebe—Watson," Catherine said with great effort, her face contorting and her eyes squeezing shut.

"Is Phoebe a friend of yours here in the facility?" Deja asked. "Or a family member? Or someone from before you were…uh …someone from before you lived here? Do you want me to find her for you?"

Catherine shuddered. She clenched her hands together and held them against her chest. Soon her whole upper body shook so fiercely it rattled her wheelchair.

Fear gripped Deja, rendering her temporarily helpless. This was not good. Not good at all. She wrapped her hand around Catherine's trembling arm to steady her. Was Catherine's behavior a regular occurrence or an emergency? No one had mentioned anything about seizures. This was not how Deja imagined her first hour of her first day on the job. She was about to run into the hallway and call for help when Catherine's shaking subsided. She opened her eyes and tears rolled down her face.

Deja grabbed a tissue from the nightstand and dabbed Catherine's cheeks.

After Catherine's troubling reaction, Deja hoped the name Phoebe Watson would never come up again.

Chapter 3

Present Day
Victoria

FBI Special Agent Victoria Heslin sat beside her colleague, Agent Dante Rivera, waiting to learn why their boss had called them into his office. Whatever he presented them with, Victoria felt confident she and Rivera could handle it. They'd faced years of challenges together. Rivera always had her back, and she had his.

Special Agent in Charge Larry Murphy entered his office carrying a mug embellished with the Georgia Bulldogs mascot, a not-so-subtle nod to his passion for college football. His military-style posture added to his commanding presence, and his stern expression conveyed the weight of his responsibilities. He was a good, fair boss who appreciated his agents.

"I've got a new assignment for you," he said. "An hour ago, we got pulled into the Jane Doe case from Rutherford County. Are you familiar with it? The woman's remains that were found buried in Madison Creek Woods."

Victoria nodded and leaned forward to learn more.

"Jane Doe's murder might be connected to a crime in another state," Murphy said. "Last year, officers in North Carolina stopped a man named Dan Sullivan for a traffic violation. They had a K-9 unit. The dog alerted them, leading to a search of the vehicle. They discovered the body of a twenty-six-year-old woman in the back. The mother of twin toddlers. She'd been sexually assaulted, beaten, and strangled. Sullivan's DNA was all over her body. The traffic stop and subsequent search were conducted properly. The evidence was solid."

Placing his mug on the desk, Murphy crossed his arms and continued, "Sullivan was convicted and sentenced to life in Virginia. Just a few days ago, he said he wanted to offer authorities additional information."

"What information?" Rivera asked.

"He wanted to give them the location of another woman's remains, and he did, implicating himself in Jane Doe's case," Murphy explained. "Her body was found exactly where he directed the police to search in Madison Creek Woods. Now, he claims to possess knowledge about the location of additional victims and wants to negotiate."

"What are his terms?" Victoria asked. "What does he want?"

Murphy frowned. "He wants his sentence reduced."

"Why do we need to be involved?" Rivera asked.

"Sullivan hasn't disclosed Jane Doe's identity, presumably as leverage. The detective who interviewed him believes Sullivan doesn't know her name. He thinks Sullivan could be lying. We need confirmation that Sullivan is indeed responsible for Jane Doe's death." Murphy directed his gaze at Victoria and said, "You'll take the lead on this, considering your growing expertise in serial killers."

Rivera gave her a slight smile.

"Jane Doe's remains are less than a year old," Murphy continued. "There are no local women missing, so detectives are checking neighboring cities and states. With normal circumstances, we should identify her soon."

"Our job will be easier once she has a name," Rivera said.

"Yes," Murphy answered. "If Sullivan's story proves credible, he serves less time in exchange for the rest of what he knows. The victims' families deserve closure, but we have to confirm beyond any doubt that Sullivan is responsible for Jane Doe's murder before any deal is made."

"Got it," Victoria said. "And if Sullivan didn't kill Jane Doe?"

"I trust you'll uncover the truth," Murphy answered. "Someone out there knows who the poor woman is and what happened to her. Find that person."

You can order *The Ones They Buried* from Amazon or your favorite retailer.

NOTE FROM THE AUTHOR

If this is your first Agent Victoria Thriller, you might not know it's part of a series. I wrote the books so readers could read them alone without confusion. Each features a unique crime investigation which resolves at the end. Victoria's personal stories continue from novel to novel. There is a list of her adventures and my other thrillers in the front of this one.

I also want to thank you for being a reader, and for choosing my book. Without you, I couldn't continue to write. Please consider leaving a review and recommending this book to others. Your continued support is appreciated more than you'll ever know.

Yours sincerely,
Jenifer Ruff

ACKNOWLEDGEMENTS

Writing is mostly a solitary process, though my dogs are my constant companions for every word I write and revise. Each time I shift my weight in my chair, they jump up, hoping for a walk or a treat. But they aren't much help. After working alone for so long, there is nothing I appreciate more than receiving constructive feedback. For that reason, I would like to mention and thank several people here.

From Charlotte, my mystery-thriller critique group, who read early chapters and always help strengthen my writing—authors Susan Mills Wilson, Reita Pendry, Alex Whitney, Dennis Carrigan, and the late Jim Boatner.

My parents, Linda and Blaise Bisaillon, and my aunt, Mary Vassallo, who have read drafts of every book and given me honest, constructive feedback on what they did and didn't like. Without them, there would be too many mentions of animals, and animal related things, I am sure.

My beta readers: Author and Journalist, Karen D. Scioscia, one of my strongest sources of encouragement, advice, and friendship since my first novels.

Bill Douglas, a retired creative writing professor and attorney, whose intellect and accumulation of interesting skill sets uniquely qualify him to offer a variety of insightful feedback. He contacted me through my website several books ago and enlightened me on sailing lingo in a manner so helpful; I knew I wanted him to read all my books before publication. And lucky for me, so far, he has agreed.

Allison Maruska, an exceptionally perceptive reader, editor, and an incredible writer. The things that she notices often amaze me.

Audrey J. Cole, whose books are fantastic, and whose friendship I cherish, and her husband, Brett Pflugrath at Rainier Designs, who creates my wonderful covers.

Nenia Corcoran, an author and speaker. Talk about lucky timing for me! Scrolling through BookTok, I saw a post of Nenia doing a book review. As a former law enforcement officer, she had excellent insight on that book's law enforcement issues. I asked her to be a beta reader, and she generously said yes!

After reading The Atonement Murders, Nenia provided me with a list of law enforcement issues that weren't quite right, along with explanations of why. I feel great about the corresponding changes I made thanks to her insight. Some parts of the investigation still aren't entirely to protocol but remain so at my discretion with the goal of entertaining readers.

My ARC team, which I'm happy to say is growing with each book I publish, though some of you have been along for the ride with me from the beginning. I'm so grateful for your support!

And finally, my husband, Mike, who listens to all my ideas when we walk the dogs, as well as listening to me go on and on about the challenges, technical issues, and highs and lows that come with writing, publishing, and marketing my books. This time around, I was stressed about learning Atticus, a new-to-me formatting program. Hope a bit of my sanity was worth the pretty dropped caps in this book. Anyway, I know I'm lucky to have Mike's support.

JENIFER RUFF

USA Today bestselling author Jenifer Ruff writes dark and twisty thrillers, including the award-winning Agent Victoria Thriller Series. Jenifer grew up in Massachusetts, has a biology degree from Mount Holyoke College and a Master's in Public Health and Epidemiology from Yale University. She adores peace and quiet, animals, and exercise, especially hiking. She lives in North Carolina with her family and a pack of greyhounds. If she's not writing, she's probably devouring books or out exploring trails with her dogs. For more information you can visit her website at Jenruff.com

- amazon.com/stores/author/B00NFZQOLQ
- facebook.com/authorjruff
- instagram.com/author.jenifer.ruff/
- tiktok.com/@jeniferruff.author
- http://bookbub.com/authors/jenifer-ruff

Made in the USA
Coppell, TX
28 September 2025